Death on Disappointment Mountain

Jeff Krogstad

This book is a work of fiction. The characters, incidents, and dialogue are drawn from the author's imagination and are not to be construed as real. Any resemblance to actual events or persons, living or dead, is entirely coincidental.

All rights reserved.

Death on Disappointment Mountain
Copyright © 2023 by Jeff Krogstad

No part of this publication may be reproduced or transmitted in any form or by any means without permission in writing from the author.

www.jeffkrogstad.com

ISBN: 979-8-218-27351-4

Author's note:

I first experienced the Boundary Waters at the age of fourteen as part of a group from my church. Canoeing at the end of May, we were ill-prepared and poorly organized. Our trip was plagued by snow, rain, bad food, getting lost, and interpersonal conflict. And in spite of it all, somehow I was hooked.

One of the great joys of my life has been hundreds of days since then spent in the Boundary Waters of northern Minnesota. This precious wilderness area, deep forests dotted with lakes and rivers, is set aside without roads or motorized boats. The full name is the Boundary Waters Canoe Area Wilderness.

The US Forest Service website describes the BWCAW this way: "More than 1 million acres, it extends nearly 150 miles along the international boundary adjacent to Canada's Quetico Provincial Park and is bordered on the west by Voyageurs National Park. The area contains more than 1,200 miles of canoe routes, 12 hiking trails and more than 2,000 designated campsites."

Like the characters in this book, I have found challenge, renewal, and perspective in that landscape. Gliding through remote lakes and rivers by canoe, portaging all my gear, living without electronics–these things bring me to life. I've introduced many others to that place, including my children and good friends. Whether I go as part of a group or solo, I always find myself in a new way there.

Many years ago my family took a layover day on Gaskin Lake. We camped a couple nights on what my daughters named Raspberry Island. During an idle August afternoon I found myself wondering what it would be like to experience the sudden onset of winter in the Boundary Waters. This story grew and blossomed from those imaginings. The places named in the book are real, from the waterfall between Ashigan and Cattyman Lake to Disappointment Mountain. If you go, please treat them well.

Jeff Krogstad
Summer, 2023

Chapter One

Mac clicked off his headlamp. Another day. *The* day. The final day. He could see the jagged outline of trees against the brightening sky. There was light enough to read his own handwriting now.

He'd heard the wolves last night off to the southeast of Parent Lake. That was good. They would tend him, care for him as he wanted to be cared for, with efficiency and without words. He trusted them to find him in a timely fashion. There was a time for a man to go, and he knew it was his time. Yeats had it right. "I will arise and go now," he'd written. In the end, the timing was mostly out of his hands. Dylan Thomas be damned, he had made peace with this. Maybe he wasn't going gentle into that good night, but close enough. Another decade or two might have been nice. Sadly, that wasn't an option. It was time.

Fear. He dreaded the pain.

He looked up and scanned the pines across the clearing. The dark silhouettes of the trees stood like sentinels around the snowy wetland. His camp lay at the southwest edge of the open snow where the ground started to rise to the summit of Disappointment Mountain, a grandiose name for what in Colorado or Montana would be a nameless hill. Still, if the geologists were right, once upon a time this had been the backbone of a respectable mountain range, far older than the youthful Rockies. He pondered for just a moment the ages and ages of wind and water, moving mountains of ice, the snow, heat, and drought that turned a mountain range into a few hills and lakes. Was it the Cheyenne who used to say "only earth and sky last forever"? Maybe just the sky, he thought wryly. A billion years wasn't a bad run for a mountain range. The life of a man was far shorter.

It had been a cold night, and Mac relished the crisp morning. He was glad for the clear air. At least it wasn't a hazy, warming humid day. The crisp morning gave a man the idea he could make decisions and act on them. Reality had firm, hard edges on a day like this.

Out of the corner of his eye he caught a movement. He imperceptibly turned his head to the right. A wolf. Big one. Hunting across the clearing on the other side of the creek. It was a hundred yards away, nose to the ground. Mac held his breath and watched it zigzag in and out of the brush for twenty, maybe thirty seconds before it disappeared back into the trees, looking for mice and chipmunks. That had to be a good omen.

Chapter Two

Many days later and a hundred miles away, Kim Norby sat in her car in the Ma's Coffee parking lot. She stared at nothing for a long moment, fighting the grief that swelled up in her throat. Six days since she learned about Mac's death. A stranger walked into the reception area at the McPherson Foundation and asked for Kim by name. He handed her the manila envelope that turned her orderly world into chaos. "My name is Brad Swenson. I'm sorry to tell you that Mac is dead. He committed suicide, up in the Boundary Waters. On February 24th. Before he died he asked me to give you this." *This* was the sealed envelope, with Brad Swenson's name and cell number written in pencil on the outside.

She had trusted Mac. Admired him. She believed in him. Without doubt, she possessed a clearer picture than just about anyone what he was really like, warts and all. Kim knew she would stop at nothing to carry out his wishes. Almost all of them.

So here she sat, preparing to meet with Brad Swenson and hear his story. Usually her mind was methodical, but today her thoughts tumbled around like ping-pong balls dropping on a tile floor. Why had Mac specified she meet Swenson offsite? The Foundation had perfectly good meeting spaces, high-tech conference rooms, comfortable chairs, excellent coffee. Why a coffee shop? But that's what Mac's note demanded.

She could imagine his voice reading her the various documents he'd placed in that manila envelope. Some of them were simple, even elementary. The numbered list, however, was another matter. This meeting was number two on the list. Each item on that handwritten page seemed stranger than the last, and as to number seven… it was a stretch, even for Mac.

She swallowed her grief and checked her eyes in the rearview mirror. Mac said once that pretty as she was, she was tough like wire. She'd need that toughness for this meeting. She was old enough to have some well-earned self confidence. Wise enough to give Mac the space he so often needed. Bold enough not to walk on eggshells around him. She knew she was an effective asset in the ventures of the Foundation. But this assignment was uncharted territory.

Brad Swenson walked across the snowy parking lot and up to the coffee shop door just as she did. He held the door for her. "Ms. Norby."

"Mr. Swenson. Thanks for meeting me." They ordered and found a table in a quiet, out-of-the-way corner.

Once they were settled, Kim took the initiative. "I'm not sure if you know this, but for the last twelve years I've served as Mr. McPherson's executive assistant. His death creates a massive disruption for us at the McPherson Foundation. The whole organization was really his baby. Hearing your story is a critically important part of tying up the loose ends."

He sipped his coffee, watched her face, and didn't say a thing. She continued. "It's not just that, of course. Part of it for me is personal. I worked closely with Mac for a long time. His death leaves a huge gap. I'm eager to know what your interactions with him were like. The materials Mac sent with you suggest that the two of you had extensive conversation." Silence. "Some of Mac's comments make it sound like your time with him in the Boundary Waters was a way for you to deal with some personal issues in your own life. Would you be willing to start wherever you like, and tell me a little about yourself and your experience with Mac?"

Brad stirred, and considered. Finally he spoke. "Red lights made me wait longer than anybody else. That's how I knew my life had really gone bad."

This was not at all what she expected. Kim took a sip of her cappuccino, then considered the man across the table, the man who had delivered unwelcome chaos into her life. Early 40's. Thinning light brown hair. Weekend ensemble of faded jeans and an untucked flannel at 10 am on a Tuesday. She took another sip. Damn Mac and his harebrained ideas, anyway. She knew he would insist she play along, listen well, be professional. To start with. "Red lights? How did you know?"

"I timed them. Seven seconds longer on average, but there was one down by the West End, right next to Costco there, that made me wait fifteen seconds longer. Every time. If I wasn't waiting for the light, average was twenty-two seconds. If I was waiting at that light, thirty-seven seconds. Didn't matter if I was in a car or on foot."

Kim looked out the window at the ice on Lake Superior. Last night's dusting of snow made it sparkle under the cold March sun. "Seems like an odd thing to notice. Everybody hates red lights."

"It's funny what you pay attention to when your life is collapsing. When you're in enough pain, sometimes it feels like it has to be on purpose. Like the universe is out to get you. I was pretty far down by that time. Red lights seemed like something I could test. Objectively." He sipped his coffee, then added, "More or less."

"This would be when? Last summer?"

Brad looked away and took a deep breath. His eyes squeezed shut, just for a second. "June."

She watched all the physical tells. Part of her sympathized with this man, but if she was going to do this last strange job Mac had asked her to accomplish, she needed to get through these questions, and many more, with just a hint of measured mercy. "Can you tell me about your life last June?"

Brad Swenson looked straight into her eyes. Kim had a sense she was being evaluated. She returned his gaze while he made up his mind. Without breaking eye contact, he lifted his coffee cup (dark roast, no cream or sugar) and drained the last gulp. "Mind if I get a refill before I try to answer that?"

"Of course. They're free here."

"Want anything else?"

"No, thank you."

While Brad got his refill, she checked her phone. Nothing urgent. She left the ringer off, but set an alarm for her next appointment. Brad came back with a fresh cup of coffee.

"How much time do you have? If you really want to know this, I probably need to give you a little backstory."

"I have an appointment three blocks away at 11:30, so I have an hour before I need to leave."

"Okay. Let's go back to March, a year ago. I was working for a big retailer, commuting into downtown Minneapolis every day on the light rail. A little bit of phlegm in the corporate hairball."

"Sounds like you weren't thrilled with your job."

"It was a job. I'm okay with numbers, and I'm okay with people. What killed me was being part of the Borg. You know, Star Trek? 'Prepare to be assimilated'?"

"I'm familiar with the Borg."

"I was somewhere around what you'd call middle management. It's that level where you're so indispensable that you can't be fired. I was making decent money, salting enough of it away in savings, living the suburban routine, managing to stay mostly out of debt. Completely assimilated."

"You were married at that time, right?"

Brad made a point of testing the temperature of his coffee and taking a deliberate sip. "Yes."

Silence.

"Mr. Swenson, I'm sorry to ask these questions, but these things are all related to the envelope Mr. McPherson gave you. The one that you brought to me. He wanted us to have this conversation, if you're willing."

"Mac." Brad gazed at the radiance out the window. "Yeah, I'll keep talking. I owe him a lot more than that."

"I want to hear about that, too, but I'd like to get through some of these preliminaries first if we can."

Heavy sigh, and Brad launched in. "Yes, I was married. Lauren and I met in college. She was smart, and beautiful, and we seemed like a great match. Both good students, both enjoying college life just enough without going off the rails. Upwardly mobile. We dated, got engaged, graduated. Seemed the most natural thing in the world to get married. We'd have been married twelve years last summer."

"Kids?"

"We debated early on, but after a couple years of not taking precautions and not getting pregnant, we both kind of heaved a sigh of relief and decided we'd get a dog. I wanted a lab, she wanted a terrier. We got a terrier. Never could stand that dog, and the feeling was mutual."

"So what happened between you and Lauren?"

"I came home from work one day. It was March sixth a year ago. Found a note. 'Brad, I'm divorcing you. I'm taking the dog and half the bank accounts and equity in the house. Papers should arrive this week. Don't be an ass about this.' Twenty-nine words. She didn't sign it."

"Was it that simple?"

"A divorce is never that simple. But her lawyer talked to my lawyer, and they each made a few thousand dollars. The real estate market was hot so we had no trouble selling the house. One day half our joint savings and checking accounts disappeared, and boom. The divorce was finalized June 20th. Except for the sleepless nights and the guilt, it was almost that simple."

"You memorized the note, Mr. Swenson. That doesn't sound like it was simple to you. Did she have a boyfriend?"

"I'm Brad, okay? Honestly, I don't know. I never heard about a boyfriend. A couple of my friends wanted to speculate, but… I guess I just wasn't that interested anymore." Deep breath. "Here's the deal, Ms. Norby. We had been roommates for a very long time. She had her life, her friends, her career, I had mine. It just seemed normal. I think she actually enjoyed her life. We did things together with a few other couples, but mostly that was her and her friends getting together and the husbands just tagged along and made small talk. We didn't share much of a life. Not for years."

"Doesn't sound like the two of you had much heart-to-heart conversation."

"Oh, we talked. About everything except heart stuff. How was work? Chinese or burgers tonight? She was good at pointing out stuff I did wrong in a condescending way. A good blow up a couple times a year just to clean out the carbon. Once a year about finances, around tax time, and once a year about getting together with her extended family, around Christmas. It was a script."

"Was that how you wanted it?"

Brad looked out at the harbor for a long moment, then turned back and she couldn't read the expression on his face. "I'd never been married before. For all I knew, this was normal. I did a little reading and a little counseling while the divorce was in process, trying to figure it all out. One of the authors used a term–'normal marital sadism'–to describe all the stuff we do to each other day in and day out that keeps us from having healthy relationships. I guess we had settled into normal marital sadism. I was just going through the motions, and I didn't have one damn clue what I really wanted."

She let that moment pass, then changed the subject. "I'm curious about that 'Don't be an ass" comment. Was that pretty typical?"

"I am quite sure that Lauren wrote that note after a couple glasses of wine. She never came close to swearing unless she'd had a couple drinks. That way of putting me down was pretty typical once she'd had a couple."

"So between March 6th and June 20th your divorce is proceeding. What's happening in the rest of your life?"

Brad laughed unhappily and sipped his coffee. "Remember all those middle management types that knew their jobs were protected? Yeah. I was part of the massive layoff last spring that made all the papers. Whole departments gutted. I was better off than most. I wasn't up to my eyeballs for a new boat or a lake place. I had money in savings, a pretty good cushion, even after the divorce. I drove a Toyota Tundra that had been paid off for a few years."

"Sounds like you're pretty conservative financially."

"I watched my folks scrimp and save to get out of debt half a dozen times. They were farmers, and lots of years they couldn't afford to put in a crop without borrowing against their life insurance policies, things like that. I learned a lot watching them, and I hate being in debt."

"Did you find another job right away?"

"Didn't even look. I knew a guy with a sleeping room above his garage. Got that for a couple hundred a month and rented a storage unit for most of my stuff."

"Is that where you're living now?"

"I've still got the storage unit in the Twin Cities for forty bucks a month. I've been in Duluth for a while now. Sleeping at a friend's place, mostly."

"What did you do with your time?"

"Drove myself crazy, to start with. Man was not meant to sit around all day doing nothing. Got pretty depressed."

"When did you get the idea of going to the Boundary Waters?"

"It started with going to church."

Ms. Norby raised her eyebrows, but said nothing.

"I got depressed enough I couldn't stand myself, and I thought about all those years sitting through Sunday School classes. My parents were good Swedish Lutherans, donchaknow. One Sunday morning I happened to be out getting groceries and drove past a church. I parked and walked in just in time for the sermon."

"And?"

"The text was from the gospel of Mark, where it says that Jesus was driven into the wilderness and he was with the wild animals and the angels took care of him. Pastor Bob preached about the transformative power of wilderness, and how God uses the wilderness moments in our lives to work for our good and his glory."

"Sounds like Pastor Bob made an impact. You remember that pretty clearly for a sermon almost a year ago."

"I was hooked. I went up to him after the service and asked if we could talk. He invited me over to his house for lunch, and I told him about the note, and the layoff, and the traffic lights. The whole deal. I said I couldn't even begin to describe what was going on until I heard him talking about being in the wilderness."

"Did Pastor Bob have some good advice?"

"He mostly listened. But it felt so good to talk to someone about it, I asked if he had any time that week that we could talk. I met with him three more times and just bent his ear. Finally I stopped in the middle of a sentence and said, 'Pastor, you've listened to me for about five hours now, all told. Don't you have anything to say?' He laughed and said it seemed like I needed to talk."

"Did he have any advice for you?"

"He did. He said that sometimes dealing with an emotional wilderness requires going into a physical wilderness. He talked about

Elijah after his conflict with the prophets of Baal and Moses after he murdered the Egyptian. Even Jesus went into the wilderness after his baptism. It made my brain hurt. I hadn't thought about these stories since Sunday school. And I never thought about them on an adult level, like they mattered in my own life."

"So then you went into the wilderness."

"Not so fast. Yes I did, but it took a long time to get there. Turns out Bob used to lead men's groups into the Boundary Waters through his church. He saw a lot of guys find something special out there. But, he said, it seems like you might need more than just a long weekend with the boys."

"What did he suggest?"

"He said he wondered if it would be a healing thing for me to do a solo trip. He said he'd done one once, for four nights, and it was a really challenging thing for him."

"What was so challenging?"

"I asked him that. Just being alone with himself, he said. He learned more about himself in those few days than he'd learned in four years of seminary. Honestly, he said, it almost killed him."

"And this sounded appealing to you?"

"Hell, no. I laughed in his face and said I was a full generation off the farm and way too entrenched in the suburbs to go play Daniel Boone. But I couldn't get the idea out of my mind. There's an REI. You know, big outdoors store..."

"I'm familiar with REI."

"...not far from the place I was staying. So I went in there and looked at their canoeing stuff, and camp stoves, and all the rest. I was completely clueless. But I felt stupid walking out without buying something, so I bought a book. It was written by a guy who solo canoed the Mississippi."

"That's not exactly wilderness once you get past the first couple towns."

"I never finished the book. I read the first two chapters, where he was making the decision to do it, how he got outfitted, and then how he got completely lost for a week in the swamps up near Bemidji, just downstream from Itasca Park. It was right after ice out so the water was high and it was cold. He said that week was the crux of the trip. If he could survive that week, he could do anything. I decided I'd go to the Boundary Waters."

"Did you work through an outfitter?"

"That first trip I did. I talked a lot with Pastor Bob about where to go and what gear to use and stuff like that. I did a little research online and went through an outfitter out of Grand Marais, off the Gunflint Trail."

"Which outfitter?"

"Place called Bear Trap Outfitters, on Poplar Lake. Turns out the owners were a couple 70's rockers and they got a big kick out of having 'BTO' logos on all their canoes. You know …"

"Bachman-Turner Overdrive. My older brother used to love them."

A half-smile crept into Brad's face. For the first time in the conversation Kim saw a light come into his eyes. She watched him as he looked across at her, imagining her as a younger sister. "How much older?"

She smiled and shook her head. "You said your 'first trip.' How many have you made?"

"Three, technically, though the papers never seemed to get that right. That first one… I booked the outfitter, got the permit, had them supply all the gear, talked on the phone with Pete, one of the owners at BTO. Explained what I was doing and he was a little cautious about sending me out alone. But it was early August, the Boundary Waters was full of campers, the weather was good, and I was going on easy routes."

"Where did you go?"

"Paddled right off BTO's dock into Poplar Lake. Got myself thoroughly lost in among the islands and bays and learned to use those Fisher maps and my compass in the first hour. Finally found the south side of the lake and the portages into Lizz and then Caribou, down Horseshoe and eventually into Gaskin. Did a base camp and explored a little bit on the lakes around there."

"How long were you in the Boundary Waters that trip?"

"Four nights. That's what Pastor Bob had done, and it seemed about right."

"Was it stressful?"

"Yes. And no. It was like I had the most peaceful time, externally, and all the pain and garbage inside was just churning the whole time."

"It must have turned out positive. You went back."

"Something in that experience caught me. I wanted more. It was this weird combination of hard physical work and absolute kick-back relaxation. I thought, this must be what it was like to be a hunter-gatherer before we invented farming. Kill a mammoth and you don't have to work for a month."

"Not many mammoths around anymore. And you had a pack full of freeze-dried food, I assume."

"Yeah, that bothered me some. I started wondering what it would be like to be in the wilderness away from the Boy Scout troops and the weekend warriors. What would it be like to go in long-term? The idea got stuck in my head and I'd find myself daydreaming about it pretty much constantly. How much could you legitimately find your own food? What would that even be like?"

"Is that why you went back the second time?"

"Pastor Bob gave me an old, dog-eared yellow book called *Camp and Trail Methods*. It was written back in the early 1900's before the invention of anything lightweight. This was written by a guy who got what it was to live in the woods, or at least to go in for a few months at a time."

"You wanted to go in without any modern gear?"

"Not at all. But the attitude is different. Those REI campers, they're trying to take all the conveniences with them. Butane curling irons and espresso makers and freeze-dried blueberry crumble dessert. I realized there was something about just going into the woods and being there without all the trimmings that appealed to me, deep down."

"You know, most people see a wilderness canoe trip as a vacation."

Brad chuckled. "That's exactly it, though. I wasn't looking for a vacation. I could have run off to Vegas or Costa Rica or pretty much anywhere. I was looking for something else. Healing? That's not exactly it. I was looking for something more than just a chance to relax. Restoration. Looking for myself, maybe. Identity. I saw a T-shirt that says, 'I've gone out to find myself. If I should return before I get back, please ask me to wait around as eventually I'll check in here again.' I felt like that. Like I needed to go find myself in a really literal kind of sense. Like maybe on one of those backcountry lakes, I'd paddle around a corner and there I'd be."

Kim's cell phone buzzed. Without looking away from Brad's face she said, "The Boundary Waters is a good place for that kind of searching." She glanced at her phone. "Mr. Swenson, we are starting to get to the parts of the story I really need to hear. Can we get together later this week?"

"My schedule is flexible. What works for you?"

She surveyed her cell phone. "Thursday, late afternoon? 4 pm?"

"How about we just make it dinner?"

She hesitated, then smiled. "Okay. You know Betty's in Canal Park?"

"Of course."

"Let's say five, then I'll have time to listen to the rest of your story. Thank you, Mr. Swenson."

"Looking forward to it, Ms. Norby."

Chapter Three

A half hour later, Kim Norby sat across the desk from a fifty-something man, lean, with dark brown eyes, a thin mouth and dark hair going gray around the temples. "What do you know about him, Kim?"

"His story is that he ran into Mac by accident up in the Boundary Waters. Mac befriended him somehow. I'm still digging into that. Then before he committed suicide, Mac gave this Brad Swenson a sealed envelope to hand deliver to me. He walked into my office with the envelope a few days later. The documentation in the envelope is unusual to say the least."

"Unusual is no surprise if it really comes from Mac."

"I know. I'm tempted to believe him, but there are some big 'what-if's' in this story."

"So what do you need from me?"

"I need to know what you can dig up about Brad Swenson. Is he who he says he is? Any history of suspicious activity? Any likelihood that he created the documentation and made it look like Mac's idea? Everything I could put together from our meeting this morning is in my notes." She handed three sheets of paper covered with her neat handwriting across the desk.

"Are you wondering if Mac's death was actually a suicide?"

"Of course. Mr. Swenson is the only witness."

"What about forensic evidence?"

"I don't know. What's even possible?"

"Pretty challenging at this point. You might find the campsite, and even the remains. But how much you can tell from all that, even if you had some high powered lab working on things, is anybody's guess. NCIS is mostly fiction unless you want to pour a lot of money into it, and everything from freezer burn to wolves is going to have made a mess out of Mac by now."

Kim looked down. "I know. But to be thorough I probably need to get someone in there, don't I?"

"Seems like the natural thing to do. You have anyone for that kind of work?"

"Maybe. It's kind of a long shot. If that doesn't pan out, I'll get back to you."

"Works for me. I'll do the standard background check and see what else I can dig up. Should be some good documentation down in the Cities to start with."

"Thanks, Al."

"Take care of yourself, Kim. And look hard at this guy before you let him get too close."

Kim looked hard at the older man. "You know something about this?"

One side of Al's weathered face rose in a lopsided grin she'd seen dozens of times over the years. "I know Mac's sense of... humor? Maybe destiny. When Mac got on a roll, he thought he was as powerful as God, and sometimes he was. But even Mac could make mistakes. All in all, though, that man had a gift, and he was usually right, even when he shot from the hip."

"Believe me, Al, I know." She was silent a few seconds, then added quietly, "That's what scares me."

He raised one eyebrow and watched her walk out into the cold March sunshine.

Chapter Four

Back in her office, behind closed doors, Kim made a phone call. The number on the far end rang, and rang, never going to voicemail, and just when Kim was about to hang up, a wispy female voice finally answered. "Hello?"

"Hi. I'm trying to reach Misty Jacobs."

"Misty? Hang on." There were muffled sounds of conversation in the background, an engine, what sounded like a dog barking, and several bumps and clicks. Finally another voice came on the line.

"This is Misty."

Kim cleared her throat. "Misty, this is Kim Norby. It's been a really long time."

A second of silence, then laughter. "Kim! How in God's name are you? You calling to tell me you're on your way up to visit?"

"Not right now, at any rate, though we might get there. I wasn't sure this number would even connect with you anymore."

"You should call more than once every decade, Kimmy. People move. Die, even."

"Actually, that's kind of why I'm calling."

The voice on the other line was flat, guarded suddenly. "What."

"Nobody you know. My boss died. He was winter camping in the Boundary Waters, and I'm not sure if anyone has been in to try to recover the body. You still do any of that kind of work?"

Silence. Then, "Not for a long time, Kim. That stuff all goes to the BCA or the FBI these days."

"I'd rather be a little more directly involved."

"Has the death been reported?"

"Not yet. I learned about it two days ago, and I've got no reason to believe there's any foul play involved."

"But you don't know for sure, do you." It was not a question.

"That's honestly why I want a look at the remains, whatever's left."

"Boundary Waters, a couple weeks back? Kim, you know that's not going to be pretty."

"I know. Wolves and crows and whatever else. But I'd like to get in there and take a look before things thaw."

"Going to have to make it fast, then. Any idea where exactly?"

"I should find out Thursday. You got any time to make a winter camping trip?"

"You know you ought to be going to the police. Forest Service, if it's in the Boundary Waters. Someone official. I'm not, not anymore."

"Misty, I'll explain all this if you'll see me. I need more than some sanitized report, for a couple reasons."

"Can you drive up on Saturday? With my hectic schedule, I'm not sure I can free up time for a drive to Duluth."

"Seriously?"

"Of course not. But I don't know if I trust my truck right now. Alternator's going bad."

"I can be there. What time?"

"Saturday. You remember how to find it?"

"Pretty sure I remember. I'll probably be there late morning. And, Misty?"

"Yeah."

"I'm sorry for not calling you for so long."

"Like hell you are, Kimmy. You're doing the upwardly mobile thing and got busy. And now you need me. See you Saturday. You got gear?"

"Yeah."

"Bring it."

19

Chapter Five

Kim pulled into the parking lot at Betty's at a quarter to five. On a Thursday evening it was still fairly quiet, though this was a popular spot. Tourist traffic on weekdays wouldn't become a real annoyance for another couple months, when RV's and oversized pickups pulling enormous boats filled the North Shore of Lake Superior. Duluth was still a fairly quiet town in March, though the college students always kept a place like Betty's buzzing. She got a booth out of the way–the head of a respectable bull moose hung on the wall overhead–and positioned herself to watch the door. Brad came walking in out of the sunshine a couple minutes before five, and she waved him over.

"How are you, Ms. Norby?"

She smiled and said, "One more day until the weekend, right?"

He shook his head. "I don't miss those days. I remember that whole idea that you organize your week around how much you dislike your job. I hate Mondays. Wednesday is hump day. Thank God it's Friday."

"Sad to say, that's the reality for most people. How do you organize your time these days?"

He grinned and shook his head. "It's a challenge, strange as that seems. Last summer it was terrible, and I've learned a few things since then. Processed a lot of junk. I had a counselor for a while who said life is like a room where we live. We all work hard to keep it more or less presentable, but we all have a closet. That's where we keep the things we can't control, the things that make us uncomfortable. He said counseling is a way to process those piles of stuff that aren't presentable."

"Interesting answer. So you organize your time around processing uncomfortable things?"

"I've spent a lot of time that way over the past year. You remember that old Paul Simon song? 'Fat Charlie the Archangel filed for divorce. He said, "Well, this will eat up a year of my life."' I guess for almost a year I've had a really interesting back and forth between stuff going on inside me that needs to be processed, and things that are happening externally that I need to deal with."

"Like what kind of externals?"

"Like being in the Boundary Waters, for one. So much in the wilderness involves things that need to happen externally. That's what makes it restful for so many people, I think. You go away from all your internal battles. At the same time you get away from all the electronic noise that keeps you from using your internal time. And with all the turmoil–losing my marriage, losing my job, figuring out the what and the why behind all that, I've had plenty to chew on inside."

"You've put some thought into this."

"I don't keep a television on for background noise anymore. That alone has freed up dozens of hours a week that I can use for honestly thinking about real things. I am very selective about how I medicate my pain. And along the way, just for fun, you have to decide trivial things like where you're going to live and whether to get a job or not."

The waitress came over just then and introduced herself as "Rosie" and asked if they wanted drinks. "I'd like a glass of Pinot Noir, and a water, please," Kim said.

Brad flashed Rosie a boyish grin and said, "You have Surly Abrasive?"

"Sorry, Furious is the only Surly we've got right now."

"How about Bell's Two Hearted?"

"Yep, we have that one on tap. Tall?"

"Sure."

As Rosie spun away toward the bar, Kim turned to business. "You told me a little on Tuesday about your first trip to the Boundary Waters out of Bear Trap Outfitters. If there's more I need to know about that trip, I'm all ears. Otherwise, I'm curious about what made you go back in the fall, and how you met Mac."

Brad considered for a moment. "I guess that first trip was pretty average. The only thing that really stood out aside from the whole first-time-in-the-backcountry experience–which was amazing–is a day trip I made that really got the wilderness hooks into me good. I was camped on Gaskin, and paddled west for half a day into some of the little narrow lakes off the beaten track back in there. Hensen, Omega, Kiskadinna Lakes. All long and narrow and not traveled much. I paddled and fished and on the way back, sun setting behind me, I stopped and watched a moose for about half an hour."

"How close were you?"

"About a hundred yards away, just pulled up on the shoreline in the shadows. It was on Omega. I hadn't done anything like that since I was a kid on the farm, and maybe not even then. It was powerful. Magical."

"Is that what made you want to go back?"

"No. Watching that moose was delightful, peaceful, life-giving. But what made me desperate to go back was the Christmas displays in the stores."

"What?"

"October 12th, I went shopping to get a few things. I was living pretty simply, volunteering some time at Pastor Bob's church, picking up a few odd jobs here and there, mostly bookkeeping for a friend who has an accounting business. They had the whole damn Christmas train wreck set up in the back quarter of the store, music playing on the loudspeakers. Paul McCartney, 'Simply Having A Wonderful Christmas Time.'"

Rosie appeared with their drinks. "Are you ready to order?"

Kim nodded at Brad. "I've been asking too many questions since you got here. I know what I want, but you haven't looked at the menu yet."

"You go ahead and order. I can figure it out by the time you're done."

Kim turned to Rosie. "I'll have the steak kabobs, medium rare."

"You want to upgrade to a whole surf-n-turf thing with a walleye fillet?"

"No, but I will have a cup of French onion soup."

"You want that out first, or with the meal?"

"First, please."

"And for you, sir?" Rosie turned to Brad, who was still scanning the menu.

"How is the lake trout?"

"Excellent. People rave about it."

"I'll have that, with sweet potato fries, please."

Rosie collected menus and bustled away. Kim turned back to work. "You don't like Paul McCartney?"

Brad laughed. "That's like saying I don't like Jesus, right? No, it's just that song. The Beatles are fine. Even most of his solo stuff is fine. I'm not big on Christmas pop in the first place, and that song is the worst of the worst. So I turned around and walked out of the store. I guess it was in that split second I decided to go back into the Boundary Waters for a fall trip."

"That's late in the year to go in."

"Last fall was so warm, remember? And October was about as summery as I've ever seen it. Gorgeous colors, warm days, cool nights, but no hint it was ever going to get really cold. I figured I could go in for two or three weeks and get inoculated against the Christmas season."

"Back to Bear Trap again?"

"Nope. I'd been doing a lot of thinking about it, and some talking to Pastor Bob. I picked up a used canoe from one of the outfitters on the Gunflint. They sell them off at the end of the season sometimes."

"What kind of a canoe?"

The question seemed to surprise him. "Souris River. A Quetico 17. Kevlar. The guy I bought it from said it's a good all around canoe and you can use it for solo paddling. That sold me right there. I looked at a couple of the little solo canoes, but I knew I might want to come back in for a longer trip sometime, and I wanted the capacity to do that."

"So you're living in the Cities, storing a new-to-you canoe in your storage unit, and one day Paul McCartney pushes you over the edge. What happens next?"

"I'd been dreaming about going back ever since August, so all along the way I'd started picking up some odds and ends. I got one of those cook stoves that you can operate just with twigs and sticks, and tried that a couple times to get used to it. I'd bought a life vest and paddles with the canoe, and I got a couple used Duluth packs from the same outfitter."

"You were thinking ahead that far?"

"I knew I was hooked on wilderness canoe trips, and it just made sense to start buying gear. I looked for deals: used canoes and packs, tents, that kind of thing. It didn't actually cost that much, and this wasn't just a fling for me."

"Are you normally prone to flings?"

His eyebrows went up. "No. Uh–no. I've always been pretty cautious. Well, not cautious. I like an adrenaline rush as much as the next guy, but I'm deliberate. Maybe that's a better word. And if I commit to something, I stick with it."

Kim thought about Lauren's note to Brad, and the silence began to stretch. Brad went back to his narrative.

"It took me a week and a half to get ready to go. Dehydrated a bunch of meat, bought some flour and salt and baking powder and a few other odds and ends. Did a little research on fall fishing and bought a few lures and a couple new maps."

"Where were you going in this time?"

"I looked at a few different lakes, but I'd only been in through Poplar, right? I looked farther up the Gunflint, and I called Pete at

BTO. He said if I wanted to be alone, there was still some late season traffic up on the Canadian border, so maybe avoid Saganaga. If I wanted to fish for walleyes but avoid crowds, probably enter through Seagull and then get into the backcountry south of the border. But really, he said, this time of year you can just write your own permit. No application process after October first. So drive around to the entry points and check out the parking lots. If you're looking for solitude, just go where you don't find cars. So I drove up on October 24th, stayed overnight at BTO, and paddled in on the 25th. I drove up to Seagull, almost at the end of the Gunflint, and there was one other car in the lot. That lot is made for at least two dozen cars. I figured those are good odds."

"How long were you planning to stay in?"

"About two or three weeks. I was going to watch the weather a little, of course, and play it by ear."

"Did anyone know where you were?"

"Pete from BTO knew what I was thinking. Pastor Bob had a vague idea. But no, nobody knew to come looking if I didn't show up."

"Seems a little … rash?"

"Yeah, looking back it does. At the time I just wanted to get away. And to be fair, I had a pretty good idea that I was taking on a huge challenge, and I was willing to deal with the consequences." That hung in the air for several seconds, and Brad continued. "My folks are both gone. I don't have kids. Nobody is really depending on me. Free as a bird, right?"

"Sounds lonely, to be honest."

Brad nodded slowly, watching her face. "That's the flip side of the coin."

She weighed that for a moment before she spoke. "You paddled in on the 25th. When did you meet Mac?"

"I'll tell you all about it. But I'm curious. What was your relationship with Mac?"

Kim looked into Brad's intense eyes for several seconds. This was not the script she intended to follow, but the question was clearly important to him. Fair's fair, she thought. "Mac was my boss. He was the founder and CEO of the McPherson Foundation, which he set up with his family's fortune thirty years ago, when he was in his late twenties. I was his Executive Director for the last twelve years."

Brad waited, but she didn't say anything more. "Well, that's important information. But what was your relationship with Mac?"

Kim nodded slowly. "Mac was a challenging guy to work for. You apparently spent time with him, so you maybe know what his personality was like. Brilliant, but always ready to go off like a firecracker, and then the explosion is over and you move on. Absolutely intense and committed to causes and people he cared about. Mac had a deep sense of responsibility to do good with his family's money. I respected him and cared about him."

Brad watched her face as she said this last, and his eyebrows climbed ever so slightly, but he didn't speak.

Kim finally went on. "Cared about him as a friend. And as someone committed to his work through the foundation. Mac could work himself into the ground, and I learned early on that he needed an intense way to get away from the stresses of work. I fully supported his need to get away and do solo wilderness trips. I would mind the store while he went away to recharge, most often to the Boundary Waters. Sometimes other places that were more remote."

Brad didn't speak, and he never looked away from her eyes. It was a little disconcerting, but Kim had worked with Mac's intensity for a long, long time. She held his gaze, and didn't flinch or look away.

"I'd been getting more and more worried about Mac lately. He seemed to be pushing harder when he was at work, but it wasn't just a healthy go-for-the-gusto kind of pushing like before. He was urgent about something, and I could never figure out what that was. Until I saw the contents of the envelope you delivered, I could only speculate about what that urgency might have been."

"You know that I don't have any idea what was in that envelope, right?"

"Yes, though to be fair I should tell you that the foundation will fact check your story, just to be thorough."

"I've been backgrounded before. And I would expect that. I'm delivering the last communique from the head of a massive non-profit. You people need to do your due diligence."

"Exactly. So one step in that is, I need to know your story. If you're okay with it, I'd like to record our conversation from here on in so I don't have to take so many notes."

"That's no problem by me. Honestly, Ms. Norby, I'm just the delivery boy here. But I get that you need to be thorough. Record away."

Kim worked with her cell phone for a few seconds, then set it in the middle of the table. Brad's response was perfect. But she was not yet sure if that meant he was exactly who he claimed to be, or if he was an exceptional actor. "Thank you. Just for the record, this is Kim Norby's conversation with Brad Swenson at Betty's Restaurant, March ninth. And Mr. Swenson, you consent to this recording?"

"I certainly do."

"Mr. Swenson, can you tell me how you first met Mac?"

"I paddled in through Seagull Lake on October 25th last fall. I loaded all my gear in the canoe. Three Duluth packs plus a smaller day pack. Put in at that nice boat landing on the east end of the lake, then southwest down the lake and across the big open part of the lake at the far end. It was a beautiful fall day. Most of the leaves were off the trees by that time, and there wasn't much wind. Sunny and pretty warm. I suppose almost sixty degrees. Beautiful. Portaged into Alpine. Took me three trips for each portage. Heavy clothes, lots of food, heavyweight sleeping bag. Bulky. Navigated my way through the twists and turns on Alpine and portaged down into Jasper, a couple more. I forget the names of the lakes. Then into Ogishkemuncie. It was a long day, and really hard work. I paddled halfway down that long, narrow lake and camped on one of the sites in the narrows. I knew I didn't have to worry about finding a site, since I was almost alone out there. I paddled until the sun started to head for the horizon, and then set up camp. It got chilly at night. I slept hard and woke up incredibly sore the next day, so I took a couple Advil and a rest day. Figured that's the luxury of a solo trip with no agenda, right? So I napped and fished and explored. Climbed up to the waterfalls on the slope south of Ogish. Beautiful. I'd read about them in a guide book. Absolutely gorgeous. And I had it all to myself. It was a little like a fairy tale, or like being Jeremiah Johnson."

"You didn't see anyone else?"

"I thought I spotted one other canoe far off on Alpine. There were a couple fishing boats on the east end of Seagull, in that part of the lake where they allow motors. But other than that, nobody."

"And did that frighten you? It doesn't sound like it."

"You've got to understand. I was so desperately hungry to deal with my pain by that time. Anything that seemed like it had any promise looked like a huge positive to me. So this solitude was like an angel calling my name."

"Most people just want the pain to go away."

"I know. Me, too. But I've been around that roundabout enough to know that you need to actually deal with it or it won't go away. You'll just numb yourself and do more damage later."

Kim nodded. "We're up to October 27th."

"That day I paddled out the west end of Ogish, through a bunch of little portages down to Kekakabic. That's a big lake, a long one. I was still pretty stiff and sore, and I got tired pretty easily. So I camped on the east end of the lake that night, just sort of set up camp and collapsed into bed.

"The next day was getting a little windy out of the south, but I loaded up my gear and started paddling. As I got farther out into the lake, I started having trouble keeping the canoe on course. I realized later that I'd loaded it too heavy in the stern, and the crosswind was catching my bow. At the time, though, I didn't have a clue why it was so difficult. So the wind pretty much wrenched me around the lake. There's a little bay on the north side, almost like a lagoon, with some islands protecting it from the south. I paddled in there and rested my arms for a while. The wind blew me in toward shore. There was a campsite there on my map, and it looked deserted. Fire grate and tent sites were high up on some rocky cliffs, maybe fifteen feet above the water, with a little canoe landing down below. I figured I'd pull in. There was a fallen tree just under the water by the landing, and I got hung up on it. About that same time, I saw back in the trees, away from the landing, that there was a canoe pulled up in the brush. Somebody was camped there, and I figured I'd better leave them in peace. I guess I twisted around too fast or something at the same time I was trying to get my canoe off that tree, and next thing I knew I was in the water, my canoe was upside down, and my Duluth packs were bobbing all around me. I started floundering around, even right next to shore, the water was too deep for me to touch, and finally swam all my stuff into the landing and dragged it up on shore. The water was cold. It had been cold enough at night, the water was down in the 40's, maybe. I was chilled bad, and started shivering like mad by the time I got my canoe pulled up. I fell down a couple times, broke some branches. Made a bunch of noise.

"All of a sudden, here comes this old guy down the trail from the top of the rocks, face red and yelling at me. 'Ass! You incompetent ass! What the bloody hell are you doing?' He waded into my dripping wet mess and stood there like an elementary school principal chewing out a student."

Kim couldn't stifle a smile. Brad did a pretty fair imitation of Mac. "Sounds like Mac in one of his moods."

"Yeah. He railed at me for a while, up one side and down the other, and finally stopped himself. Then he said, 'Leave most of your gear and get up by the fire grate. We'll have to get you warm. Which pack are your dry clothes in?' So I pointed out the right Duluth pack and he just looked at me. 'Well, haul it up on top, dammit! Get your heart pounding, get some warmth going. You're not hypothermic yet.' So I hauled my gear behind him up to the top of the cliff, and he was right. It started to warm me up. Eventually he built up his fire, I got dry clothes on, and wrung out my wet stuff."

"Did he kick you back out on the lake?"

"He thought about it. Talked to himself the whole time. Had a pretty good debate going, too. Finally he decided I'd better get my stuff dry before he 'evicted' me. So I ended up hanging my wet gear, pitching my tent, and staying over that night."

"Mac let you stay on his campsite?"

"Against his better judgment, he made very clear."

"That seems strange from what I know of him."

"I had never met Mac, so I don't quite know how to judge, but I think he wanted the company."

"That definitely doesn't sound like Mac."

"Not to say he was pleasant. He was rude and gruff and as difficult as possible. But every time I talked about packing up and getting out of his way, he'd tell me not to be a damned fool and to stay put. So I got dry, eventually, and got my tent up and such, and Mac made supper."

"*He cooked for you?* "

"Yeah. Fresh lake trout and instant mashed potatoes. Tasted like heaven."

Kim's jaw was still hanging open a little, and her eyebrows stayed on the top floor. "He cooked for you."

"I take it that's not like Mac."

"Not the Mac I knew. I've worked for the man more than a decade, and I've never known him to cook a meal outside a wilderness situation, and never, never for anyone else."

"He was a good cook."

"Mac was good at everything he did. That doesn't surprise me. It's the social part of things that I find shocking."

"To be honest, Ms. Norby, it seemed to me like he was struggling a little bit. Like he wanted the company, but he was so used to being gruff and antisocial that he couldn't let anyone know. He didn't quite know how to say what he really wanted."

"And how did you deal with that?"

"I had an uncle growing up that was a little like that after his wife died. He'd always made a growth industry of putting people off, but after she died he got desperate for human contact. I was his favorite nephew, and I learned to read his moods pretty carefully. He still had to come across like a porcupine, but there was something else, too. I used to call it his 'go away a little closer' mood. He needed contact with another human. Mac seemed kind of like that those first few days."

"Wait. How long did you stay on Mac's campsite?"

"That time, four nights, I think."

Kim sat back and shook her head, staring at Brad. "What did the two of you do for four days?"

"He educated me, to start with."

"Educated you?"

"Talked me through what it was like to be in the backcountry this late. Partly talked about tourists. That's what he called them. And how much he hated them. Seemed like he had a pretty clear picture of traffic patterns in the Boundary Waters, all with the idea of avoiding contact."

"That's how he'd go. He'd go in for a week or two at times he thought he could avoid seeing anyone."

"Yeah. He talked about that. Said bear hunting season was closed as of mid-October, so those damn fools were gone. Late season fishermen stayed closer to the entry points, he said. Distance paddlers stayed mostly to the border chain of lakes where they could make better time. Not many (here he'd give me a withering look) came into this area to bother him, and those that did just paddled right on by if he kept his camp hidden."

"Did he seem to resent you being there?"

"Sometimes, but again, that seemed like the porcupine thing. He didn't really want me to leave. I could tell."

"Do you have any idea why he might have wanted you there?"

Brad sipped his beer and shook his head slowly. "I think this is easier for me, Ms. Norby, than it is for you."

"How do you mean?"

"All I knew of Mac started that day he helped me out of the water. So I don't have his past patterns to get around. He just seemed like a man who was hurting and looking for company and didn't have a clue how to ask for what he really needed. I dealt with that. I got the impression he was somebody who knew how to get things done out in the world. A CEO type or something. Executive. He knew how to give orders and how to make his opinions known. But I knew he would never have survived in middle management where I used to work.."

A genuine smile started to grow across Kim's face. "No," she finally said, "I don't think he would have gotten very far in those annual review processes."

"He had a lot of opinions, and that's death in the corporate hairball."

"Lots of opinions. And more often than not, he was right." Kim took a sip of her wine, and seemed to hold that idea in her mouth for a few moments.

"How's the wine?"

"The wine? Oh. It's good. Decent. I'm no connoisseur, but I like it."

"That's what matters."

Rosie showed up with Kim's soup. "I'm going to try to eat this without getting it all over my clothes. I love French onion soup but it's a mess to eat. Would you please continue your story?"

"Gladly. So the first few days, it was just Mac playing Bear Claw Chris Lapp to my greenhorn Jeremiah Johnson." In response to Kim's blank look, Brad shook his head. "You might need to watch that movie. 'Jeremiah Johnson.' With Robert Redford. We actually talked a lot about it."

"About the movie?"

"Yeah. Every so often Mac would throw out a line from the movie. First time was when I scorched a flannel shirt I was trying to dry out. It started to smoke and I pulled it off the line over the fire really fast, slapping it against my leg to put out the sparks, and he just mumbled, kind of to himself, 'Didn't put enough dirt down. I seen it right off.' So I knew he knew the movie."

"Wait a minute. What about putting dirt down?"

"It's a line from the movie. Bear Claw is teaching Johnson how to survive in the wilderness in the winter, and they each put down a bed of coals, cover it with a layer of dirt, and stretch their furs out on it to go to sleep. But in the middle of the night Johnson wakes up and he's catching fire. Jumps up, smoking to beat the band, tearing off clothes that have caught fire. Bear Claw opens one eye and says, 'Didn't put enough dirt down. I seen it right off,' and he rolls over and goes back to sleep. He was a rough teacher."

"You're saying Mac was like that?"

"A lot like that. His lessons could be pretty hard, but he really wanted me to get it, really wanted me to learn what he was trying to teach."

"I've seen him treat people that way, now that you explain it. He always said if people weren't ready to learn, they couldn't be taught."

"Yeah. A couple times when I got things he was trying to teach, he'd quote that old Buddhist saying, 'When the student is ready, the teacher will appear.' That was about as close as he got to giving a compliment."

"I've heard him say that a time or two as well," Kim mused, poking at the layer of cheese on top of her soup. "What kind of things did he teach you?"

"Mostly how to respect the wilderness so it doesn't kill you."

"Specifics?"

"Don't overextend yourself if you don't want to deal with the consequences. Leave yourself some margin so you can deal with unforeseen circumstances. Don't work yourself into exhaustion. Plan ahead and prepare based on your planning."

Kim nodded, and Brad continued. "Understand, those are my words, summarizing things that got communicated over a day of fishing or repacking gear or telling stories around a fire while the rain fell. Mac never packaged those lessons in easy-to-digest bits. He'd tell a story, and leave you to puzzle out the moral."

"Sounds like Mac."

"We would not speak for two or three hours, just sitting or working on gear or fishing or whatever, then suddenly he was telling some long-winded story about the time he broke his leg on a portage because he was trying to carry too much gear and he slipped on a wet rock."

"Is that how he broke that leg? I always wondered. He came out of a two week trip three days early, and I'd never seen him do that before. Hobbled around in a cast for six weeks and he was absolutely insufferable. Even I didn't dare ask for details."

"He said he was six portages from his entry point when he fell. He had to rig a splint himself to get out, then have the doctors re-set his leg when he got to the hospital. That was another of the lessons he talked about without ever getting it tied up neatly. When things go bad, you just have to get plumb mad-dog mean and tough it out. If you give in, you neither live nor win."

"Jeremiah Johnson again?"

"No, that's me, quoting 'The Outlaw Josey Wales,' actually. I don't know if Mac knew that movie, but it's a good way to summarize the lesson he taught. It wasn't about being physically strong as much as it was about being mentally tough, able to keep going when you have to."

"Again, this sounds familiar."

"And I am convinced that's why he was so concerned about leaving margin. So that you didn't have to push yourself so hard except when it really mattered."

"Later, you got into situations where it did really matter, if the papers had it right. Can you tell me about some of your adventures after you and Mac split up? And how did you decide to leave him if he didn't want you to?"

"One day it seemed like Mac had made up his mind about me, and he started talking about places I might want to spend time on my solo trek, places he'd seen alone and enjoyed. It was a whole new kind of conversation. I don't know if he'd decided I was suddenly capable, or that I was ready to strike out on my own, or if he was just tired of company. But we spent a day talking about things I should do, or not do. I asked a couple times what he was planning, and the next morning I headed north, into the South Arm of Knife Lake. Alone."

"After, I assume, he shut down your questions about what he was planning?"

"No. He was actually quite forthcoming about where he was headed."

"What did he say?"

"He said he was headed down to the hills east of Disappointment Lake to get a place ready for his winter trip. He said that was usually part of his fall routine, was to get a spot prepped so he could hike in and winter camp for a couple weeks."

"He usually took a couple weeks late January or February. He loved winter camping."

"I asked if he wanted me to come along and help him out, and he said he figured I'd better get on about my solo trip, that he'd gotten in the way enough already. So I paddled north into Knife Lake, climbed up Thunder Point like Mac said I should. I puttered around for a few days, fishing for walleyes and lake trout and avoiding the main part of the lake along the Canadian border because Mac said there would be paddlers still coming through there from time to time, even though it was starting to get well below freezing a lot of nights. I was thinking one evening about paddling down to see Disappointment Lake, since Mac had mentioned it, and made up my mind that I'd leave the next morning. But that morning, just as I was ready to load my gear, Mac showed up."

"Mac came to see you?"

"Sure seemed like it. I asked him if he was lost, and he just looked back the way he had come and said, 'Maybe.' I told him I was about ready to head southwest, and he said, 'How about south? There's country down there that is pretty deserted this time of year.' I said that sounded just fine, and he said, 'Well, make us a pot of coffee and then we can hit the trail.' So that's what we did."

"You and Mac traveled together?"

"For two more days. We paddled south down to Fraser Lake, then east. We were camped on the west end of Little Saganaga. It's a beautiful lake! The next morning, Mac started packing his gear. 'Where now?' I asked. He took a long look at me and then said, 'I'm headed out, Pilgrim. Got some things back in civilization I need to do. If you're up this way around the second week in February, I might be on Disappointment Mountain.' And he left, paddling east."

"Any idea what the date was?"

"I went back and worked the chronology when the Forest Service people and reporters were questioning me later. That must have been November 5th."

Kim thought a moment, then pulled out her phone and spent some time on the touchscreen. "Mac came back into the office on November 7th, so that makes sense. Then the 8th we had that big snowstorm. But I suppose you know all about that."

"Yeah, I had a front row seat for that. But the 6th was a pretty critical day for me. That was the day I wrecked my canoe."

"I read about that. How did it happen?"

"Stupidity, mostly. Temperatures had been dropping and most mornings there was a little ice in the shallows. I realized I needed to start heading back toward civilization. So I started moving east, in no hurry. I portaged around the rapids between Little Sag and Mora, loaded my gear into the canoe, and stepped back up on the rocks to grab my paddle and life vest. It had been windy for a few days, so I tried to be cautious, but I let my guard down and a gust caught my canoe. Pushed it out away from the landing. My canoe floated out into the current while my back was turned. It all washed down the rapids. The canoe caught sideways on a couple rocks and the force of the water just folded it in half. A couple big punctures and a pretty serious tear where it folded."

"What about your gear?"

"Mostly it washed down the rapids back into Little Sag. I found pretty much everything, but it was beat up and wet and torn, and I had to get soaked and really, really cold to recover it. So I gathered it all up and got dry clothes on and carried my gear up through the woods to a campsite on Mora. Spread everything out, built a big fire. Knew it would take me a couple days to get everything dry, and I'd have to figure out if I could patch the canoe or if I was walking out somehow. I wrecked mid-morning, I suppose, and it took me the rest of the day to get my gear out of the lake and up to that campsite. By that time I was exhausted. I set up my tent and dried out my sleeping bag as best I could. It had stayed pretty dry in my pack, and that probably saved my life. I spent a miserable night trying to sleep and trying to stay warm. I had gotten pretty chilled. The next day I built up my fire, strung clotheslines, and started drying things out. There was a stiff east breeze blowing right into my campsite. At first I figured that was a helpful thing. The east wind should have been my first clue. The next morning, the 8th, the bottom fell out of the temperature, and the blizzard hit."

"What did you do?"

"I guess I was fortunate or blessed, or something, that I'd spent the day before drying things out. When the first snowflakes started I pulled most of my gear into my tent and got my warm stuff out, reorganizing, stuff like that. I could tell the temperatures were dropping, and I grew up in Minnesota. Figured it might get nasty. That day I mostly hunkered down in my tent. Each time I stepped outside the snow was half a foot deeper than the last time. The wind switched to the northwest, so I was a little more sheltered, but it started drifting pretty heavily, too. Blew and snowed for three days solid, and the temperature dropped to about fifteen above."

"I can't imagine what that felt like, being completely alone, many days from any kind of help, stuck in a tent, with the snow piling up, and a wrecked canoe."

Brad smiled, and Kim thought the smile looked more than a little haunted. He looked out the window toward Lake Superior as he began to speak. "The fear came in waves," he said. "I'd be fine for a few hours, and then I'd start to feel the walls closing in, like the wind and the ice were coming for me. I've never been prone to panic attacks, but I suppose that's what happened. My heart rate would just skyrocket. I'd work through a wave of fear, fighting it off or just enduring it until I could breathe again, then I'd be fine for a little while. Then we'd do it all over again. Rinse and repeat. I can understand how the Ojibwe came up with the idea of the 'windigo,' the ice monster that freezes your heart. It felt like I met him out there during that blizzard."

"How did you get through it?"

"The stories say that in order to kill the windigo, you have to become the windigo. There's some wisdom in that. You have to turn your heart to ice to kill the windigo. Looking back I think that meant I had to put down my fear and just do what needed to be done. I had to turn my heart to ice rather than give in to the fear."

"But what needed to be done in that blizzard?"

"I needed to not go insane. That was my biggest problem. I started trying to remember things. Lyrics to old songs, all the words to the Lord's Prayer or the Apostles Creed from church services when I was a kid, the preamble to the Constitution, the theme song from

Gilligan's Island, stuff like that. Anything I could force myself to remember, just to keep my mind busy. And it would work for a few hours at a time. I started to get hoarse from singing to myself. I started trying to remember every word from Pastor Bob's sermon that first Sunday, about Jesus going into the wilderness. I went through every single word of Lauren's note to me, forward and backward."

"I can't imagine."

"I'm glad. Nobody needs to go into that place."

"You did."

"It's like Mac had been teaching me. If you lose control at a moment like that, you neither live nor win. You have to be willing to do the hard thing, to push yourself. And in that blizzard, the battle was a mental fight to keep a hold on my mind. People who have never done anything like that don't get it. I read a Tom Clancy novel once that included the Soviets using sensory deprivation tanks to torture people. I think my mental battle was a little like that."

"That lasted three days?"

"Roughly. Sometime the third night the wind dropped, and the snow must have stopped. I fell asleep. I was exhausted, and I hadn't slept much during the blizzard. I woke up in a full-out panic because I couldn't breathe. It's a miracle I didn't tear the zipper out of my tent getting out of it. The snow had drifted in a few inches over the top of my rain fly, and it was cutting off most of the air exchange. Kept me warm, but I needed to get out and push the snow away from the top of my tent, at least a little, so I could breathe inside."

Kim was wrapped up in the story, hanging on every detail, when Rosie appeared with their food. "Sorry these took so long, folks. The kitchen messed up your steak kabobs, I'm afraid, so I just had them remake both orders so you'd get your food at the same time. I hope that's okay."

They both busied themselves for a few minutes with silverware and condiments and napkins. Brad was peering at Kim, brow furrowed just a bit, as she tasted the first of her kabobs. She noticed his expression, swallowed carefully, and finally asked, "What is it?"

"I'm just wondering. You said Mac came back to work on the 7th of November. Did he seem different at all? Odd?"

Kim considered, remembering. "He seemed preoccupied, I guess. There were a couple important funding questions we needed to work on, and he didn't even seem interested in them. He had something else on his mind."

"He didn't seem more... I don't know, tender, maybe, than usual?"

Kim laughed out loud. "In a million years, I would never use the word 'tender' to describe Mac. No, he certainly didn't seem tender. But preoccupied, definitely."

"Do you know what was on his mind?"

"I have a couple theories, based on the contents of the envelope you brought to me last week. At the time I had no idea."

"Care to share?"

"I am afraid I can't, not right now. There are some items in that envelope you delivered that need to remain confidential for the moment."

Brad laughed. "Maybe I should have steamed it open. I'm a terribly curious person."

Kim grinned, just a little. Brad saw the grin and leaned in, his eyes crinkling at the corners. She retreated behind her professional facade. "You mean you didn't open it up and read it?"

"It was none of my business. I was just the courier. I figured Mac sealed it for a reason. And as you know, I owed him a great deal."

"Of course. You seem to be an honorable man, Mr. Swenson. I spend most of my days dealing either with lawyers concerned with crossing i's and dotting t's, or with people seeking money from the Foundation. Honor is a rare pleasure."

"That's sad."

"I'm afraid it is."

They ate in silence for a few bites. Kim put down the tangle of thoughts that kept trying to get to the surface of her imagination and forced herself back into the past. "Back to your story. You're camped on Mora Lake, the blizzard is over, but now you're dealing with a couple feet or more of snow. What happens next?"

Brad took a sip of his beer. "I wasn't able to patch the canoe enough to keep it watertight. I had some duct tape in my pack, but not enough to take care of both gouges and the tear. Besides, the lake was starting to ice up in a big way, and I worried that trying to paddle through the ice would tear any patches off. And the tape is great stuff, but it doesn't stick well in the cold and wet."

"Mora is quite a ways inside the Boundary Waters. What were your options?"

"I figured I needed to go northeast, somehow. I spent time looking at my maps. That's one of the things I did during the blizzard, until I used up one of my flashlight's batteries, and that scared me a little bit. So I left the maps alone until I could look at them in daylight.

But it just made sense to try to get back to the Gunflint Trail if I could. The only question was, paddling or walking?"

"Doesn't sound like paddling was an option."

"Right. Once I figured that out, I had to think about whether it was reasonable to wait for the lakes to ice over so I could walk on the ice, or if I needed to fight through the woods."

"How long would it take for the lakes to freeze?"

"That's just it. I had no idea. Maybe it would take another month, if the temperatures climbed. But it seemed like it was staying cold, and at least along the edges of the lakes the ice was getting pretty sturdy. I suspect all that snow falling into the water acted like a lot of tiny ice cubes, among other things. I started looking at my gear, trying to decide what I needed to bring out, or if I could leave some things there. In the end, I weaned myself down to two packs worth of gear. My food supplies had been dwindling anyway, so there was a lot less weight to carry there. But I still needed all my warm gear, for certain. I could have left my equipment pack, but I'd have needed some of that, even walking out. In the end, I used the canoe like a sled and took everything with me."

"Did you wait for the lake to freeze up?"

"I took a day to work on my gear and to plan a route. The ice seemed to be forming pretty well, but I knew I wouldn't be able to walk across the middle of the lake for quite a while yet. So I started working my way around the shoreline. It was frustrating. The route was so indirect. I had to start out working my way northwest when I wanted to go east, following every little bit of the shoreline, things like that. Mostly I walked on the land and dragged the canoe across the ice that was forming. Mentally it was incredibly challenging. But the air was clear and cold, so if I could be patient, here and there I could walk along the new ice. The shore itself was full of snow. Pulling that loaded canoe through two or three feet of snow was about impossible. After I played with that, trying different things and watching the ice growing stronger, I decided to stay put for another day or two. I caught a few fish and ate them, and made up a bunch of pancakes that I could eat on the trail. I organized my gear so I could hopefully make as much progress in a day as possible. I finally started circling the lake on the ice three days after the blizzard ended, on the 14th."

"And did that work like you hoped?"

"I didn't fall through the ice, though I had a couple near misses. Very quickly I learned to watch for creeks emptying into the lake and keeping water open near their mouths. I'd have to float the canoe past those, and it would take on water through the holes I hadn't been able to patch. Where the ice was thicker I would try walking on it. I had read somewhere about carrying a long pole just in case, so a couple hours into dragging that canoe along the ice, I stopped and cut myself a pole. I was careful. Took my time. That first day I only made a couple miles."

"Sounds challenging."

"The ice was nerve-wracking, and the portages were exhausting. I finally got the portages down to a system. I'd take a pack and walk the length of the portage through the deep snow, leave the pack at the far end, then walk back. Then I could load the remaining pack in the stern of the canoe and drag it along the trail I'd broken. That was the easiest way through."

"Doesn't sound easy."

"Nothing in the Boundary Waters is easy, especially not in the winter. After two days I'd come as far north and a little east to Brant Lake, right on the edge of the Boundary Waters proper, but there were still a couple lakes to travel to get to a resort or a road. It was the 17th that I walked into Tuscarora Outfitters and thankfully, there was someone there when I came tugging my broken canoe up off the lake."

"The news reports said you had some frostbite, but otherwise you were okay. Is that true?"

"I actually didn't have much frostbite. A little bit on my toes, I guess. I didn't really have good footwear for winter camping. I think the amount of physical work, and the fact that I was moving most of the time and my blood was circulating, helped. After an overnight stay in the hospital, they pronounced me fit to travel and let me go."

Rosie returned just then and asked if they had saved room for dessert. "Not for me," Kim decided, "but Brad, feel free. I would like a cup of coffee, though. Black."

Brad considered the dessert menu, but said, "I think I'll have black coffee as well. Thanks." Rosie took the dessert menus away and promised to come promptly with coffees.

Brad turned his attention back to Kim. "Thank you."

"For what?"

"You finally called me Brad. Thank you."

"Sorry. I didn't intend to. Must be the wine." Kim held up her empty glass as if it was Exhibit A in evidence.

"Thank goodness for Pinot Noir, that's all I have to say. You keep calling me Mr. Swenson and I keep feeling like we're doing my quarterly review."

"I'm sorry. There are just some dynamics to this situation that are easier for me if I keep a sense of professionalism."

"I'm all for professionalism. Just call me Brad while you're being professional."

"I can live with that."

Their coffees arrived, and Kim continued. "You may be interested to know that when your story made the news, Mac was extremely attentive."

"I would imagine so. He'd just spent days with me in the Boundary Waters."

"He never let on about that, though. That's part of what surprises me now. He never told me he knew you. He followed the news stories and got his maps out to see where you'd been and pieced together what the different press releases and newspaper and TV stories told. He would look at the maps like he was putting together a jigsaw puzzle, and he'd ask me what I thought of the whole thing."

"What *did* you think of the whole thing?"

"That varied based on the day. When your story first broke, it sounded like just another overconfident weekend warrior who got lucky, surviving the consequences of their own hubris."

"Don't sugar coat it, really, I can take it."

Kim looked down at the table and grinned self-consciously. "Sorry. But you know what I mean. Every fall there's the deer hunter who wanders off into a swamp and comes out like a hero two days later after the rescue crews and the helicopters have spent thousands of man-hours looking for him. Or the guy who wanders off a hiking trail because he doesn't know how to tell direction in the woods, and if he comes out alive everyone is thrilled. Initially I figured you were the same story all over again, just without the rescue crews and helicopters."

"No one knew I was missing. Why would they look?"

"That was one of the first things about your story that caught my attention. Mac actually pointed it out to me. There was no search, no public investment in finding you. You just survived and walked out, and then it seemed like you were wondering what all the fuss was about."

"That's exactly what I was wondering. Honestly, if it hadn't been for that reporter with the Duluth *Tribune* getting a head of steam about what a great story this was, I don't think anyone would have payed attention. Based on his writeup, the Forest Service decided they needed to question me, and the DNR got involved, and then the TV stations in the Cities picked it up."

"Was there any fallout from your fifteen minutes of fame?"

"A little. Not much. Pastor Bob just shook his head about the whole thing, said he was glad I hadn't died out there because he'd have felt responsible."

"Pardon me for asking, but did you hear anything from Lauren when all that broke?"

"Not a thing. I doubt she even noticed, and if she did, she didn't care."

"That seems sad."

"Maybe. I wouldn't have expected anything different."

Kim absently looked at the time on her phone, and was suddenly startled. "Oh, my word. It's nearly eight pm!"

Brad grinned. "Time flies."

"Okay, Brad, I'm sorry. I really need to get to the part of the story where you find Mac later in the winter."

"Are you sure you don't want to just set up another time to talk next week?"

"No, I–I can't. I have some things that ... Please, can you just give me an overview? I'm enjoying all the details, but I'm sorry for dragging this out so long."

"You're a great listener. It's a pleasure to have someone genuinely want to know the story, and not for a news article."

"I do, but I have a sense this next part will be critically important in a couple ways. Can you tell me about finding Mac later in the winter?"

"Short version?"

"Please. Maybe we can go back later and fill in some of the details."

"I'd like that. Short version is, I came back to civilization, endured the media attention, calmed the Forest Service down when they realized they hadn't done anything wrong and I hadn't left a mess for them to clean up, and then Christmas hit me in the face like a baseball bat."

"I sense a theme here."

"I love Christmas, don't get me wrong. My hangup is the one you always hear: I hate the commercialism, the jingles, the hypocrisy of it."

"So you went winter camping."

"I gritted my teeth and got through the holidays. I was house-sitting for a guy here in Duluth. Actually, the same place I'm staying now. He winters in Tucson, and he invited me to keep an eye on things for him for a few months. All the while, though, the beauty of the Boundary Waters in the snow kept playing like a movie behind my eyeballs. Constantly. After New Years I made arrangements, invested in some better cold weather gear, and made plans to go back in. I had some obligations in January, and I needed to get used to the snowshoes and the other gear I'd bought. So that took a couple weeks. Plus, I wasn't excited about being around during the run-up to Valentine's Day. And Mac's words about the second week in February rang in my mind, too. I thought it would be fun to see him again, fun to surprise him."

"Valentine's Day. You have holiday issues."

"No doubt."

"And you knew where Mac would be?"

"He had told me he'd be on Disappointment Mountain. So I did a little research and decided to go out of Ely this time. I made arrangements to leave a car at an outfitter on Snowbank Lake, so it was just a couple miles across Snowbank and one portage to Disappointment Lake, then across that one to the mountain."

"It's not really a mountain."

"You know it?"

She nodded. "I've seen it."

Brad considered this a moment and nodded. "No. It's not a mountain. It's the biggest hill around, though, and there are hiking trails that cross it. So I got in, set up a camp on the east side of Disappointment Lake, and started snowshoeing the hiking trails. There had been several inches of fresh snow, so I didn't have any tracks to follow. I just wandered the woods for a couple days. The third day, I saw a plume of smoke rising up out of the trees up on the southeast side of the mountain. I hiked as close as I could and bushwhacked my way up the slope the rest of the way. Once I was in the trees I couldn't see where the smoke was, but eventually I'd find a clear spot where I could get my bearings. Eventually I found the fire, and there was Mac, pointing a rifle at me."

"A rifle?"

"A Ruger Mark VII .30-06. Beautiful gun. Stainless steel barrel, laminated stock, variable three-to-nine power scope. Pointed right at my chest. Then he recognized me. Seemed almost disappointed to put the rifle down. 'Swenson' was all he said."

"Was he surprised to see you?"

"Didn't seem like it. He had invited me, you recall."

"Months before. And you had almost died in a blizzard since then. Why would he think you would come back, in the winter, and show up in his camp?"

41

"I didn't almost die in that blizzard. I got a little bit of frostbite."

Kim just looked at him for several seconds. She felt perplexed, and a little bit annoyed. What was that all about, she wondered? Why the strong emotional reaction, right here, right now? She commanded her face to return to at least the appearance of calm, and met Brad's eyes. He finally cleared his throat and glanced down at the table, then back at her.

"Mac seemed distracted, to be honest. But I don't think he was displeased that I showed up. Once he put the rifle down, I asked him how he was. He just shook his head and turned back toward his campsite. He'd set up in a little clearing southeast of the summit, kind of at the edge of a little marsh. It was still a couple hundred feet above the lakes, and it was far off the hiking trails, so he was pretty well concealed."

"Tell me more about where his camp was located."

"Thinking of taking a trip?"

Kim met his eyes once again. He did not look amused, or angry, but in a way she couldn't quite place, there was some kind of intensity to his face. "I need to know as much as possible, to cover all the contingencies."

Brad nodded slowly. "Southeast of the summit, there's a swampy area. It looks on the map like a small lake or a pond, but that's set in a swampy depression. At the south end of that swampy area, the beginnings of a creek flow off to the south. I imagine even in the summer it's just a trickle, but there's an opening in the trees where that creek heads southward out of the swamp. Mac's tent was set up on the southwest side of that opening, right at the edge of the swamp, up against the treeline."

"Can you sketch what the opening looked like, and where the campsite was?"

Brad took the pen she handed him and began to draw on a napkin.

"Mac was camped on the north side of the trees, then?"

"No, his camp was facing east, just a few yards." He pointed with the pen. "Right here. I don't think he'd get much sun there, if that's what you're thinking. Just a couple hours in the middle of the day. That seemed odd to me. I tried to set up my campsites so the sun would hit it and at least warm things a tiny bit during the day."

"I'm just trying to get a sense of where exactly the campsite was. That's very helpful. Thank you."

"Listen, I know you have to do your due diligence. I will admit, I've done a little poking around on the web, and I understand that Mac had more money than I ever imagined. I'm sure his death causes some pretty big legal issues."

"The hope is to prevent any such legal issues. Mac left his matters very carefully structured in case anything happened to him. There were just a few key decisions that remained to be made. But legally, those things shouldn't be any problem. They just complicate matters for the Foundation during the transition."

"Will you take over for Mac? Or does he have other family members that will manage the non-profit?"

Kim shook her head slowly, watching Brad's reactions. "I'm not wired for the executive job. I'm a strong number two, but I don't want the corner office. And Mac had no close family, certainly none he wanted running the foundation. He was crystal clear about that. And his succession plans are drawn up, legal and otherwise, to make sure of that."

"Sounds like Mac was pretty good at planning for contingencies."

"He was, and where he missed details, I helped him out. I'm confident this transition will go smoothly, if we can, as you put it, complete our due diligence."

"Ms. Norby, I want to help any way I can. This conversation has already taken up the lion's share of your evening. What else do you need to know tonight?"

"Can you sketch for me what happened next, until you discovered Mac's body? I really appreciate the time you're taking to fill me in. This is incredibly helpful. And personally, it gives me some closure as well. As gruff as he could be, Mac was my friend."

"Grieving is hard work."

"It is. And, Brad?"

He looked her full in the face for a long moment. She could feel the wine making her a little lighter than normal, not enough to do any of the dangerous things alcohol does to decision making, but just enough that she could feel a little bit of the edge in what she said next. "Fair is fair. If you're Brad, I get to be Kim."

The lines at the edge of his eyes crinkled, then the corners of his mouth turned up a tiny bit. "Okay."

She sipped her coffee, which was lukewarm by now. "Well. Now that we have that figured out, tell me: What happened next?"

"I spent a few hours with Mac that day. He told me about coming into the backcountry early in the month, pulling a sled with some of his gear, and finding the cache where he had left supplies back in the fall. He seemed pretty content, like he was enjoying the solo time. But like I said, he seemed distracted. Not weak, exactly, but ... well, maybe a little bit weak. As weak as a man can be who just pulled all his gear on snowshoes five miles into the backcountry in a Minnesota winter."

"I saw that same distraction in him all winter, until he left for that solo trip. Until you brought that envelope, I had no idea it was anything more than burnout, fatigue, what have you."

"What did you find in the envelope?"

Kim shook her head. "I'm afraid it's best if I don't share anything from what Mac sent me until you've finished your story. I want to get your experience, your memories, without them being affected by what I've read."

"Fair enough." Just then Rosie swept by with coffee refills, and Brad continued. "When I left to go back to my campsite that night, Mac was looking out over the clearing. He didn't look at me, but he said, 'Swenson, I hope you'll come back tomorrow. It pains me to say so, but I'm craving company.' I offered to move my gear up closer to where he was, but he shook his head. 'If it's okay with you, I'm looking for a neighbor, not a roommate.' I said that sounded just fine, and I'd see him the next day.

"For a couple days it was like that. I'd hike up about mid-morning, we'd talk, or just sit, or whatever. Then an hour or so before sunset, I'd excuse myself and head back to camp."

"What did the two of you talk about, when you talked?"

"Winter. Wolves. Why the moose numbers were decreasing. The advantages of different kinds of gear. The way the full moon looked on the snow when there was no street light for twenty miles. What it must have been like for the ancient Greeks to stare up at the stars and make up all those stories about the constellations before Edison invented artificial lights. Fishing. Poetry. What it was like for the natives on this land before the whites came. Movies."

"Sounds like a wide variety of topics."

"Mac was looking for a neighbor. Not a soul-mate. But he could carry a hell of a conversation."

"So you came by each day, and you were neighborly. How many days did this go on?"

"Nine, ten days. A couple times I told him I was taking the day off, going to make a day hike some other direction. I got the sense he was a little disappointed when I took a day for myself. When I showed up the day after being gone, though, he didn't say anything about it. Just seemed relieved to see me."

Kim felt a knot in her stomach. "That doesn't sound like the Mac I knew. Or maybe it does, but it sounds like he was in tremendous pain of some kind."

"Maybe. Other than being quiet, he played it pretty close to the vest. Then we get to February 24th. I had spent the last three days with Mac. I just had a sense he needed the company, I don't know. But that afternoon he seemed up, almost cheerful. A little more alive than he had been. As I was getting ready to head down the mountain to my own campsite there was a light snow falling, nothing much, just flurries, and he clapped me on the shoulder and said, 'Swenson, you're an awfully good neighbor. I'm not a social guy, but I want to tell you it means a lot to me, you coming up here like this. Have you seen the waterfall up on Cattyman Lake, where it empties into Gibson? It's a good day trip. Head up there tomorrow and have a look around. The waterfall gets pretty spectacular in the winter, with all the ice. Take some pictures.' I said that sounded like a good idea, and maybe I'd do that, depending on the weather, but I'd see him the day after. He didn't say anything to that.

"I was halfway down the trail when I heard the shot. I knew those woods by that time, and I knew it couldn't have come from anywhere except Mac's camp. I turned around and went back up the trail, back up to his campsite. There, sitting next to his tent, I found Mac sitting against a tree. He had set the rifle out in front of himself, stock on the snow between his knees, and put the muzzle under his chin. It hadn't made a terrible mess."

"Was he dead when you found him?"

Brad was silent a long moment, eyes fixed on his coffee cup. "Yeah. He was dead. Still warm, but dead. I checked him to see if there was anything I could do, laid his body down next to the tree. That's when I noticed the note."

"Note?"

"A folded piece of paper sticking up out of the chest pocket on his coat. I pulled it out... well, here." He reached in his back pocket and pulled out his wallet. From it he extracted a folded piece of paper and handed it to Kim. She unfolded it slowly, looking carefully at it, caught somewhere between the emotions she would ascribe to a forensic pathologist, a penitent praying before a holy relic, and a bereaved widow.

She opened the sheet and saw Mac's handwriting, but weaker and threadier than she remembered. It read,

Swenson,

A man's death may be the most personal thing he possesses. Talking with you about this decision would have made me doubt myself, and put too much on your shoulders, so I figured I'd do it this way. Sorry to put the aftermath on you like this. I'm taking the coward's way out, I guess. If you're willing, there is a sealed manila envelope in my tent. Whenever you head back to civilization, please hand deliver it to Kim Norby at the McPherson Foundation in Duluth. She will take care of it from there.

I ask that you not move my remains. I like this spot, and the wolves and crows will see to my burial. Keep the rifle if you will, though I know that's a little weird now, and any of my gear that you can use. It's yours. The Forest Service will probably want it cleaned up if they learn of it, and I'm afraid I'm asking you to handle that as well. I trust your judgment.

You've come far, Pilgrim. Were it worth the trouble?

Mac

I will arise and go now, for always night and day
I hear lake water lapping with low sounds by the shore;
While I stand on the roadway, or on the pavements grey,
I hear it in the deep heart's core.

She read it three times, slowly. Tears filled her eyes, and she took a deliberate moment to wipe them away and regain control. "There's a smudge near the bottom of the page," she said. "Is that —"

"It's blood. Mac's. I pulled my gloves off when I found him and I must have gotten some on my fingers, and then I handled the note."

"There's a lot to unpack here."

"For sure."

"Brad, would you mind if I kept this and had it analyzed? Check the blood and handwriting and all? Once it's checked out I'll get it back to you."

"I figured you'd need to do that."

The silence stretched out between them. Kim searched Brad's face, wondering what he was feeling about all this. He did not show emotion readily, but she had long experience getting past the tiniest of signals to read a difficult man's heart. Mac had never worn his more vulnerable emotions openly, and frankly the note surprised her in its frankness. Its tenderness. She felt an undercurrent of jealousy rising up in her, an ugly bilious thing that envied Brad his connection to Mac's heart. She'd only briefly wondered about a personal relationship with Mac, early on, and quickly set that aside. He had been a powerful, enigmatic man, a strong man, and she respected him deeply. But he was not a safe man, emotionally speaking. And so she had kept her distance. But Brad had obviously connected to him in a few brief days in the wilderness, and she felt like she was on the outside of their conversation, on the outside of this note. As she searched his face, she realized his eyes were calm. An openness, a striking lack of self-protection gazed back at her. Some of his walls were down, and that presence, that immediacy, pulled her strongly. But she still had work to do.

"You had gone quite a ways down the trail before you heard the shot and came back. It must have been close to dark by then. What did you do?"

His eyes never left hers, and she willed herself not to look away. "Once I figured out what Mac had done, I just stayed there with him."

"All night?"

"All night. I pulled his sleeping bag and pad out of the tent and stayed there next to him through the night. Sometime in the middle of the night I got chilled and built up a fire."

"Did you sleep?"

"I dozed a few times, but not really. I was starting to drift off as the fire burned down, and a pack of wolves started howling to the east. I woke up and listened to that for a while, and an hour or so later the sky started to get light."

"And the next day?"

"I straightened things up as best I could. Put Mac's gear back in his tent. Puttered around the camp for a while. Finally realized I really didn't want to leave, so I just stayed there again that day, and the next."

"And Mac's body was just laying there?"

"I wrapped it with a blanket from his tent, but yes." He looked down, looked out the window at the lights on the harbor, looked back at Kim. "I guess I felt like I was bound by his request not to move his body. I wanted to do something different, but what to do? He wanted to go back to the earth, and who was I to deny him that?"

"Did you think about bringing his body out?"

"Of course I thought about it. Have you ever read that Jack London book, *White Fang?*"

"No."

"It starts out with two guys with a dog sled in Alaska bringing another guy's body out of the wilderness in a coffin strapped to the sled. He was some important man, apparently, Lord somebody, and they felt like they needed to bring his body out. A wolf pack ate all their dogs and one of the men. The last man survived, but just barely. But the wolves didn't get the dead man."

"You were worried about the wolves?"

"No. Not really. But I think the point of the story, at least that part of the story, is the foolishness of catering to the dead when they're beyond care. The living have to tend to the living."

She said nothing, and Brad continued with an intensity that surprised her. "Maybe that's what Jack London is getting at in the whole book: There is a brilliance, a vibrance, to relationships of living beings. Love–and loyalty, and action and connection–it's what makes this existence meaningful. It's what makes healing possible. But so often we throw effort after foolishness, giving our love and loyalty to dead things. We try to change the past or guarantee the future, and we completely miss the present. We live on anxiety instead of joy."

Kim pondered those words for a moment. There was a lot going on behind Brad's face, behind those guileless eyes, obviously. Was he telling her the truth? She had a lot of work to do before she could answer that question in any definitive sense. Mac had been a shoot-from-the-hip judge of character, and he was very rarely wrong. He had trusted Brad deeply. Of course, Kim didn't mention that the letter from Mac in the manila envelope Brad had delivered to her began with the caveat that if the envelope showed signs of tampering or had been opened, she was to pursue a very different course of action. The envelope had been intact, with no signs of damage she could see. That was a mark in Brad's favor, she supposed.

"You sat with Mac's body for two days after you found him. What then?"

"I had slept in Mac's tent the second night, as it got pretty cold. And I suppose some of the shock had worn off, but I still didn't feel quite right about leaving Mac alone. But that morning I woke up with my mind made up that it was time to bring you that envelope."

"You left Mac's camp intact?"

"I took the rifle, because Mac said I should. The rest of his gear and his tent I packed up and left there. Then I headed down to my camp and packed my things up in my sled and walked back out, across Disappointment and Snowbank and back to civilization."

"Not the trip you had expected."

"Maybe not. But that's the thing about living in the present. You don't control it. It happens, and you experience it, and live in it, and make your choices in it. Then you live with your choices."

The silence again stretched between them.

"Brad, I'm so grateful for all the time you're taking to share your story."

"Under the circumstances, I'm glad to be able to do it."

"I need to wrap this up for tonight. Can I get in touch next week if I have more questions?"

"I'd like that. Please do."

Chapter Six

Thirty-six hours later, Kim was in her Forrester, turning left off Highway 61 along the North Shore onto Minnesota Highway One, a two-lane highway which wound up into the iron-rich hills above Lake Superior. She had patched her phone into the stereo and listened to each word of her interview with Brad. The back of the vehicle held gear for every contingency she could foresee. She remembered this drive, climbing up from the big lake, in many seasons—lush green summers with trees a thousand shades of green; the crazy cacophony of colors in the fall as the maples exploded in brilliant oranges and reds; the tender buds of spring against the last melting snowdrifts. Now, however, she followed miles of winding forest-lined highway, but there was no color. Her sunglasses shielded her eyes from the dazzling sunlight on the March snow. Trees stood like twisted skeletons on either side of the road, leafless and bare. The stands of pine felt like some comfort to her as they stood pale "evergreen" and relatively unchanged.

Mac's death had rattled her, she realized, and she was uncomfortable in her own mind. Restless. Uneasy. Eventually she came to an unmarked gravel road that headed vaguely north. She drove a mile, then turned west onto a smaller gravel road that was mostly covered with packed snow, and finally about 11 am she pulled up in front of a weary double-wide manufactured home. Three or four decrepit cars in various states of cannibalization dotted the yard, snow covering each one like a shroud. A clutter of debris, muted by snow, filled the space between the house and a detached garage. There were fresh tire tracks in the driveway and smoke coming out of a chimney amidships on the roof, but no other sign that anyone was home. Kim sat for a minute, checked her cell phone, and was vaguely surprised that she had two bars of cell signal.

She remembered coming here on weekends a lifetime ago, when she and Misty had worked together on the Gunflint. She wondered if life was still the same here. Deep breath.

She slammed her door, harder than strictly necessary, to let anyone inside know that she was there. She walked up and knocked on the screen door. No answer. She tried dialing Misty's number, and she could hear the phone ringing in the house. No answer.

Now what?

She heard a vehicle approaching up the gravel road, and soon a pale-green Ford F250 pickup with a snowplow on the front turned into the driveway. It rolled to a stop and Misty climbed out. A cigarette perched on one side of her mouth, and an enormous German Shepherd clambered out of the cab after her. Misty took a last inhale from the cigarette and reached back into the cab to grind it out in the ashtray. She kept looking at Kim, then looking away. The dog had started barking when it saw Kim.

"Shady. Hush," Misty said. She made eye contact with Kim again, and finally said, "Hey, Kimmy."

"Hey, Misty. It's good to see you."

"Hell." She looked away at the trees, her eyes sweeping the debris in the yard and the shoddy paint on the house and the vestigial cars.

"You smoke now?"

"I try. I'm trying to find something I can do that's just for myself, you know? These damn cancer sticks are the best thing I've found so far. I hate 'em. Looking for a better habit, but there aren't a lot of options. Getting too old to spend every weekend drunk and pregnant."

"Misty, I—" Kim began.

"No." She held up a hand like a traffic cop, stopping Kim's apology. Kim stirred to speak again, but Misty closed her eyes and kept her hand up, palm out. "Kim. Just shut up for a second." Her dark eyes looked out at the trees again, then up at the blue sky, then back at Kim's face. "I'm sorry. I'm sorry I was a bitch on the phone, and I'm sorry to be burned out and bitter when you finally come see me." A mischievous smile crept across her face, and for a moment she looked twenty years younger, the bright, dark face Kim remembered. "Deep breath, right? I'm going to go slip into a better attitude, make a pot of coffee, and let's talk about this dead man that's making your life complicated."

Kim smiled sadly, but she had no idea what to say to that. Misty came up and gave her a quick hug. "Thanks for coming up. It's good to see you, too. Come on in the house. You do still drink coffee, don't you?"

"Better believe it, baby." They walked up the two steps made out of stacked concrete blocks and into the unlocked front door.

Walking into the house, memories washed over Kim. About fifteen years earlier, she and Misty met when they were both on staff at Wilderness Christian Adventures, a Bible camp and canoeing outfitter that specialized in taking church kids on guided week-long trips into the Boundary Waters. Three summers they'd worked together, and on free weekends it was an easy drive down to the Dairy Queen in Grand Marais and then another hour southwest to stay with Misty's family. Kim's family was another five hours south in the Twin Cities, and staying with Misty's family (a mix of Ojibwe and Finnish blood that seemed perpetually perched on the edge of ruin, but never toppled over into the abyss) was a pleasant break from the life of camp counselors. Kim remembered a family in chaos and in love, fights breaking out over supper, babies and cousins, picking blueberries in the pine-covered hills above the house, sharing a double mattress in Misty's room and whispering late into the night. It had been a delightfully different life from her carefully scheduled suburban upbringing, both parents working professionals and community-minded.

Misty busied herself making coffee in the kitchen while Kim looked at photos all over the wall in the living room. Some dated back to the times she had been here; others looked newer. Here and there she caught a glimpse of Misty as a girl, as a young woman, aging bit by bit, and showing just a hint in a couple photos of the bitterness that had erupted momentarily in the driveway.

"How is your mom, Misty?"

"Getting old. Too soon. She's sixty, but she's been having some trouble with her memory. Physically she's fine. But she's a little timid these days. She's okay, though. I brought her down to stay with Jeannette for a few days. She doesn't like to be alone."

"Are you thinking we can try to head into the Boundary Waters this weekend?"

"Seems like the thing to do if we can. Going to be a mess in a few weeks. Better to do it now while the ice is still good and the ground is frozen. You did bring your snowshoes, right?"

"Them and pretty much everything else we might need."

"Figured."

"Toboggan and tent and sleeping bags, too. Might need to stay in a night or two."

"Shovels?"

"The ground is frozen."

"Snow, dummy. When did this guy shoot himself?"

"February 24th, if I have it right."

Misty considered. "We've had maybe three or four inches of snow since then. Not too bad. You figure we're bringing a body out?"

"Mac didn't want his remains moved."

"Forest Service isn't going to like that."

"He's way up on the east side of Disappointment Mountain someplace, off the hiking trails. He figured the wolves and the crows would take care of things."

"They very well might have."

"Brad–that's the guy who found the body–said he heard wolves howling the night Mac shot himself."

"Brad, huh?" Misty leered at Kim, who just smiled and shook her head.

"Okay, Misty, we should probably do the 'I haven't seen you for a decade, so what's your life like?' questions. I'm not married. Never been. I've dated a few guys but mostly my life has been about work. Most of the man-energy I have had for the last dozen years has gone into managing my boss, Mac, and his Foundation. Big non-profit that funds education and wells in Africa and stuff like that. My folks are still living and they bought a lake place north of Brainerd when they retired, so I drive down and see them for a weekend three or four times a year. I bought a little house in Duluth five years ago. Pretty boring. How about you?"

Misty laughed and shook her head. "How do you do that, Kimmy? How do you piss me off when you're just trying to tell me about your life?"

"What?"

"Try this on. I focus on taking care of Mom and plowing driveways to make a little extra cash. Mostly I work security shifts down in Silver Bay at that big taconite loading plant. Ever since I got out of the sheriff's office, I've been in the rent-a-cop business there. Same job. No raises, no promotions. Five years ago we got broke into here at the house and whoever it was knocked Mom down and broke her ribs. Never caught the son of a bitch, even though I rode the department about it for a month and they had a pretty good idea who had done it."

"Did they tell you who?"

"Didn't need to. I knew who they figured, and they were probably right."

"What did you do?"

"Bought a pistol and got a dog. And put in a deadbolt."

"Why wasn't the door locked when we came in?"

Misty rolled her eyes. "I was only gone a couple hours. Give it a rest."

Kim was quiet for a few seconds. "Kids?"

"I have managed, somehow, not to end up pumping out kids like every other pre-menopausal woman in the Arrowhead. Those years after Wilderness, I had a couple near misses with guys that had 'trouble' tattooed across their foreheads. Had a miscarriage when I was twenty-five that scared me to death because I knew the guy would have run if he found out I was pregnant. So I swore off babies and everything that goes with them."

"And took up cigarettes." Kim stopped herself. "Look, I'm sorry. And I'm sorry about the miscarriage."

"Cigarettes came later. But yes. Does my smoking bother you?"

"No. Yes. I don't know. It surprises me."

"Why?"

Misty poured two cups of coffee and they settled in at the kitchen table. Kim noticed that the table was clean, and the kitchen was worn but tidy. She made a point of looking around as she sipped her coffee. "Misty, you've always been a quality person. I've always respected you and looked up to you."

A bitter laugh escaped Misty and she shook her head. "Kimmy, you are too much to be believed. All the times I brought you here, and you could never see what a trashy life this is, and how anyone with an ounce of sense would cut and run somewhere else."

"Everybody has crap to deal with."

"Some more than others."

"Some just hide it better."

"Well, mine is on display. Just look at the front yard."

"So clean up the yard if it bothers you."

Misty sipped her coffee. "Maybe I should."

"Do you do any writing these days?"

Misty's eyes widened a little, and she quickly looked at Kim's face. "How—" she began, then bit down on it. "Oh, yeah. Oh, damn. I forgot I showed you that stuff."

"We were pretty drunk that night. You more than me."

"Yeah."

They both sat as the memories came drifting back, three years' worth of friendship that had quickly faded as their lives took very different turnings. "No, Kim, I never wrote anything. Well, not that went anywhere."

"But you still write?"

"Not for years."

"Why not?"

"Too many useful things to do."

"Shit. Misty, I'm going to say this and then I'm going to drop it unless you bring it up—but your poems, the things you showed me that night, that one story you let me read—those things still haunt me. In a really good way. I loved your writing. It was like you were an artist using words instead of paint brushes, painting these beautiful, intense pictures."

Misty just looked out the window and said nothing for a long time. Finally she turned back to Kim and said, "So tell me. Tell me about Mac and his death and what we need to do."

Chapter Seven

By early afternoon, they loaded Misty's gear into the Forrester and drove to Ely, a bustling town built largely on summer tourism, especially the kind that related to its proximity to the Boundary Waters. Kim called ahead and reserved a room so they could get as early a start as possible the next day. They spent the drive to Ely listening to the transcript of the interview with Brad. As they pulled into the hotel parking lot, the audio came to an end.

"So is this Brad Swenson a decent guy, do you think? Or are we looking for evidence that he's lying through his teeth?"

"He seems decent. But he might just be a really good actor. I don't know. Mac seemed to think he was the real thing, and Mac was usually a good judge of people. In fact, most of the papers that Mac sent me in that envelope have to do with Brad, directly or indirectly."

"Like how?"

"Like Mac wanted to bring him into the Foundation and put him to work. Brad doesn't know that."

"What do you think?"

"I think I want to see the place Mac reportedly killed himself and then make up my mind."

They checked into the hotel room, got supper at a local hotspot called the Insula Restaurant, named for a lake in the Boundary Waters that was a crazy maze of dozens of islands. Over supper they reminisced about their days as canoe guides. "Did you ever spend time on Insula?" Kim asked.

"I went through a couple times, but we usually didn't get that far west. You?"

Kim giggled. "I took a group of high school girls there once. We stayed two nights because the girls couldn't figure out how to read the map."

"You didn't show them?"

"I tried, but this was one of those we've-got-it-all-together groups that thought they knew everything. From one of the rich suburbs in the Cities. Edina or someplace like that. Somehow they'd been able to navigate through the simpler stuff, but the tangle of islands on Insula was just too much, and they couldn't figure it out. What a mess."

"What happened?"

"They finally asked for help."

"Did you rub their noses in it?"

"No. By then they had been through a few crying jags and arguments and they were pretty well busted up by the whole experience. I just pointed out a few landmarks and helped them figure out where they were. From then on they wanted to check every turn with me, but they did okay."

"I remember a lot of groups like that. One way or another, they'd get broken by their own pride."

"Good life lesson, huh?"

"Even for you, Kimmy?"

Kim saw the challenge in Misty's eyes. "My life might look perfect on the outside, but that is far, far from reality."

"Maybe so. But I gotta say, from where I sit it looks like you've got it together."

"Professional camouflage."

"Darn good job of it, then."

"I've got my own heartbreaks. And longings. Burned bridges and broken dreams, Misty. And a whole pile of 'what if' thoughts to sift through when I can't sleep."

"You might just be human after all."

Chapter Eight

The next morning they were up early. The night before they'd gone through and put together gear for the most likely scenarios, choosing what to bring and what to leave behind. They had food for two days and emergency rations–Clif Bars, mostly–for a couple more. They stopped at the Forest Service office on the east side of Ely, but the doors were locked and the place was dark. "Probably getting a late breakfast in town," Misty said. "Nobody comes through here in the winter."

"Maybe they just don't open up until nine," Kim offered generously. "It's barely eight now."

"You're so kind, Kimmy."

They drove another fifteen miles east to the string of resorts that covered the south side of Snowbank Lake. Kim had called ahead to a resort called "Roger's Outfitters" and arranged to leave the Subaru there if they had to. They parked out of the way against a snowbank, got their gear out of the back, and packed up the sleds Kim had brought. Each was attached to twenty feet of rope looped through a pair of eight-foot PVC sections to prevent the sled from creeping forward on downhills. A simple harness slipped up around each woman's shoulders. After a bit of loading, adjustment, and double checking everything, they worked their way down the bank, past the dock that had been pulled up on the shore last fall, over the swelled ridges of broken ice where it had pushed up against the land over winter, and out onto the ice. The lake stretched out, flat and cold and sparkling white, to the east of them. The rising March sun had a little more power to warm these days than it had in January, but the morning was still cold. Snow was drifted in long, low ridges that felt like concrete under their feet.

"Probably don't need to worry about the ice, at least," Misty observed. "It's been plenty cold. You could drive a tank across this."

"I like this better than fighting whitecaps," Kim murmured. "I had to cross this lake into a high wind once. That was ugly."

"It's a big lake."

They started walking, each wearing a high-tech pair of lightweight snowshoes that gave them a little more flotation on the windswept snow covering the ice. For the first couple miles, the going was easy. Off to their left, they could see a few ice fishing houses clustered around a point, but they didn't see anyone else crossing the lake.

The portage to Disappointment was a challenge. The snow under the trees was softer, and pulling the sleds required balance, strength, and determination. Twice they had to work their way over fallen trees, and twice more they could simply work their way around trees that had fallen across the portage trail.

"Forest Service guys are going to have some work to do this spring."

"Yeah. How you holding up, Misty?"

"I'm good. This is a lot easier than taking care of Mom and everything else I normally do. Like a vacation. Can't wait to make camp and have you mix up a few margaritas."

"Sorry. Left my blender at home."

"What? I'm heading back to paradise."

"Okay. See you later."

They walked on in silence across Disappointment Lake, a long, curved body of water with bays and islands enough to keep navigation challenging. Halfway across the south end, Kim pulled up and drew out the Fisher map, folded up to show this section of the Boundary waters and protected inside a clear gallon Ziplock bag. She held it up so they could both see, and pointed to a spot on the east side of the lake. "Brad said Mac was camped up here, near this little pond. Supposed to be a clearing there. Looks like it might be easiest to go north through the narrows and catch the trail going east up and over the crest, then drop down into the clearing."

"Lay on, MacDuff."

"Don't you mean 'lead'?"

Misty snorted. "Hah! Everybody gets Shakespeare wrong. The quote is really 'lay on, MacDuff.' It's a challenge to battle. Not an invitation to walk in front of somebody else. So maybe it's not the most appropriate quote at the moment."

Kim chuckled and shook her head, but took the lead anyway. A mile or so north, after skirting the east edge of an island and working their way up the shoreline, they turned into a small bay, crossed it, and climbed laboriously up the east bank of the lake into the woods. The toboggans fought them as they pulled up over the broken ice along the shore, then up the rocky shoreline itself. The slope rose ahead of them through the dark pines, and it took their eyes a few minutes to adjust. After a difficult hundred yards or so, they came to what looked like a snow-covered trail.

"Hold up," Misty said. "There have been people here. See the tracks?"

They were not fresh, but Kim could see, too, the dim impressions of snowshoe prints that had been covered with a few inches of new snow. "That makes sense, according to Brad's story. He camped down here and used this trail to go visit Mac's camp." They turned and followed the trail north, paralleling the shoreline. "Should be a fork where we want to take the right hand trail, going east up the hill," she said. "Then we're going to have to climb."

They almost missed the turnoff, as the trail to the east was blocked by a downed fir tree. They worked their way around that obstacle and started climbing. The next three quarters of a mile was challenging enough that neither woman spoke. Finally they came out on level ground in a spot where the trees were a little thinner and they could see just a bit to the south and east where the slope of Disappointment Mountain gradually fell away below them.

"That might be your clearing over there," Misty pointed to the right of the trail. About a quarter mile farther on they could see an opening of some kind in the forest.

"Probably makes sense to follow the trail east, then cut across. I don't want to bushwhack more than we have to."

"Sounds good to me."

It was a relatively simple matter to follow the trail eastward until they could see the clear space in the trees straight to the south. There was a kind of natural saddle over the top of the hill, and a few deer trails crossed up and over this natural funnel. They led downhill toward the clearing. The women followed the most likely of these, but the going was still hard. The sleds got hung up in brush, and they went through a patch of small poplar trees that grew thick as hair along the trail. Misty swore quietly. "Maybe we should have left the sleds up on the trail."

"Fine time to think of that. I'm thinking we can camp in the same clearing. That will make it a lot easier to try to find any sign of what happened."

Another hour of pulling and pushing through the tangles and they heaved an exhausted sigh as the sleds pulled free into the clearing formed by the swamp. "Wouldn't want to camp here after the thaw, I'll bet," Misty observed.

Kim stared out at the opening, remembering Brad's napkin sketch. It was mostly open snow, though here and there a spindly tamarack tree poked up out of the swamp. "Over there, I think," she pointed. They crossed southward toward the opening where a creek probably flowed out of this pond in warmer weather.

As they approached the treeline, Misty spoke up. "Hold up," she said. "I think we're close. Let's leave the gear here and take a look around. If there is any sign to be found, I don't want to mess it up more than we have to."

"Good idea."

Misty took the lead now, and they left the sleds behind as they cautiously circled toward the spot where Kim thought Mac's camp must have been. As they looked at low angles across the snow, they could see it had been trampled and disturbed, but then covered with a few inches of fresh flakes that softened and obscured most of what was there.

"So Brad said he packed up Mac's stuff and left it, isn't that right?"

"Yeah. That's what he said."

"Did he say where he left it?"

"No. I didn't think to ask."

"Look there, Kim, about twenty yards back in the trees, in those poplars." Misty pointed off to their right.

Kim looked, and she could see what looked like a platform up in the trees. They walked over to it. Four trees grew in a rough square three feet across. Each had a trunk about three inches in diameter that had been cut off ten or twelve feet above the ground, forming pillars that now supported a platform built of more pieces of cut poplar and lashed together with parachute cord. On top of this platform rested a large bundle covered with a gray tarp and lashed down with still more parachute cord. Under cover of the trees and partially obscured with snow, the whole apparatus blended in remarkably well with the stand of trees.

"I assume that's Mac's tent and gear," Kim speculated. "I don't know that we need any of it right now. Should we just leave it there for the moment?"

Misty nodded. They turned back to the edge of the trees, scanning for anything that might provide the next clue.

"Brad said Mac's body was around this corner, I think, against the trees facing east toward the creek," Kim said. "Let's look over here."

They walked another thirty yards east and turned back into the brightness of full sunlight across the snow. As sunlight on the snow slammed like a hammer into their eyes, Misty put up a hand to block a bit of the brightness. She sucked in a deep breath, and Kim quickly put her hand up as well.

"I think we found him. Or what's left of him."

Fresh tracks covered the snow, and in half a dozen places they could see bones that had been stripped of meat, standing up out of the snow like sinking ships. Frozen bits of muscle and fabric still hung from the bones, but for the most part they looked more like bones and less like a dismembered body. Kim felt an unexpected surge of relief and realized she had been bracing herself for this grisly moment. The pieces of the skeleton were scattered here and there across twenty yards of trampled snow. Misty took a couple cautious steps forward and looked around, assessing. "Wolves," she pronounced. "The whole pack."

Kim was stunned by the brutal reality of it. Mac had joked about things like this once in a while. But seeing his reddish bones scattered across the snow–a half dozen ribs still attached to a section of spinal column, a well-gnawed lower leg, the twin bones cracked and split and chewed, and a few other configurations–made her stomach churn and her heart sick. Her vision started to go dark and she could feel that last Clif Bar threatening to make a reappearance.

Misty grabbed her by the arm. "Kimmy. Come here. Turn around, baby, and come here with me for a minute." Kim allowed herself to be led back to their sleds, where Misty sat her down on a pack. "Sit here, Kim. Just breathe. Here–have a little bit of water. Not much. Just a swallow."

Kim breathed deeply, trying to get the images out of her head, making a point not to look back to the carnage in the bright snow. Misty had guided her so she was sitting facing away from it, wisely. Slowly, slowly she felt her stomach settle and her brain regain some sense of stability. Misty eyed her worriedly.

"You okay?"

Kim breathed deep again. "I will be. Thanks. It just got to be too much for a minute."

"It happens. Believe me. Even if it's not somebody you care about. Take your time."

Kim leaned forward, resting her face in her mittens. "Oh, Mac."

"Sounds like he kind of wanted this. Maybe the problem is we got here too soon. Another week the wolves would have cleaned things up a little better."

An unstable laugh, half sob, escaped Kim's incredulous lips. "Yeah. Though–and this sounds so weird to say–it's not as bad as I expected. I thought—" She stopped, unable to put words to the vision that had lurked in the back of her mind for the last few days.

"Deep breath, baby."

Kim tried to concentrate on breathing.

After a few minutes, Misty looked back to the south. "You okay here for a few minutes? I think I need to take a closer look at all that. Take a swig of that water. Not too much."

Kim stirred. "I should help you."

"Like hell you should. You sit here and breathe. And don't watch what I'm doing. I'm going to sort through things, see what I can figure out. Won't take me long."

Kim stared across the swamp, looking north, toward the top of Disappointment Mountain. Misty walked back south to Mac's remains and spent several minutes looking carefully, circling, but not trampling the scene. She eased back into the trees a bit, then down toward the frozen creek, then back up to the trampled snow. Finally she returned to Kim, who had glanced back at her a few times, but finally busied herself getting a tent and groundcloth out of their packs. Misty came walking up, a grim expression on her face.

"How you doing, Kim?"

"I'm okay. It was just too much for a minute. I'm okay. What did you find?"

"Looks like they've been back more than once. Probably means the hunting hasn't been good, or it took them time to pick the bones clean. There's not a lot of meat left. I think I found most of the skeleton, except—" She fell silent.

"Except what?"

"I didn't find a skull."

Kim just stood, arms hanging useless at her sides, looking over toward Mac's remains, then looking away. "It's got to be there, right?"

"I would think so."

They both stood silent, gathering reserves, looking at each other, looking back toward Mac, and looking away. Kim finally spoke. "Let's get our own stuff set up. We can look for Mac's... we can look some more in the morning. It's getting late enough in the day we should get the tent set up and gather some wood."

They pulled the sleds back to the north side of the clearing, about a hundred yards, wordlessly agreeing that they didn't want to camp too close. Kim set up the tent, and Misty gathered a prodigious stack of firewood. Using her snowshoes, she trampled down an area about ten yards across, alongside a massive boulder. While Kim trampled another area adjoining and pitched the four-season dome tent on it, Misty methodically prepared a sizable fire, waiting only to be set ablaze. Then she cleared snow off a flat rock next to the boulder and rummaged in the packs until she found Kim's camp stove.

"Can you eat?"

"I think so. Something hot would be good, huh?"

"Yeah. Beef stroganoff?"

"Sounds great."

As the sun dropped below the horizon, Misty busied herself cooking supper, and Kim threw sleeping bags, pads, and clothes bags in the tent. Then she filled another pot with snow and set it next to the stove to begin melting and heating for tea. Meal and cleanup and a blessed cup of hot tea for each of them occupied most of the next hour or more. They heated another pot of water to fill their water bottles to keep in the sleeping bags in case it became bitterly cold overnight.

"Misty, I just realized. You haven't had a cigarette since we were standing in your driveway."

"I told you. I hate the damn things. It's just a way to do something for myself. Right now what I'm doing for myself is going off having adventures with you. I'm not sure I'll go back to being a smoker when we get back. Doesn't fit me somehow."

"Must be a recent habit."

"Very recent. I don't think I'd call it a habit yet."

The stars began to appear overhead as the sky went from blue to indigo to black. By the time they finished their tea the sky was stunning, from treeline to treeline. The Milky Way glowed like a sash above the western horizon, and Orion perched overhead. A million other stars stood out above their heads.

"Didn't see a lot of that, not even back at Wilderness," Kim whispered.

"Nights were pretty short back in the summers. And we always had a fire going at night, right?"

"Yeah. There were a few times, though. Remember that night at the end of our second summer, out on the ridge?"

"That was the night you almost proposed to Josiah, right?"

"I did propose. He laughed at me."

"His loss."

"Better believe it, baby."

They fell silent for a long time, staring upward, soaking in the stars. Then the hair on the back of Kim's neck stood straight out and her back went all gooseflesh as a long, sonorous wail rose just across the clearing, just where Mac's scattered remains lay cold under the starlight. Unseen and unheard the pack had returned, and many voices joined in and began to sing just a hundred yards away. Neither woman was able to breathe for several seconds. The unearthly choir seemed to go on and on, individual wolves joining in and falling silent in a greater chorus that rose and fell, encompassing the clearing, the trees, the hillside, and the women. There was something in that song, in the nearness of the wild choir, that forbade intelligent thought. Neither woman spoke. Without words the song rose and fell like a great invitation, a declaration of purpose, a warning. Finally as the voices died down Kim whispered, "We should light that fire."

"They won't bother us. I think."

"You don't sound too sure."

"Wolves don't bother people. You know that."

"They just bothered Mac some, Misty."

"He was dead already. That's different."

"Mmmm. Delicious. Maybe we're next on the menu."

Misty considered. "Might not hurt to light the fire. And just so you know, I do have my pistol on my belt."

"Good to know. Figured you might."

Kim found a lighter in their day pack, and Misty got the fire started. Very quickly it leaped up, feeding on the spruce twigs Misty had set up at the core of a stack of larger wood, and soon the blaze lit their campsite and far beyond.

"Well, now they know we're here," Kim chuckled.

"They knew we were here before they started singing. In fact, they were probably serenading us just to let us know they were there."

"Breeze is out of the west. They wouldn't catch our scent."

"We left scent all over the place exactly where they are. They know we're here."

"And now they're off to hunt a moose, hopefully."

"Maybe. I don't think we'll have any problem if we stick together and stay close to the fire."

"Funny how you can think about winter camping in the Boundary Waters and read about people having wolves close by and back in Duluth it doesn't seem like any big deal. It's a little different having them singing across the clearing."

"They come by our place sometimes. Mom got a little dog about ten years ago–a Pekinese that she kept mostly in the house. Wolves got that one."

"Really?"

"Well, I'm pretty sure. She let it out one night and never saw it again. Doggie disappeared and wolf tracks all over the place. Not hard to figure that one out. Never found as much as a tuft of fur."

"You hear more and more stories like that in Duluth–people in the edges of the city that lose dogs."

"A wolf has got to eat, I guess."

"Yeah. Let's build up that fire a bit."

Chapter Nine

Misty had gathered plenty of fuel, so they stoked up the fire and straightened up their sleds and packs and equipment. The moon, a few days past full, was rising over the east end of the clearing, its left side a clear, beautiful curve, its right margin ragged as it waned. It hung huge and bright above the horizon, and the snow began to shine with that strange blue light that seems so powerful in the frosty north country nights. They crawled into the tent and settled into the safe darkness inside the tent. Kim had provided a four-season tent, thick sleeping pads, and sleeping bags that were rated to twenty below zero. The air temperature outside was hovering around zero or a little above, so the women were comfortable enough. She'd also brought a small propane heater to take the edge off the cold in the tent, but they still gasped and swore and didn't waste any time getting stripped down to base layers and under wraps. Once they were in their sleeping bags and the lights went out, they shivered for a few minutes but very quickly Kim was able to turn off the heater and they were quite comfortable, their stocking cap covered heads peering out the openings of their mummy bags, warm water bottles tucked in next to their sides. On the dome of the tent above them they could see the glow from the moon shining from the east as a counterpoint to the flickering shadows cast by the flames to the west.

"Quite a light show," Misty murmured.

"Yeah. Been a long time since I went winter camping."

"We did that trip together up on Rose Lake. Have you done much other than that?"

"Just a few short trips. You?"

"I was out on assignment a couple times with the sheriff's department and ended up camping out. Nothing recreational, really. Slept out in ice houses a couple times when we were fishing. That's the Arrowhead's version of a hot date, you know?"

They lay quiet for a while, watching the lights move across the dome of their tent. A great horned owl hooted somewhere at the edge of hearing. The wolves had been quiet for quite a while now, and Kim wondered where they were. Still in the clearing, perhaps, or a mile or more away, trotting through the forest, sniffing out the trails of their prey? She was suddenly oppressed by the weight of the wilderness. She had a sense of hundreds and thousands of lives, prey and predators, existing independent of her own, each life nothing more than a shooting star illuminating the night for a brief moment. In the quiet it seemed miraculous to her that when she was far away, living out her own existence in man-made cities, driving on concrete highways and living and working in artificially heated buildings, the wild things lived out their lives here, in the harsh and glorious days and nights. And that was true across the globe. For a moment that sense of the weight of the entire world filled her consciousness.

Misty spoke, calling her back into the present, into her sleeping bag in this tent. "Kimmy, do you listen to much music these days?"

"Some. Not like we used to. But yeah."

"I've been listening to a song that keeps running through my head."

"What is it?"

"It's kind of haunting. Talks about once I die, letting the wolves enjoy my bones. Can't get it out of my head."

"Thank you very much for that, Misty. Can't imagine why that would be in your head right now. I'm glad I haven't heard it, at the moment."

"Yeah. Pretty vivid." She was quiet a moment. "I've worked a lot of deaths, when I was a cop. Saw a lot of cops get calloused to it, just close off. But for me it was always a heartbreaking thing, deep down. No matter what the body's story was, somebody was left crying, or angry, or depressed. Guess I learned that it's pretty important, what we do with the death of someone we care about."

"How do you mean?"

"Well, I figure Mac's beyond caring. Whatever's true after death. If he's in heaven with Jesus or if he's just dead or whatever, it's not his problem now."

"I suppose that's true."

"Thing is, Kimmy, it's your problem, in a way. You've got to figure out what to do with Mac's death."

"That's why I dragged you up here. I've got to figure this out. That's part of my job now."

"More than the Foundation, though. More than figuring out what to do next. This was somebody you cared about."

"Yeah." Kim breathed in, and let that breath out in a long sigh. "Oh, yeah. I haven't really let that in a lot."

"I understand that. But you've got to, at some point. Not all at once, and maybe not right now. But you can't just be teflon through all this."

"Misty, I want to tell you something, but I need to know you won't talk about it except with me."

"I can do that."

"In the sealed envelope Mac sent back, the one Brad brought me, he explained a few things. Not completely, and I've still got a lot of questions. But one of the bits of information he shared in that packet was that he had pancreatic cancer. That's why he decided to kill himself. He knew that statistically, there was something like a ninety-five percent chance he'd be dead within a year."

"So he committed suicide to get ahead of it?"

"Something like that. Mac wasn't good at being weak. I think he decided he didn't have a lot of choices."

Silence stretched out between them. Finally Misty spoke.

"I guess I can see that. Not sure that's the way I'd handle it, but I can see that. Did you know anything about it?"

"I'd noticed a change in Mac over the last six months or so. Not sure quite when it started. But I didn't know anything about cancer. I thought maybe he was just going through a phase."

"Why are men so full of locked doors and secrets and closed off rooms? Kimmy, that pisses me off. Why wouldn't he talk to you about it?"

"The last thing he wrote, probably, was a note to Brad. He said he was worried that if he talked to Brad about this decision, it would make him doubt himself. And it would make Brad carry too much responsibility. Both of those things sound exactly like Mac. He didn't want anyone to make him question himself once he'd made up his mind. He always wanted to take responsibility for his own decisions and issues."

"So he makes a decision to kill himself without getting any second opinions."

"He'd gotten the medical tests done, and gotten doctors' second opinions. He'd done that."

"But I mean the decision to commit suicide."

"Yeah, that was all Mac."

"Why here? Why like this?"

Kim considered. "I know he loved it up here. The Boundary Waters was his getaway, his escape. A few times a year he'd come into the backcountry, always alone."

"Would you say he was a lonely man?"

"Maybe a little. He was incredibly strong-willed. He was probably the most forceful personality I've ever known. And growing up in a family with money, an only child, I think he was a little isolated.

He never, never talked about anything like that. But he didn't have many friends. He had tons of associates, relationships that were good for the Foundation, good for his work."

"Did he go through outfitters when he came up here? Did he have his own gear?"

"Oh, yeah. Mac was a gear-head. And given his money and the way he was wired, he would never work with an outfitter. He knew the CEO's of most of the equipment companies. Wenonah, Souris River, REI, all of them. So he'd get a deal on some kind of pre-release when they were coming out with new stuff. He had the best of the best equipment. Not always the most expensive. Just quality stuff."

"Remember how we used to laugh about that kind of stuff? We'd see the guys with the expensive canoeing shoes, and there we were in our canvas sneakers. And our shoes were better than theirs for most of what we were doing."

"Oh, I remember. And Mac got the difference. He talked about that a lot. He didn't want expensive gear just for the sake of spending money. He wanted whatever worked best, no matter what it cost, cheap or expensive."

"I guess if you've got the money, that makes sense. Seems kind of ironic, I guess, a guy like that getting taken down by cancer."

"He got taken down by a rifle bullet."

"You know what I mean."

"So what are we going to do tomorrow?"

"I guess that's up to you, in a way. Do you want to bring Mac's bones—what we can find of him—out with us?"

"I know the Forest Service would have a fit, but I want to leave him here, at least mostly. We're going to need something that verifies his death. The skull would be ideal if we can find it. But he was a blood donor, and I think we can do a DNA match to verify that it's him if we just bring something out they can test."

"And do what with the rest?"

Kim took a deep breath. "Leave it. Once it thaws, not many people are going to come down into this clearing. It's well off the trails. And where his bones are, it's going to be pretty swampy through the summer, looks like. Between the wolves and the crows, like he said in his note, they'll scatter him pretty effectively."

"Ashes to ashes, dust to dust?"

"I guess. It's what he asked for."

"Nobody back in Duluth that's going to want a funeral?"

"I don't know. We'll probably do some kind of a memorial service at some point once word gets out. We'll want to think about how to handle the press on that."

"For the Foundation's sake."

"Of course. The Foundation was his life. That and these wilderness trips."

"What about you, Kim? How are you going to grieve this thing?"

She sighed. "This trip is a big piece of it. I'm really grateful you were willing to do this with me, Misty. I'm not as teflon as I look, and it means a lot to have you here."

"I get that. You're welcome. It's funny, I figured some man would have snapped you up a long time ago. In some ways that might make this easier. Might be nice for you to have a guy along who could keep things all compartmentalized."

"Never found a man I could camp with. That was always a deal breaker. Let alone winter camping. They always want you to be the squeamish girl they can protect, or else they're the squeamish ones and need you to protect them. I guess I never found the partnership I was looking for. And you're doing a damn good job of helping me through this."

"Well, bringing a guy out here is a sure way to find out what's under the surface. We saw that often enough back in the day. I think tomorrow we should criss-cross the area where Mac's bones are. We can track the wolves a ways, see if we find things they've carried off. That will take some time, maybe the whole day. You don't need to spend more time in among the bones than you want to."

"Okay. I don't think it will be so bad. Today was just a lot to take in at once."

"Understandable. Get some sleep, Kimmy."

"Good night."

The silence grew inside the tent until the tiny night noises outside sounded loud. A breeze rustling the pines. The squeak of some night creature jarred Kim for a moment. Logs settled in on the coals as the fire burned down. Ice down on the pond creaked as it cooled down. The night deepened. Kim woke up a few times in the darkness, shifted herself slightly, listened to Misty's even breathing, and drifted back into sleep.

Chapter Ten

They woke as daylight was slowly filtering into the clearing. Kim remembered from their Bible camp days how Misty, who so often seemed brooding and serious, almost always woke up cheerful. "See?" Misty chirped. "No wolf attacks."

"Count your blessings, I guess."

They waited a few moments for the propane heater to warm up the inside of the tent, then made short work of getting bundled up for the frosty air outside. As they exited the tent, the sun rising behind them gave the pines and poplars a soft, golden glow. It grew increasingly bold as the sun cleared the horizon. As Kim was about to step forward toward the mess kit, Misty threw out an arm to block her way and pointed with her other hand at the ground around their camp. "Look," she breathed.

"Wolf prints," Kim said. "Looks like they must have been pretty curious."

"Must have been early this morning, after the fire had mostly burned down. They came within twenty feet of the tent."

"Still carrying that pistol?"

"Bet your ass."

"I think I'll stay near you today, then."

"Probably a good idea. I still don't think they'd bother us, but I don't want to be stupid either."

They looked long and hard around the clearing, but saw no visible sign of the wolves aside from their plentiful tracks. Misty took a closer look at the prints while Kim fired up the stove for coffee. She brewed it strong and hot and handed Misty a cup as she walked up.

"It's hard to tell, but I don't think there were very many of them here. Just two, maybe, or three."

"That's plenty for me."

"Might be the alpha pair checking us out or something. I don't know enough about them to have any sense how they might deal with this situation."

"You mean how wolves will behave when they've just eaten a corpse and then somebody else comes and camps on the same site in the middle of their home territory? I doubt many studies have been done on that particular circumstance."

"Good point. Let's keep an eye out today."

"Yes ma'am."

They made a hasty breakfast, had a second cup of coffee each, and policed up their packs. They left the tent set up, unsure whether they'd spend another night here or not. By the time the sun had been up a full hour, they strapped on snowshoes and headed south across the frozen swamp. Misty took the lead. The plan was to make a rough circle around the obvious remains they could see, and follow any wolf tracks that headed away from Mac's bones. They hoped in this way to locate whatever might have been carried off, including Mac's missing skull.

They quickly saw that the wolves had crossed and recrossed their snowshoe tracks from the day before. It was strange to see the wolves' tracks atop their own. Once they got past the disturbing fact that the wolf pack had been sitting right here and singing last night, they settled down to business. As they circled, starting to the west, then veering south up the slope and back east through the taller trees, they found several sets of wolf tracks looping out into the trees and back. They didn't find any more bones until they got back almost to the creek and found where the pack had traveled back and forth through that open area to the south. There they found the remains of a well-chewed leg from the knee downward. Kim looked off into the trees while Misty carried it back into proximity with the rest of the bones and laid it gently on the snow.

When she came back, she said, "I think we're going to have to work our way down their track a bit. Wolves don't make trails like deer do, but it looks like they've been back and forth down this waterway a few times. Lots of traffic. We might find something else if we go a ways down here."

"Want to finish the circle, or do that now?"

"Let's do it now. Not sure how far we'll follow it, but we can finish the circle when we come back up."

They began slowly working their way southward through the corridor between the trees. After the wide open clearing of the swamp above them, this seemed a little claustrophobic, and though neither mentioned it, they were both watchful for wolves in the darkness under the pines to either side.

The wolves had obviously been back and forth through this opening many times. Crisp tracks indicated where the wolves had walked the night before. Less distinct tracks had frozen and thawed a few times. Dim depressions of tracks that had been snowed on mixed together with the more recent impressions. "They've been here every day for the last week, looks like," Misty stated.

"Any guess how many?"

"Hard to say. At least a dozen, I would think."

"Small wonder there's so little left of Mac."

They found no more bones, at least in the first quarter mile of gently decreasing elevation. Then the slope dropped sharply, and the two women stood atop a cut where the creek bed fell fifty or sixty feet over a very short distance. "That would be a pretty rapids during the spring thaw," Kim offered.

"It would at that. I wouldn't want to try to get up here during the thaw, though. We had it easy, walking across the lakes. And it's another kind of easy when you can paddle and portage. But traveling during the thaw and during the freeze-up, that's another story."

"Brad got stranded east of here, over by Little Saganaga, during the freeze last fall. That big blizzard in early November. He wrecked his canoe and ended up walking out."

"Your Brad did that?"

"He's not my Brad, Misty."

"Touchy."

"You might have seen the news stories about him. The Duluth paper and a couple Twin Cities TV stations made a big deal out of him surviving the blizzard and walking out in the snow."

"I don't pay attention to those stories. Unless I have to go hunting for someone, and I'm not in that line of work anymore. So is this guy one of those idiots that gets himself lost in the woods?"

"I don't think he was ever lost. Had a rough time when that blizzard hit, but he handled it okay."

"I maybe did see that news story. Last November? Didn't seem like much of a story. I figured it was a slow news day."

"That's kind of what Brad figured. He didn't see what all the fuss was about."

"So from the conversation you replayed for me, he was up here when Mac shot himself. You believe it went down the way he says?"

"He seems honest enough, but I'd feel better if we could piece things together a little more clearly."

"Piece things together? You mean if we could find Mac's head."

"Yeah. I guess that's the important part."

"Well, I don't think it's here. And I'd rather not have to climb down and then back up this rapids on these icy rocks."

"Let's go finish that circle."

They turned and worked their way back up the slope to Mac's remains, turned east by northeast, and began working their way around the circle again. There were several sets of wolf tracks going off eastward, across the creek bottom, into the trees on the other side. Misty suggested, "Let's take a turn up here and see what they're doing off in the woods." They climbed up into the trees, following the tangle of wolf tracks here and there but finding no more sign of Mac's remains.

They turned and were about to head back toward the clearing when Misty hissed, "Hey–look up there!" She pointed northeast across the bright, sunny clearing where they could plainly see, a few hundred yards away, a human walking across the snow, moving westward along the treeline. The figure pulled a sled loaded with gear.

"What the–?" Kim had not, not by any stretch of the imagination, expected to see other winter campers. Maybe on the lakes, possibly on the trails. But not here.

"Who do you suppose that is?"

"Maybe we should go find out."

"Not so hasty, friend. Let's think about this."

"Okay. What do you think?"

"If Mac didn't die like Brad said, the most probable idea that comes to mind is that someone is coming to clean up their mess."

"Could it be Forest Service, or DNR?"

"Doubtful. Why would they be coming through here in the winter? On the trails, yeah, but not back in here. You said the death hadn't been reported yet. There's nothing here to concern them."

"Wolves."

"So you think it's a doctoral student who's doing an internship with the DNR and is out here to continue his thesis research into pack behavior?"

"That's it exactly."

"If that's the case, I'll buy you dinner when we get back to Ely. Possible, but not likely."

The figure across the clearing had progressed almost to their campsite, and they saw them stop. The silhouette stood still a while, apparently looking at their tent.

"Let's go confront this whoever-it-is. You still have your pistol?"

"Yes, but I would rather exercise some caution."

"How hard is it to get at?"

"It's in an outside pocket on my parka. Not too hard."

"Let me lead, then if we get into a confrontation, you've got me screening you while you get the gun out."

"I don't like it. What if I shoot you in the back by mistake?"

"Don't."

"If I say 'Get down,' you drop, baby. Right now."

"Deal."

"Ready?"

"As I'll ever be."

"Lay on, MacDuff."

"I hope we're not really heading into battle."

"Me too. Let's go."

Chapter Eleven

Kim walked out of the trees into the sunshine and started on a line across the clearing toward their tent. Misty followed in her tracks, looking like she was taking advantage of the trail Kim was breaking. The figure at their campsite was now looking around, surveying the clearing, and quickly spotted them. Kim could see the figure clearly, though they were too far away to make out features. The person was wearing sunglasses, which made sense on the bright snow. To her surprise, the standing figure shrugged out of the harness, took three steps back, and sat down on a pack to wait for them.

Misty spoke just loud enough for Kim to hear. "Our guy is playing it cool as a zucchini. But don't let down your guard."

A hundred yards away, then seventy. Fifty. The figure sitting on the pack watched them come closer and still closer. When they were thirty yards away, it stood. Misty inhaled sharply. The figure casually reached up and pulled back hood and stocking cap.

"Hi, Kim."

Kim stopped short. "Brad?!"

"In the flesh. I wondered if I'd find you up here." Brad craned his neck to look past Kim at Misty. "Hi. I'm Brad Swenson."

"Hi." Misty's right hand stayed in her parka pocket and the silence stretched.

Kim asked the obvious question: "What are you doing out here?"

"After the questions you asked, I guessed you might come up here. And after all that happened here, I wanted to come back and get it straight in my head. Another of those difficult things to process, you know?"

"So you're just here for the emotional follow-up?"

"Kim, Mac killed himself right over there. That evening I was talking to him, and then a few hours later he was dead. It shook me, bad. Even though I hung around for a couple days, I really didn't get my head around all that happened. I was kind of in a fog. So that's one reason to come back."

Misty spoke. "Got any others?"

Brad stared at her for a second, hearing the challenge in her tone. "Well, for one, I know Mac's death puts me in a difficult light. I was the only person here. So there's the question of murder and whether my story is true."

"I've heard the recording of your conversation with Kim, so I know your version. Let me ask you, is that the way it went down?"

"Pretty much."

"So you didn't kill Mac."

"You heard the conversation. You know my story."

The tension wasn't going away at all, and the silence seemed awkward and dangerous. Brad finally broke it. "What did you guys find over there? Did you find Mac?"

Kim answered. "Parts of him. The wolves have torn him up and scattered the bones pretty thoroughly."

Brad looked across the clearing, toward the area Mac's bones were scattered. "I'd like to see."

Misty, still behind Kim, said, "We can do that. Here's how we'll do it. You go in front, following that snowshoe trail there"–she pointed–"and Kim and I will follow you."

"Okay. Look, just so you know, I'm not armed, and I'm not here to cover my tracks. I'm not here for trouble. Honestly, one reason I came up is that I was worried Kim might come up alone, and I figured it would be an ugly scene if the wolves had gotten to Mac."

"So you were hoping to find a woman in a crisis alone up here?"

"No! God! Why are you twisting things I say?"

"Just trying to understand, Mr. Swenson."

"Then understand this. Mac committed suicide. I was the guy on the scene. He asked me to do something for him before he died. I did it. I delivered that envelope to Kim. So I'm involved. And in our conversation, I could tell she cared about Mac and she was probably going to come up here to see what she could find out. I didn't know how much she knows about the woods. A little, at least. I could tell that from the questions she asked. But I was worried."

"Now you're the guy on the white horse?"

"It's complicated, all right? There's more than one reason I'm up here. Closure. Worry for Kim. Concern for myself, and the possibility I'd be accused of something I didn't do."

"Just so you know, Kim can handle herself just fine in the woods."

"Good to know."

Kim spoke up. "Let's get going across the clearing. Brad, probably best to leave your gear here for the moment. Anything you need?"

"No, I should be good."

"Let's go. Doesn't do us any good to argue."

Brad led off on his snowshoes, and Misty followed a few yards behind, hand in pocket, with Kim bringing up the rear. A few yards from the scattered bones, Brad stopped, surveying Mac's remains, the wolves' tracks, and the signs of the women's investigations. He looked up toward the trees, then back to Mac's bones, then back toward the cache. Kim stepped off the trail three paces to the left, and Misty to the right. Both stayed a little behind Brad. After a few moments, he began to speak quietly.

"His tent was right over there, next to that big pine, just on the far side of it. He was sitting up against that big tree when he shot himself. You can see the bullet hole in it, if you look." He took his right glove off, then his sunglasses, wiped his eyes, and put his sunglasses back on. "I laid him on his back just this side of the tree, and that's where I left his body, wrapped in that blanket." He scanned the bones. "They must have dragged him over this way. Thirty feet, I suppose. Or maybe they were just fighting over the parts and moving out where there was more room when they got hold of something."

Brad inhaled deeply, and the breath came out as a long sigh. He walked over to the spot he'd pointed out where Mac's tent had been, scanning the ground. "Did you find his blanket? A mostly-green print polarfleece."

Kim spoke up. "No. But we haven't looked around much over there. It might be just under the snow a bit."

"You're right–here it is." Brad bent down and pulled up a blanket, torn and stained, that had been hidden under a couple inches of snow. He shook it out and stretched the ragged thing out, and they could see that the wolves had not been gentle.

Misty asked, "You took his tent down and put it up in the cache?"

"Yeah. That and most of his gear."

"What about the rifle?"

"I took that out with me. It's locked up at the place I'm staying. Like Mac said, it was weird to carry that around, but I was trying to do what he'd asked me to do. I left him here, and took the rifle. Figured I could come back and pack out his other stuff if need be."

Misty had been watching Brad closely, and Kim watched them both. A tiny bit at a time, she saw her friend begin to relax, at least a little bit. Still, Misty's right hand kept returning to that slash pocket on her parka. Kim felt an urgency to get this train moving in the right direction. "Brad, Misty, it seems to me we should try to collect what's out here and see how much of Mac's remains we've got."

Misty considered, eyeing Kim. "Seems reasonable. You up for that?"

Brad was looking back their direction now. Kim said, "I'm fine. And if I need to go sit on a log for a bit, I can do it. I'd like to have a sense of how much we're still looking for."

All three began the grisly task of reassembling Mac's remains, making a rough skeleton in the snow. Aside from the missing skull, they had the majority of the bones. They couldn't find the lower part of the right arm, and many of the ribs were broken up or missing.

"No head, huh? I wonder where that ended up. It seems odd that the bones are already so clean," Brad commented. "And all the inner organs are missing. There's very little here you'd call muscle or skin."

Misty shook her head. "It's a big pack, and they're hungry. Signs are that they've been spending a lot of time here the last few days, cleaning up exactly that. Taking the soft tissues and organs, the muscles, and chewing the bones. Pardon my saying so, but my guess is that most of the damage to the skeleton happened in the early stages, when they were going after the organs. Tore things up and scattered the limbs, and the wolves farther down the hierarchy gnawed the muscle off what bones they could pull away from the pile."

Kim shuddered. "Okay. That's enough forensic detail."

"Sorry."

"No, I suspect you're right. But now, what do you think, Misty? Do we go looking for the lower right arm and the head, or do we call this good?"

"If you're leaving most of his remains here like he wanted–which by the way, you should never mention to anyone so the Forest Service doesn't hear about it–we just need to take out enough of him we can do the tissue typing and DNA match or whatever to verify it's him for the purpose of getting him declared dead. That will be important for your foundation and all the legal processes."

Brad looked around a bit, thinking. "I think it might be smart to move the bones we have a little farther toward the swamp. My guess is this clear area gets pretty wet and grows up into cattails and sedges all around the edges. You can see some of that right over here"–he pointed westward to a patch of brown cattail stems reaching up out of the snow about fifty yards away–"and once it thaws, that soft ground will prevent any wayward hikers from discovering Mac's bones by accident."

"Why bother? The wolves will just take the bones where they want to."

"Yes, but if they start out in the swamp, they're less likely to be moved out of it. Things will be thawing in the next month or so, and if you don't want people running across Mac's bones by accident, the swamp is a better place than the higher ground. It's pretty remote here, but you don't want some adventurous hiker running across Mac's bones."

Kim thought about it, then said, "Sounds like it might help. I don't think it would be a huge issue if someone found a bone or two this summer and brought it out, but I'd rather not have to deal with it."

They used Mac's much-abused blanket to pile his bones together, and they dragged them a few yards farther out into the lower ground, near where the creek ran out to the south.

"Do you think it would help if we buried them down in the snow a bit?" Brad asked.

"Couldn't hurt," Misty said. "There's a folding shovel on our sled."

"I've got one, too. I'll get it." He headed back north on what was becoming a well-packed snowshoe trail.

Once Brad was out of earshot, Misty turned to Kim. "Well? Anything striking you as suspicious?"

"Not really. You?"

"Him being here right now is plenty suspicious for me. And I notice he hasn't once said he didn't kill Mac."

"He already told me the story of how Mac committed suicide. Why would he have to say he didn't do it?"

"I almost came right out and accused him—and he skirted the issue."

"So you think he killed Mac?"

"After Bible camp, I worked as a cop. That's where my training came, Kim. I was taught to be suspicious. I believe people are sinners, just like the Bible says, and every last one of them acts like it."

"That attitude won't get you many free drinks at the local bar."

"No, I usually have to buy my own. But that attitude also keeps me from losing my purse."

"You carry a purse?"

"Metaphorically speaking. I don't go to the bar much either, but you get my point."

"You're saying we still need to keep an eye on Brad."

"Better believe it, baby."

"By that logic, you could have come up here and killed Mac."

81

"Motive and opportunity. That's what Brad's got."

"I see the opportunity, obviously. What's his motive?"

"Whatever is in that manila envelope he brought out."

Kim thought hard about that. Misty continued. "Are you convinced those papers are genuine, that Mac wrote them and that he wasn't coerced?"

"I'm pretty well convinced. They seem like genuine Mac. And there's enough of his sarcastic sense of humor in there that I'd be really surprised if he wrote those documents with a gun to his head."

Misty looked at the bones on the tattered blanket. "I wish we'd had a chance to test for the cancer," she said. "Not much left to determine if the pancreatic cancer was the real deal."

"Might be able to get something from his doctor."

"Maybe, but it will take a court order. HIPAA has that stuff sealed up pretty tight."

"We've got lawyers for that kind of work at the Foundation, if it comes to that. At the moment, I have to say Brad's story looks like the most likely truth. Doesn't seem like he's trying to protect himself, as far as I can tell."

"Just keep your eyes open is all I'm saying."

"Well, don't shoot him just because you were trained as a cop. You seemed pretty tense when he first showed up."

"I *was* pretty tense. He's acting a little better now, but I'm still a little uneasy."

Brad came back with the shovel, and working together the three dug a deep hole in the snow, down to the brown swamp grasses along the hard-frozen ground. They tried to be gentle about the quasi-burial. But in the end they mostly dumped the bones down the hole. The entire process seemed like a macabre version of a funeral, but no one joked about it. Mostly they worked in silence. When the hole was filled in, they wrapped the pelvis and several lumbar vertebrae that were still attached to it in the blanket and turned to go back to their camp.

"Oh, Jesus," Misty breathed. "Look over there." She pointed across the swamp to the east. Standing out from the treeline, dark against the snow, they saw two wolves, alert and watching them, but not seeming concerned. "So much for keeping Mac's location a secret."

"Well, at this point it is what it is," Kim said, resigned. "They could just as easily come back tomorrow and dig him up after we're gone."

They turned and walked in file to the north, back to the campsite. The sun was descending toward the trees. None of them had been particularly hungry while they dealt with Mac's bones, but now their stomachs were growling. While Brad pitched his tent thirty yards east of the women's camp, Kim put together a supper of rehydrated chicken chow mein and rice. Misty gathered firewood to replenish what they'd burned the night before. A half hour later, they sat by the fire, eating piles of steaming food from their plates and watching the sky fade to black.

"You sure you don't want your tent a little closer to the fire?" Kim asked Brad.

"No, I'll give you ladies a little privacy. Besides, I might snore."

"Kim snores. No big deal. Not worried about wolves?" Misty asked.

"No, they don't bother me."

"What do you mean, I snore?"

"Not bad. Just cute little snorey breaths. Not enough to keep me awake."

"I don't believe it."

"Better believe it, baby."

Brad laughed. "I've got to get my sleeping pad inflated and sleeping bag rolled out, but I can do dishes first, if you tell me where the soap is."

"Don't worry about it," Kim said. "We'll get it."

"Okay. Thanks. Supper was delicious."

They all turned in early, tired from a long day in the cold air. A haze of high clouds covered the sky. The clouds obscured the stars. The haze diffused the moon's light when it rose. By the time the moon began to climb above the pines to the east, all three were asleep. About four a.m., when the hazy moon was at its zenith, a cow moose crossed the east end of the clearing, moving south to north. The wolves were long gone, far afield on the trail of other game, and she trotted through the moonlight undisturbed.

Chapter Twelve

The next morning they all emerged from their tents. The sun was climbing above the eastern horizon to a glorious day. The snow-covered forest fell away to the southeast of them. They could see in the distance the openings of lakes here and there like pearls strung in a net before them. The soft light of dawn created long, stark shadows and ice-rainbows along the eastern margin of the clearing. The morning was cold but not painfully so. The previous night's haze had blown away, and the day promised to be brilliantly clear.

"With that sun, I'll bet we'll see the snow melting off the tree branches this afternoon," Misty observed.

"You ladies headed out today?"

Kim nodded. "I think we've found what we can find for the moment. Now I need to get some proof of Mac's death back so we can start the legal processes, get a death certificate, that kind of thing."

"That will mean the Lake County coroner in Two Harbors," Misty offered. "His name is Brad Nelson. Not a bad guy."

Kim turned to Brad. "Would you be willing to go with me to talk to him? I think if we have a bone and tissue sample and your first hand story, that should be enough to get a death certificate started."

"I can do that. Sure."

Misty added, "I don't know how much weight my involvement will add, but I might be able to help. I worked with Nelson on a few death investigations back in the day. Like I said before, though, if they know there's more of Mac up here, they'll demand that his body be collected and removed. So it might be better to let him have the impression what we bring in is all we found."

"Okay. Your mom will be alright if you're gone today as well?"

"Jeannie will take care of her. Mom's okay, just a little forgetful. A few more hours won't make a difference. Once we get back to Ely we'll have to call ahead and make sure Nelson's available. We should be able to see him this afternoon if we make good time getting out of here."

"Thanks. That means a lot, Misty."

"No problem."

They packed up sleeping bags, tents, and the rest of their gear, loading it all carefully on their sleds. "What about Mac's gear?" Kim asked, looking back to the southwest corner of the clearing.

"It's cached up on the poles," Brad thought aloud. "We could try to haul it out now on the sleds. Or I can probably get in here early this summer and hike it out."

"Makes sense," Misty said. Nothing there we need to bring out now?"

"Nothing I can think of," Brad said.

Kim looked dubiously northward at their backtrail through the heavy brush. "I'm not looking forward to hauling this load up that slope."

"You guys came in that way?" Brad asked. "Saw where your tracks left the trail."

"Yeah. Why?"

"That dog-hair poplar is way too thick. That stuff will kill you. Come up to the northeast corner of the clearing and you can get through those mature pines, and there's very little underbrush. Then once you connect with the hiking trail, you head west. It's a little longer, but believe me, it's a lot easier."

"Wish we'd known about that," Misty groused.

They followed the route Brad recommended, and though they were still breaking a sweat by the time they reached the hiking trail, it was far easier than the women's original route down through the poplars had been. "I got to know this trail pretty well when I was visiting Mac up here," Brad said quietly. "Lots of trips back and forth this way during those days."

They turned west and crossed the top of Disappointment Mountain. Then they began descending toward the lake. They had to be cautious not to let the weight of the sleds push them downhill, but they made good time. By the time they emerged onto Disappointment Lake, the sun was high and felt warm on their backs. They paused to strip off a couple layers and worked their way south and west, crossed the portage to Snowbank, and followed the last couple miles across that massive lake.

As they walked on in slow single file, Kim reflected on the odd sensation she'd felt so many times, seeing buildings across the lake after being in the wilderness. The hard edges and angular lines of lake cabins and resorts stood in stark contrast to the sweep of branches, the graceful curves of snowdrifts, the irregular outlines of boulders, islands, and hills. Even after just a couple nights in the backcountry, returning to man-made structures felt at the same time comforting and, well, disappointing. Part of her had been jealous of Mac's wilderness adventures over the years. She loved the Boundary Waters, but something in her was wired to achieve, to keep her nose to the grindstone. Why didn't she do a better job of taking time away? She'd banked weeks of vacation, and Mac had often told her she needed to get away. She'd rarely done so. She knew the intricate legal and procedural work demanded by Mac's death would dominate her life for weeks and months to come. She resolved, however, that this summer she was going to squeeze in a canoe trip. Reconnecting with Misty reminded her of a long-ago Kim. That younger version of her had loved the adrenalin and challenge of the wilderness. And frankly, she had handled it well. That version of herself needed to re-emerge in some way without negating her professional life. Ambition and hard work needed balance.

Brad interrupted her reflections. "Where are you guys parked? I need to veer a little south, toward the boat landing."

"We're a little to the right, at Roger's Outfitters," Kim pointed. "We'll meet up with you in Two Harbors. Do you have your cell phone along?"

"In my glove box, powered off. I'll make sure to turn it back on when I get back to Ely. Call me when you get to Two Harbors and I'll just meet you at the coroner's office."

"It's at the hospital, up the hill from the highway. Take a right after the golf course when you get into town," Misty advised.

"Sounds good. See you there in a few hours."

Brad's track diverged from the women as they angled toward the north end of the peninsula that jutted out like a giant thumb into the south end of Snowbank Lake. Kim glanced after him as he walked into the distance.

"Well, Kimmy, he didn't ask you to bait his hook. And he didn't offer to bait yours. And he offered to do dishes. Points for Brad."

"You liked him?"

"If Mac's death went down like he said, he seems like a good guy. If he's lying about that, all bets are off."

"Yeah. That's the rub, isn't it?"

"Just a minor detail."

"So what do you think about that detail, Misty?"

"I think I wish we could have found the skull, and maybe the vertebrae from the neck. I didn't find a few of the top vertebrae."

"Why are those important?"

"Okay, TMI here. But if Brad killed Mac, the bullet wound in the head is probably not going to look like a suicide. For Mac to shoot

86

himself in the head with that rifle from a sitting position the way Brad described it, the bullet would go in under the jaw, likely, and come out the top of the skull somehow. If Brad shot him, it would be hard to get that angle, and the skull would show that."

"Okay, I'm tracking. But what about the neck bones?"

"Let's say you're Brad, and you realize all this. He's a smart guy, and realistic. He knows the skull can mess up his story. So he has to get rid of it. But cutting off a head is hard, grisly work, and any way of doing it out here will likely leave marks on the vertebrae–knife marks or saw marks or whatever."

"That's gruesome, but I get your point."

"It stands in Brad's favor that the bullet hole in the tree where he says Mac was sitting is in the right place, and angles upward like it should if Mac shot himself."

"So you believe his story."

"That bullet hole could have been staged. I just don't know, without being able to see the skull itself."

"Should we have dug the bullet out of the tree?"

"I wondered about that. Even if it was staged, it could still have been fired through Mac's head after he was dead, so there'd likely be blood and bone fragments in there along with the slug. We wouldn't be able to tell anything definite. So I left it there–but if we run up against other things that make us suspicious, we'll maybe need to get that dug out. It will just have to be done by a forensic team at that point."

"I'll file that away. I hope it doesn't come to that."

"Yeah. He seems like a nice guy. You could use a boyfriend, Kimmy."

"He hasn't applied for the job. And I have work to do."

"Give him time."

"Misty, can I tell you something without you letting it go any further?"

"You're sounding kind of like a broken record with this. Another one? Okay. I know how to keep a secret."

"Without being too specific, Mac said some things in that last envelope about Brad coming to work at the Foundation."

"You mentioned that."

"And he hinted that maybe it should get more personal."

"That son of a bitch." Misty took a breath. "So he kills himself and tries to play matchmaker at the same time?"

"Maybe."

"Nothing like putting you in a tough emotional position."

"I'll admit it is a little weird. My mother never warned me there'd be days like this."

"How could she have known? Shit."

They had by this time arrived back at the car and stowing their gear took several minutes. As they were pulling out of Roger's, Misty asked, "So. Do you find yourself attracted to Mr. Swenson?"

"Oh, crap, Misty, I don't know. I just met the man. He seems like a nice guy. He's got some self-confidence. Seems like he's intelligent. Strong-willed. Polite."

"Yeah. And maybe he killed your boss."

"Right. Or maybe he was the one person Mac trusted at the end of his life to carry on his legacy somehow."

"I think you might need to do more research. Let things play out for a while. You in any hurry? That old biological clock giving you trouble?"

"No. Hell, no."

The miles and the silence stretched away.

Chapter Thirteen

The following Tuesday afternoon, Kim sat in Al's office reading through a file folder full of documentation about Brad Swenson. "Al, it looks like this is pretty normal stuff. Credit ratings, home loans, a couple parking tickets, the divorce from last year. Anything that troubles you? Anything I'm not seeing?"

"He's pretty clean, Kim. Unless he's really, really good, and the dirt is just very well hidden, very well covered. He's not a thug, and he's not an average criminal, and he's not into anything really troubling. I did a little digging and found a couple bars where he used to hang out and have a couple too many. He went through a phase after the divorce, looks like, where that got to be a little bit of a habit, but it seems like he nipped it in the bud. Or changed gears. Or something."

"So he's clean."

"Maybe. Like I said, he might be really, really good, and this whole profile is a cover. I don't think that's the case."

"So he's clean."

Al laughed. "Kim, I'm paid to look for the worst case scenario. I'm paid to poke holes in people. The guy looks okay, honestly. But there is one other possibility."

"What's that?"

"It's possible that he's basically what he looks like up until now, but the opportunity, meeting Mac and all the rest–well, maybe he just saw a chance to do something that might pay off big, and given everything he'd been through, he said 'what the hell' and made it look like it does now."

"Anything that tells you that's likely?"

"No. Just that Mac's dead and from what you've hinted at, this guy stands to benefit. Cops would call that motive."

"I don't think Mr. Swenson even knows about Mac's suggestions."

"Neither do I for that matter, except what you've said. But if Swenson has manufactured any of this story, he does know."

"How do I find out if that's the case, or if Brad is a really solid guy?"

"I'll repeat my advice from the last time we met. Don't let him into things too far, too fast. Other than that, I think you just have to let things play out for a while. Take your time. I'll keep digging if you want, see if I find any other indications."

"Thank you. I'd appreciate that, Al."

"Has Mac's death been reported?"

"We brought a tissue sample–a bone we stole from the wolves–to the coroner of Lake County after we went to the Boundary Waters. He wasn't happy about it, but between Brad's story and Misty's description of what we found up there, he didn't see a problem with signing a death certificate once the DNA tests prove a match."

"Media?"

"We put out a press release yesterday to the Duluth *Tribune*. We're not making a big deal of it."

"I imagine it will go big."

"It might. Depends on if it's a slow news day."

"It will, if they get the connection with Swenson. That was a big local story not long ago. Him involved with Mac's death–well, that would be news."

"There's nothing to indicate they'll make the connection. If they do, we can deal with it."

"I have no doubt. Okay, Kim, I'll keep digging."

"Thanks."

"Tell me it's none of my business, but was it bad, finding Mac like that?"

Kim looked at the floor. "It was okay. Misty's a friend of mine from years ago, and she's done some of that kind of work. She handled it like a pro. The bones were pretty well picked over. Quite a pack of wolves, and they'd been there a while. Brad gave us a little perspective on where exactly Mac's tent was, the tree with the bullet hole in it, that kind of thing. Saved us some looking."

"He was up there with you?"

"He came in separately. He kind of figured I'd go check it out."

"So he came up there thinking you were alone. Did you get any kind of a read on him?"

"He seemed fine. Misty was pretty tense, but she decided she didn't need to shoot him."

Al shook his head, gazing at her. "Interesting times," he finally muttered.

"Look, Al, I know this whole thing is a little bizarre. So far, though, Brad's story is checking out. I'll take your advice and take things slow, keep my distance. And if you find anything, get in touch."

"Will do."

Chapter Fourteen

Kim's house was small but comfortable. It was originally built in 1902. The petite floor plan was unusual in a time when most houses in the neighborhood were built with an eye to housing large families. Its solid construction and dark oak trim first caught Kim's eye when she decided her position with the foundation was long term. It just made sense to buy a house. Little by little she had made it her own, but she kept the woodwork intact. The house had the feel of a simple but elegant old friend. Kim thought of the house that way sometimes. It snuggled up against the forest on the hillside to the north of downtown Duluth.

Kim perched on the couch facing the picture window—a later addition—that looked out into her backyard. She sat curled up, feet under her, her favorite afghan wrapped around her shoulders. A glass of Merlot stood mostly forgotten on the table next to her along with a few slices of sharp cheddar cheese and a handful of Triscuits on a plate. She gazed out into the twilight, thinking about the turn of the seasons. In a few weeks, the snow would be melting. The days of mud would begin. Meltwater would trickle down to the big lake by a million pathways. Frost would go out of the ground. Mac's bones would settle into the swampy soil. No doubt the wolves, or something else, would get into them again. Rodents would gnaw them for the nutrients. All in all, though it was a messy process, Mac would get his wish and go back to the soil. That process was largely accomplished already courtesy of the wolves. *When I die, let the wolves enjoy my bones.*

Reconnecting with Misty had been a good call. Why the hell hadn't she stayed in contact? Ten years. Ten years with her upwardly mobile do-gooder nose to the grindstone, managing details for Mac. It had been a good stretch, and she wasn't done yet. She loved the foundation and its work, and she was realistic enough to deal with the mundane daily details in order to achieve a greater good. But the foundation needed a leader, and she didn't want that job.

Brad? Maybe. She let herself run systematically over the memories of him snowshoeing into the clearing, dealing with Misty's suspicion and pitching in to help with finding Mac's remains, then with camp chores. She appreciated his good humor and what looked from her perspective like a sort of stoic willingness to deal with challenges.

She could see the Scandinavian farmers in his background as she thought about his willingness to do whatever needed to be done. His even-keeled personality was so different from Mac's fiery hot and cold.

She tried once again to imagine the two of them camping together, spending hours and hours on Disappointment Mountain in the snow, talking about camping equipment, movies, and poetry. Each in their own way was a self-possessed man. In spite of his emotional difficulties and the bruising he carried around over his divorce, Brad owned his issues. He didn't blame or make excuses.

And unbidden, she turned back to that last day of Mac's life, to Brad snowshoeing back down the cold trail, hearing that gunshot, understanding what must have happened and doing the difficult but necessary thing, turning back up the hill to return and find Mac's remains. She pictured Brad sitting there with Mac's body through that long, cold night and the next day.

What kind of man was he, really? Al's research seemed to clear him of suspicion, but Al was still suspicious. Was she missing something critical? What had really happened up there?

Outside the window, right at the edge of the yard, she glimpsed movement. At first she thought it was a deer. They usually hung out with her neighbors who kept well-stocked bird feeders. The fading twilight didn't do a great job of illuminating the backyard. Her eyes strained to focus. With a start she realized it was a pair of wolves standing there. Timber wolves were common enough in Duluth, and stories like Misty's about pets being snatched were not unusual, but Kim had never seen them in her yard. They stood motionless for what seemed like minutes, though it was probably only a few seconds. Time stretched out. Then they were just gone–a swish of tails and two steps and they disappeared into the darkness. She wasn't even certain she'd seen them. Finally she threw a pair of boots on, grabbed a flashlight, and walked out. Sure enough, the fresh tracks followed the perimeter of her backyard and then off into the brush.

She returned to the house, mind weighted down with a sense that all the structures of civilization are just a patina laid over the deeper wilderness below. Our laws, our streets and sewer lines–all of it is a temporary etching on the surface of the wild beneath.

While I stand on the roadway, or on the pavements grey,
I hear it in the deep heart's core.

She poured the last swallow of wine down the sink, rinsed the glass, and went off to bed.

Chapter Fifteen

It took a couple weeks, but the Lake County coroner finally produced a death certificate. Kim had sent out an email about Mac's memorial service to the foundation's few employees, and of course that started the rumor mill grinding. News of Mac's passing was simply confirmation of what many people had known when he disappeared. Mac wasn't the kind of guy who just went missing, in spite of his backcountry proclivities. For the moment, anyway, the word "suicide" was kept out of things, and it just sounded like a tragic backcountry accident. Kim debated the wisdom of all that, but the Foundation's lawyers advised her that for a short window, anyway, it was important to keep the details of Mac's death out of the press. By chance or divine intervention, the day Mac's death became public knowledge, charges surfaced against a state legislator of insider trading and inappropriate kickbacks on some construction projects. There was also a gas explosion at a building in a suburb of the Cities, so the press was otherwise occupied. There were minor stories in the Duluth *Tribune* and other outlets, but the news cycles moved on as blithely as she hoped they would.

On a Thursday morning in early April, twenty people gathered in the chapel at Corvak's Funeral Home just north of downtown Duluth. A reference in Mac's envelope had sent Kim to a file folder in his desk. There she found a complete plan for the memorial service, including a list of guests to be invited, a program, and a playlist for the occasion, selections from Bach's Mass in B Minor. Most of the guests were connected to the Foundation in some way. A few were business acquaintances of Mac's from the local area. A couple had very specific roles to play in the service. An editorial note at the bottom of the page made clear that Mac wanted no freelancing, no sentimentality, no, in his words, "damned burbling eulogies."

Promptly at 10 am, the funeral home's sound system kicked in and the guests sat patient through ten minutes of Bach's choral and instrumental genius, "Kyrie eleison"–"Lord, have mercy." As the powerful piece swelled to a close, Kim stood and faced the (mostly) familiar faces. "It should come as no surprise to you that Mac dictated the details of this little memorial, and planned this service himself. He wanted very little fuss, but he also recognized that we would need a way to say goodbye. Thank you for being here." She turned to a seventy-ish man with a trim white beard who sat in the third row back. "Professor Lundgren?"

The man stood and walked in measured stride to the front of the room. He snapped to attention like a marionette being drawn to stand at his full height, looking over the heads of the small crowd to the back of the room, and announced: "Mac shared with me his reservations about importing words from an Englishman into his funeral proceedings; however, he apparently made his peace with that, and I give you the words of King Henry the Fifth, as penned by William Shakespeare." Without a manuscript, in perfect intonation and raising the hairs on Kim's arms at times, the professor (who taught at the University of Minnesota Duluth, and every few years took a role in the local community theaters) proceeded to recite, to act, to preach, the "St. Crispin's Day" monologue. When he finished, it seemed wrong not to clap, but clapping felt wrong as well. Kim and every other person present seemed to heave a deep sigh, feeling at a depth how the professor's orations had stirred and held them those several minutes.

After an appropriate silence Kim stood once again and turned to a man in a black suit with a clerical collar. "Bishop Dunham?" The Roman Catholic bishop stood and opened a heavy black Bible. "From the book of Job, the thirty-eighth chapter, through chapter forty, verse five." He read from the great black book, and the reading went on and on–God demanding of Job, asking if he knew the secrets of the natural world, challenging him in his arrogance, and finally Job answering God like a whipped dog, refusing to speak further, cowed by the majesty of the Almighty. The bishop finished the reading, closed his Bible and quietly sat down.

After a moment, Kim stood once more. Her eyes searched the faces as she began to say, "And as a final..." She saw him, then: Brad Swenson, sitting in the back row, meeting her eyes. He gave one firm shake of his head, and she paused, then almost without any awkwardness started again. "And as a final source of meditation on Mac's life and death, I invite you to listen to the last movement of Bach's B Minor Mass, 'Dona nobis pacem–Give us peace'." She nodded to the funeral director, and the strains of the choir swept into the room, starting low and swelling to fill the space with an intricate plea for mercy, for peace. How fitting, she thought. I hope he's found it.

After four minutes culminating with timpani and horns and violins and voices swelling to a triumphant climax, Kim stood once more. "Thank you again for being here today. I know it's early in the day, but Mac laid by a few bottles of excellent Scotch for this occasion, and you are invited into the next room if you'd like, for a toast in his memory."

Everyone filed into the next room where a table was set up with a deep green tablecloth, and on it two dozen Glencairn glasses, already containing a generous shot each. There was some quiet chuckling and a few under-the-breath comments, but each participant dutifully chose a glass and all turned to Kim. No one else knew the man standing next to her, but Kim, holding her own glass, faced them all and announced, "Mr. Brad Swenson—a friend of Mac's." She half-turned and looked at Brad. "Mr. Swenson?"

Brad stood next to her and took a breath. "From W. B. Yeats, 'The Lake Isle of Innisfree.'" Then he went on to share from memory the poem that had so obviously been on Mac's mind the day of his death. As Brad spoke, Kim let the words wash over her, thinking less about their content than about the spirit of a man she'd worked with for a dozen or more years, but only started to get to know:

> *I will arise and go now, and go to Innisfree,*
> *And a small cabin build there, of clay and wattles made:*
> *Nine bean-rows will I have there, a hive for the honey-bee;*
> *And live alone in the bee-loud glade.*
>
> *And I shall have some peace there, for peace comes dropping slow,*
> *Dropping from the veils of the morning to where the cricket sings;*
> *There midnight's all a glimmer, and noon a purple glow,*
> *And evening full of the linnet's wings.*
>
> *I will arise and go now, for always night and day*
> *I hear lake water lapping with low sounds by the shore;*
> *While I stand on the roadway, or on the pavements grey,*
> *I hear it in the deep heart's core.*

Several people nodded in appreciation as Brad finished. He took another deep breath, raised his glass, and said, "Ladies and gentlemen, I give you Phillip 'Mac' McPherson. May God bless his memory among us." A low murmur of "Mac" rumbled around the room, and everyone drank. A few gasps, a couple coughs, and several deep murmurs of appreciation broke the silence. Suddenly everyone was loosed from the spell of Mac's memorial service. They broke up into little knots of people to visit briefly before one by one returning to what was, after all, a workday.

Kim felt the smoky peat sensation of the Scotch that was one experience on the way down her throat and completely different as she exhaled. It was a powerful drink, she reflected, for a powerful man. She stepped forward to thank the professor and the bishop and she greeted a couple others, then turned back to Brad. "You did it. And did it well."

He chuckled and shook his head. "I was caught up in the moment during the service. I knew I couldn't do it there. That's why I waved you off."

"That was just fine. You know Mac said it was optional for you to do that."

"That's what your text said. And if I'd tried at that moment, I would have lost it. But I thought I could get through it as a toast."

"You did an amazing job. Thank you."

"Thank you, Kim, for putting this together."

"Mac did all the work."

"You know what I mean. For implementing Mac's plan. For leading it. You're a natural."

She looked down and shook her head. "I learned to fake what I need to, working for Mac. But up front is not my favorite role."

"You looked completely comfortable and in charge."

"Thank you."

"Well, Ms. Norby, once you're done greeting your guests, do you have lunch plans?"

She surveyed the room, where a few people were already moving toward the exits. She'd been looking for a good reason to touch base with Brad, and this seemed more or less natural. And timely. "There's a hamburger place just two blocks down to the south."

"Ed's Burgers? I know the place."

"Fifteen minutes?"

"I'll go get us a booth."

"Sounds good."

Chapter Sixteen

She walked into Ed's and saw Brad at a booth near the back, a good choice for some quiet conversation. They were a little early for the lunch rush—it was about a quarter to twelve—and yet she appreciated his choosing the booth like this, so that even when the place filled up they'd be able to talk easily. She walked back to join him and he stood up. She thought, how strange that this man has never yet done anything that annoys me. Except, of course, the obvious. The entire reason they knew each other, that he had been present at Mac's death: that bothered her immensely, from a couple different directions.

She sat, and spent the obligatory minute or so removing coat, scarf, gloves. April had not yet turned to spring in northern Minnesota, so she still dressed for winter like every other person in Duluth. A few days had risen above freezing, but the nighttime lows were well down in the 20's and winter still held sway.

"Feels a little like 'Always winter but never Christmas,' doesn't it?" Brad grinned.

"You're a C.S. Lewis fan?"

"Just Narnia. Read the books as a boy, and I've gone back to them a few times. I've never read his other stuff."

Kim smiled, lost for a moment in the memory of her mother working through *The Lion, The Witch, and the Wardrobe* as a read-aloud. Kim had loved the magical story, and loved most of all her mother dedicating time each evening to read to her. But for some reason after dutifully finishing that book her mother was reluctant to start another one. Kim had gone on to read the rest of the series for herself.

Brad watched her face, waiting. Finally she realized she was being rude, or at least it felt rude. Brad seemed unfazed. "I'm sorry," she shook her head and laughed. "My mother read me that book when I was young. I was reminiscing. I think I was eight."

"And you remember it well enough that you recognized the quote and immediately came up with the author's name? Must have made quite an impression."

"It did. I read all the rest of the Narnia books myself." She stopped.

Brad just sat, attentive. Listening. Paying attention.

Kim looked down, then back at Brad's face. "I loved having my mother read to me. But for some reason, and I never understood this, she didn't want to move on and read me the rest of the series. So I read them all myself. And yes, the stories made a big impression on me."

"Did you ever ask her about it? Why she didn't read the rest of the series?"

"No. No, that's not something I ever asked her."

"Are your parents still living?"

"Yes. They bought a place near Brainerd. Enjoying retirement, I guess. They're nice people."

"Then it's not too late to ask."

Kim laughed. "Sure. But I can guess what she'd say. She'd say, 'Well, Kim, you were old enough to read for yourself. I didn't need to do that for you.' My parents were very careful to make sure I was capable and did things for myself when I was able."

"And how was that for you?"

Suddenly Kim was annoyed, very annoyed, with Brad. She was smart enough to realize that her annoyance had very little to do with him, however. "It was fine. My parents are good people and I don't want to fault them. I owe them a lot."

"Of course you do."

She struggled to get past that flash of temper.

"So, Brad, how are you?"

He gazed across the table at her face for a long, long second. "My parents are both dead. Part of what I've done this past year, while I've been grieving for what my marriage should have been, is that I grieved all over again for my parents. I have this theory that grief can't be compartmentalized. When grief gets a hold on you, it brings up every hurt from every loss and they all gang up on you. So grieving for Mac this morning, I'm back in touch with losing my parents. And Lauren. And my dreams of a loving marriage. And every other death, every other grief I've ever known."

She was taken aback. "Are—are you okay?"

"Yes, but I'm grieving. I'd be less okay if I tried to stuff all that grief back into a dark closet somewhere, keep it from coming up where it makes my eyes well up or puts me in touch with my heart."

"And you think I'm compartmentalizing?"

"Kim, I don't mean to be rude, or intrusive. What I heard you start to talk about sounded like an old grief, and that made perfect sense to me after Mac's service this morning. I was just asking about it.

Making conversation about stuff that seemed to matter. If you don't want to talk about Narnia and your mom reading to you, that's fine."

Kim considered for a moment, and just then the waiter came up and took their orders. When he left, she looked Brad in the eye. "How about this. Next time I spend the weekend with my parents, I'll ask my mom if she remembers reading that book to me, and why we stopped there."

"Okay, that's brave. Tell me if this is too pushy, but will you tell me what she says?"

"Hmm. Probably. I will probably tell you what she says."

Brad grinned. "I can live with probably."

Kim cocked her head to one side, looking at Brad like a slide under a microscope. "I think you have a unique way of grieving."

"I just try not to separate it from everything else. This is new to me, understand. I've been chewing through all this during this past horrendous, hellish, wonderful year."

"I've been meaning to ask you. What do you do with your time these days? Are you working?"

"Sort of. I told you that I'm watching my friend's place while he's in Tucson. That's a pretty big job, actually. It's not just taking out the trash. He has lots of stuff going on here, and he kind of left me in charge of a lot of that while he's down south. Said he wants to relax a little more this year. So I'm kind of a business manager."

"What kind of business?"

"Well, there's his personal estate. And then he's got some interests, mostly in applied technology. I'm not really a decision maker at this point. I'm just monitoring things, and condensing information so he can digest it without having to be on top of things day by day."

"Applied technology?"

Brad grimaced. "The world is not really fair, right? So a woman who spends her whole life investing in special ed students can barely make a living. She's doing something that nobody would argue makes the world a better place. She's probably a saint of some kind. But we don't finance that. My friend invented some part of the credit card reader that gets installed on every new gas pump."

"You're kidding."

"Serious as a heart attack. So every reader that gets installed in every new gas pump in the country puts a couple dollars in my friend's pocket."

"That's it?"

"Oh, he's got a couple other things going. And he's working on other ideas. But that's his biggie."

"And you get to sleep on his couch."

"More or less."

"And manage his business and send him reports."

"Yeah. And take out the trash."

"How do you know this guy?"

"We were roommates in college."

Just then their burgers arrived, and conversation stopped for a moment while they got down to lunch.

Finally Brad spoke again. "I've been lying awake each night as I fall asleep, thinking about putting Mac's bones down that hole in the snow."

"It's a hard image to get out of your mind. It was a hard thing to have to do. I've relived it a bit myself."

"Yeah. I've started planning a trip to go in and get the rest of his stuff."

"You said you might do that."

"I figure I have to. Mac wouldn't want his gear cluttering up the woods."

"Any idea when you might go?"

"Sooner would be better than later for my mental state. I was thinking June. Maybe earlier."

"Boundary Waters, June is still spring most years. But each year is different."

"That's a long time to remember dropping his bones down in the snow. I really do want to get Mac's gear out of there, but I think I also want some different pictures in my head, you know?"

"Are you sleeping these days, Brad?"

He looked her full in the face, seemingly surprised by the question. "Some. Yeah. It's not bad. Most of the time it's not bad." Brad looked past her, out the front window, then back at his half-eaten burger. "Grief is hard. And I keep wondering if I should have done something different."

"Like what?"

"A thousand different things. Asked different questions. Camped in a different spot so I was closer to Mac. Every single action affects the future, right? So I have spent a lot of hours going back and looking at every one of my actions."

"Sounds like a lot of pressure to live with."

Wry chuckle from Brad. "I got used to it after my divorce."

"You said it a minute ago: Grief is hard."

Deep breath. "Yes. That is a true statement."

"Seems like you're taking a lot of responsibility on yourself."

"That's the question, isn't it? How much of this am I responsible for? With Lauren, it was important for me to go back and figure out what I could have done. What I should have done. Wouldn't do me any good just to blame her. That's dishonest, but you see it all the time, the guy who blames his ex for the bad marriage. And then you see that guy get into the same bad relationship, second verse. I don't want to be that guy. I figure I have to take stock of what I could have changed and what I couldn't have. It's the same with Mac's death. I know Mac made choices, and he chose his death. But I need to look hard at my own actions and see what I could have done different."

"Maybe there's nothing. Maybe it was all out of your hands, and like you said, Mac made a choice. From years of working with the man, that's not hard for me to believe. It was pretty impossible to sway Mac from a choice once his mind was made up."

"In principle, I get that. And maybe it's easy to say from where you sit." Kim's eyes went hard at this, but Brad's gaze was fixed out the window and he didn't notice.. "I was there. I... I found Mac, wrapped him up, sat with him. I have to look at what I should have done differently."

"Brad, it's not 'easy to say that' from where I sit. You think I haven't wondered if I should have done things differently?"

"Sure, but you weren't there. That changes things."

"I just emceed my boss-and-friend's funeral. Grief is plenty hard from where I'm sitting."

"I understand that."

"Do you? Because right now it sounds like you're so wrapped up in your own grief that's all you can see." She looked at the table for a brief second, then stood up abruptly. "Brad, I'm grieving, too. And I think I need to process some more of that before we talk more about any of this. I'll get the check on my way out." And she turned and walked away. Brad sat with his forehead in one hand, staring down at the French fries getting cold on his plate.

Chapter Seventeen

Over the next two weeks, winter finally began its slow turn toward spring, then seemed to suddenly turn a corner. In a matter of two days, Duluth fairly leaped into warmer weather. Snow started melting and runoff trickled, then gushed down the hills toward Lake Superior. Kim's days were mostly filled with the transition in leadership, with settling Mac's estate. His will named her as executor, which was no surprise. She spent time pondering what to do with the problem of Brad Swenson. She thought about calling or texting daily, but let it be. She knew she had spoken truly over lunch: she was processing grief. And it didn't hurt to let things sit for a while.

She checked in with Al a couple times as well, but he hadn't unearthed any more information about Brad. He still maintained that on the surface, the man looked legit. But at the same time, he continued to hold out the possibility it was all too normal and that Brad Swenson could be playing the situation to his advantage.

Kim replayed their conversation over lunch a hundred times in her mind. Did that conversation fit with a man who was playing the situation? Probably not. Was she certain? Obviously not.

Every time she ran through that abortive lunch in her mind, she felt a swelling of hurt as she approached the moment when she started to see Brad as completely self-absorbed, entirely consumed with his own grief. Obviously, she had been hurting as well. But what had she expected?

More to the point, she wondered, what was she wishing for? It was uncomfortable territory. She revisited that moment again and again. The more she lived with her awkward departure the more she realized that what she had hoped for without realizing it was that he would see her pain and show some concern for her. Not a lot. She didn't need a marshmallow. But she wanted just a little tenderness, a little understanding, from the one man who seemed to understand Mac like she did. Brad got both Mac's strength and his weakness. He saw the value in the man. And he was obviously deeply impacted by Mac's death. She had hoped he'd have some compassion for her in her own grief.

Get over yourself, Kim, she thought. Suck it up.

Chapter Eighteen

One evening late in April she perched on her couch, afghan, wine, cheese and crackers as before. It was a favorite of hers, this quiet evening routine staring out the window into the dark. The sunlight stayed a little longer each day and the yard was almost free of snow. On a whim, she picked up the phone and dialed a number from memory. She heard the ring, and then a voice: "Kim? Why, hello!"

"Hi, Mom. What are you up to tonight?"

"I'm beating your father at Scrabble. It's a near thing, though. He put up a good fight."

In the background Kim could hear her father's grumble: "Game's not over yet, Evvie."

Kim laughed into the phone, and, as she almost never did, made a decision on the spot, without deliberating. "Don't back down, Mom. Keep up your guard. Hey, are you and Dad around this weekend?"

"I think so. We don't have any plans this weekend, do we, Roger?"

Kim heard something about "rematch" and her mother's laughter. "Okay, Mom, if you guys are around I'd love to come down, just for the weekend. Is that okay?"

"Of course it's okay, Kim. We'd love to see you. Is anything wrong?"

"No, Mom, nothing's wrong. I just need to get out of town for a few hours. And I'd love to see you. I'll probably show up late Saturday morning."

"Alright. We'll see you then!"

"Bye, Mom. Love you. And on second thought, go easy on Dad."

"Not a chance. Love you too, honey. See you this weekend."

Kim disconnected the call just as another call came through. Caller ID said "Brad Swenson." She debated for about three seconds before she answered.

"Hello, Brad."

"Kim. Thanks for taking the call."

"Of course."

"Listen for a second. I need to apologize for what I said at Ed's."

"Oh?"

"Yes. I was a jerk. I'm sorry."

"Okay. You were a bit of a jerk. And you're forgiven."

"Thank you. I've spent a lot of time chewing on the details of that conversation. Thank you."

"You're welcome."

"You actually made that pretty easy on me. I was prepared to grovel more."

"Maybe we'll just save that for another time."

"Uh–Okay. Deal."

Pause.

"And ..."

"What is it?"

"Maybe this is forward, and feel free to say no. There's a winery and restaurant opening up in Two Harbors this weekend, and Saturday they're bringing in a live band that's supposed to be pretty good. I wondered if you'd like to go tour the winery and get dinner with me."

Curiouser and curiouser, thought Kim.

"Brad, I ..."

"Like I said, feel free to say no. No hard feelings."

"That's not it. I'm going to my parents' place this weekend, so Saturday doesn't work. But it's kind of you to ask."

"Oh. Oh. That's good, that you're going to your parents."

"I try to get there every couple months at least."

"Another time, then?"

"Another time."

"Alright. Thanks for understanding about me being a jerk."

"I didn't understand. I forgave you. That's different."

"You're right. Thanks for forgiving me."

"You're welcome. Again."

"Have a good night, Kim."

"You too, Brad."

She disconnected the call and pondered that conversation. Brad had obviously been edgy about asking her out on a date, but that was probably normal. She smiled a bit at his nervousness. Poor guy. She wondered, of course, what this all meant. Was it just the natural move of a man coming up on a year post-divorce to ask a woman out? Or a schemer playing into the fiction he'd created? Had he invented the tale of Mac committing suicide? Had he created Mac's notes that boldly suggested that Kim should consider getting involved with Brad? Either was possible.

Kim knew she was enough of an idealist at heart to believe Brad was a good man who was honestly grieving for Mac's death, and that he remained unaware of Mac's suggestions about leadership of the foundation and about a potential relationship between her and Brad. It would be irresponsible, though, to assume all that without considering the alternative. Al kept reminding her of that. "Be a realist," he said, "And let this thing play out a while. If he's a creep, he'll show his true colors sooner or later."

That's probably true, she thought. There was something in this whole situation that didn't feel quite right, and she couldn't put her finger on just what it was. And yet there was a part of her that very strongly wanted to call her parents and reschedule for the following weekend so she could go to Two Harbors with Brad. What was that about?

Third time's the charm, she thought as she picked up the phone and dialed. It rang four or five times, and just when Kim was prepared for voicemail Misty answered.

"Hello."

"Misty, it's Kim."

"They've got this great invention up in the north country–caller ID. Told me who you were before I even picked up the phone. It's like magic."

"You're hilarious."

"What's up, Kimmy?"

"Got a few minutes to talk?"

"Sure. I just helped Mom get in the bathtub, and she'll want to soak for half an hour at least. I've got some time, as long as she doesn't try to get out herself and slip again."

"You do a really good job of caring for her, Misty."

"Even if every twenty minutes I'm thinking about bolting for the Cities?"

"Even if."

"So what's got you calling me? New developments in Mac's case?"

"Not really. We had his memorial service, and all that. We're getting his estate settled. All that is going pretty smooth so far. No, it's not about Mac. It's about Brad."

"Oh, here we go. Did he turn out to be playing you?"

"No, not that. Well, at least I don't think so. He did just call to ask me out, though."

"Huh. Well, he'd be a fool not to."

"Ha. Thanks."

"So where's he taking you?"
"I said no."
"Oh? Why?"
"I don't know. Well, I know. I'm going to my parents' place this weekend, and he wanted to go out Saturday."
"So reschedule one or the other."
"You think I should go out with him?"
"Didn't Mac want you to?"
"Yeah. I'm not sure that's a good reason to do it."
"Do you like him?"
"Of course not."
"Of course not?"
"Oh, hell, Misty, I don't know."
"So go out with him and find out."
"Maybe. After I got off the phone I sat and thought about how him asking me out could be a couple things. It could be just a guy who's been single for a year wanting to ask a woman out, right?"
"Sure. I guess that's pretty normal. Actually up here the guys start hitting on you before the separation is complete, let alone the divorce. So maybe waiting a year is points in Brad's favor."
"Maybe. But maybe this is the right thing for him to do because he knows what was in Mac's envelope."
"Could be. Do you really think so?"
"No, I don't. And part of me—I can't believe I'm saying this—thinks going out with him might be more fun because it feels a little dangerous."
"Getting bored, Kimmy?"
"No. Maybe. I don't know."
"So the possibility that Brad's a bad boy is a little exciting."
"A little. Thing is, I don't really believe he's a bad boy. There's just that nagging possibility."
"You like the uncertainty. So go out with him. And call me before you leave on the date and when you get home and let me know the license number of his car and stuff so I can track him down if he hurts you."
"You would, too."
"Better believe it, baby."
"Seriously, Misty, am I being an idiot?"
"In a million years, Kim, you could never be an idiot. Tell me. What feels stupid: going out with him, or not going out with him?"
"Well, going out with him, I guess."

"You're a single woman, Kim, and you're smart and you're strong and you're good looking. He'd be the idiot not to ask you out. Say yes if you want to, have a good time, and then decide if you want to see him again beyond work."

"What if he ends up being my boss?"

"You mean if he takes over the foundation like Mac planned? Kimmy, if he's not good enough to keep your interest for a second date, he's not the right guy to run that foundation."

"I guess that makes sense."

"And Kim?"

"Yeah?"

"There's no rush on this thing. You're going to your parents this weekend. You don't have to say yes next time he asks, either."

"That's true."

"Just remember, though, he did offer to do the dishes up in the Boundary Waters."

"Points."

"Absolutely. Points for the man. But keep your eyes open and your heart half closed."

"Misty, I don't know why I didn't stay in touch with you all those years."

"Me, too. Hey, I think I need to get Mom out of the tub. Thanks for calling, Kim."

"Talk to you soon."

"Yep."

Chapter Nineteen

Saturday morning Kim threw a few things in an overnight bag and straightened up her kitchen. On the way out of town she hit the drive-through at Dunn Brothers to get a no-nonsense Americano for the road. In the spirit of needing a break from being all business, she cranked up the classic rock station on the radio a little too loud and let it play. "Proud Mary" got her out of the city, and Tom Petty started crooning about getting to the point and rolling another joint. She let the music carry her up the rocky hills as the sun rose above a bank of clouds in the east and warmed her through the car window. Her coffee was finally cool enough to drink when she made the exit onto Minnesota 210 headed west. Most of the snow was already gone, and buds were forming on the trees. Spring was arriving with the accelerator all the way to the floor.

Without intending to, she found herself thinking about grief and Brad's theory that all grief gets jumbled together. She thought about Brad and his grief for the loss of his marriage, and then getting all wrapped up in Mac's death. She didn't want to obsess about that this weekend. She needed a break. So she thought instead about Misty. What was Misty grieving? Kim thought back to working together as counselors at Wilderness Christian Adventures. She'd always believed Misty was going to be the kind of writer who rocked the world. Her ability to describe things so vividly, to crack open your heart with just a few words... it was something that Kim didn't understand, but deeply admired. And here Misty was, driving a snowplow truck and getting her mother out of the tub, fending off losers who hit on her between beer and pull-tabs. Was that a source of grief for her? It sure sounded like it. Sounded like she was ashamed, in some way, of the clutter in her front yard and the life that went with it. As if, Kim thought, a person couldn't write from a trailer house in the woods of northern Minnesota.

So what about her own grief? What are you grieving, Kim?

Mac, of course. But there's more than that, isn't there?

She thought back to the eruption in her at Ed's Burgers that day. What had Brad said? It was easy where she sat? Why had his dismissal hurt her so badly? She chewed on that for a few miles. She had missed this kind of windshield time. How many times back and forth between Duluth and the Cities, or after her parents moved, between Duluth and Brainerd, had she used the drive to chew on a problem and come up with some new insight, some creative solution? Routine can be such a rut, she thought.

As she flew west and south on the two-lane highway, mile after mile between towering pines and still-drab potholes and swamps, she started to feel that grief welling up. Part of her was tempted to shove the hurt back down, to deny it a place in her thoughts. Unbidden images of Mac started to drift in and out of her mind: A satisfied look on his face when she brought him news of a tricky situation handled well; a seemingly casual question about how her weekend had gone; the furrow in his brow when they sat together at a work table pondering the best strategic course for the foundation, and then a quick glance at her and a nod when she said something that moved them forward. As the images cascaded through her memory, her throat closed up a bit and her eyes welled up. Behind all his bluster, behind his curmudgeon rants and his explosive temper, she knew he valued her and what she brought to their work. She realized early on Mac was not someone she'd look to for intimacy, but they had shared—what? Cooperation. Respect. *Partnership.*

Instinctively she checked the mirror, making sure no one was close by. As if another car passing on the highway would notice her crying, and if they did, as if that would be somehow shameful. No, she was alone on this stretch of road with the pine trees and willow brush and rocky rivers flashing past. She let go and wept for a couple miles, tears dropping from her face onto the seat belt and her sweatshirt, memories of working with Mac running around in her mind. And other images began to intrude: helping her father change the oil in their family car when she was fourteen years old; plotting secretly with her mother to find the perfect Christmas gift for her father; paddling hard through the border lakes in the moonlight with Misty.

She rested on this last image. Queen's "We Will Rock You" had just come on the radio; maybe that's what made her think of that trip. The song had been their theme for that twenty-four hours and its aftermath. It was a memory she hadn't trotted out for a long, long time. A crazy trip, but they had done it, in spite of everyone else on staff who said it was impossible for the two of them. The partnership she shared with Misty had been a powerhouse, and at the time they both knew it. It was so good to be back in contact with her. Better believe it, baby.

Deep breath. She reached across to the passenger seat and found a tissue in her purse, cleaned up her face and checked herself quickly in the mirror. No lasting harm done.

That evening she sat with her parents at their small kitchen table. Her mother had prepared one of Kim's favorites from childhood, cheesy potatoes. These days Kim would have chosen something different, but she appreciated her mom trying to honor her. They laughed at a few stories about what Kim had been like as a girl, and talked about the neighbors on the lake, and the state Department of Natural Resources bureaucrats and how they wouldn't let Kim's dad clear out the weeds from the lake in front of their house. All pleasant, all easy, all far too shallow to tap into that reservoir of grief Kim had discovered on the drive. A few times during the meal she debated about Brad's advice. Did she really want to take the lid off her old hurt about not having her mom continue to read to her? It seemed like such a trivial thing, but she knew there was more attached to it under the surface somehow.

Her dad was in the middle of recounting the story of the first fish Kim ever caught. "Do you remember that, Evvie? Not even a real fishing pole, just a four foot long piece of willow I cut for her in the backyard with ten feet of line tied onto one end," he repeated as he had dozens of times before. "And we're getting our stuff unpacked in that tiny resort cabin. What was the name of that doggone resort?"

"Was that when we stayed at Sunset Bay?"

"No, that was with Thompsons. Must have been that year we were at West Wind. Why didn't we ever go back there?"

"Probably because of that cramped little cabin."

"I guess. Anyway, we're unpacking, and Kim's already down on the dock with a line in the water. Just a bare hook. Didn't even have any bait on it. And she pulls in a perch. Little five inch perch, and she comes carrying it up to the cabin and demands—*demands* that I clean it and you cook it."

Kim grinned and finished the story. "It was the best tasting fish you ever had."

"Because you wouldn't eat it! Of course, those two little fillets were not even a mouthful."

"Dad, I never told you this, but I actually did have bait on that hook."

"You dug your own worms? I always thought you caught that fish on a bare hook!"

"No, I stole a little piece of Spam out of Mom's macaroni salad that was in the fridge while you guys were unpacking. A nice little bait cube already cut to size, and I stuck it on that hook all by myself. I certainly wasn't going to dig any worms."

"Good golly," Roger snorted, barely able to speak. "You caught that perch on Spam? Oh, that's too good. That's my girl."

"Good memories," Kim smiled. "Mom, was that the trip when you started reading me that C.S. Lewis book? We started that on one of those vacations, didn't we?"

Kim's mother smiled. "I do think it was that trip. You were pretty young. Seven?"

"I think I was eight."

"Pretty young."

"Yes. I remember laying in my sleeping bag and having you read me that story. Then when we came home after that week, you'd come sit in my bedroom at night and read me a chapter. I loved that, Mom."

Evelyn smiled, and got up and started clearing the table. "Like you said, Kim, good memories."

Roger pushed back from the table just a bit. "Well, what should we do tomorrow? We can't fish yet. Season's not open. Besides, we're out of Spam. And I don't know where I put that classy willow pole of yours."

Kim laughed. "I'm sure it's long gone. Tomorrow I think I'd like to sleep until I wake up and sit around and have coffee and breakfast with the two of you. We can figure it out from there. It's a relief to come see you guys once in a while and not have to follow a schedule."

"That's what they call retirement!" Roger thundered.

Evelyn looked up from loading the dishwasher. "How's work, honey? Have they figured out who is going to take over for your boss?"

"There's a lot of legal stuff that has to happen, but no, they haven't declared who's going to be in that CEO slot. For now I can take care of most of the workload, but we're coasting, not moving forward."

"Nonsense. You're a capable woman," her father harumphed. "You could lead that organization, and do a fine job."

"Could, maybe, but I don't think it's what I want to do. I kind of like being the second-in-command."

"Hmph. Better choose the right boss, then. Or maybe it's like that movie. What was that movie we watched last weekend, Evvie? That Greek wedding thing."

"Yes. That's the one. My Big Fat Greek Wedding."

"That's it. It's like the lady says in there, the boss is the head but you're the neck, right, Kim?"

Kim smiled and shook her head. "If I wanted that kind of power I'd just apply for the CEO job. No, I need someone I can work with, but I want a strong leader in that position."

After an hour or so of chit-chat, Kim excused herself and went to bed. She loved her parents, but there was always a little tension when they talked too much about her work. Her father was a man of strong opinions, and he was obviously a firm believer in Kim's capabilities. And yet, she thought, he still seems to be trying to convince himself. Like he was wondering if Kim could really handle it because she was a female. He would never, never say that out loud, of course. Kim had learned not to run headlong into that issue. And maybe that was the chip on her own shoulder. He had never said that he didn't think she could handle anything at all.

She lay in the guest bedroom, ready for bed and listening to the quiet sounds of her parents getting ready for bed and shutting down the house. She imagined how her parents would relate to Brad. What would they say? Would he feel comfortable? Finally she laughed silently to herself and shook her head in the dark.

Chapter Twenty

The next morning she woke before her parents. She crept into the kitchen and started coffee, and returned to the guest bedroom to don sweats. In a few minutes she poured a cup and stepped out into the three season porch. It was cool, and she wrapped a heavy blanket around herself. She sipped the black brew and watched dawn break over the lake, letting her mind stay pleasantly blank.

The door latch actually startled her, and her mother came into the porch carrying her own cup of coffee. "Thanks for making coffee, Kim. Oh, my word! It's freezing out here. Why didn't you turn on that space heater?"

"Morning, Mom. I had the blanket. It's not so cold."

Evelyn turned up the heater and its tinny electric whir broke the silence, and the dusty smell of the electric coils throwing off heat mixed with the smells of the lake, the slightly musty smell of the porch furnishings, and the other smells of spring. Kim's mom settled in her own chair and reached into a drawer. "I've been trying to read these each day," she said. "Jinny got me started on it. It's a devotional book, with one for each day. It's called Christ in Our Home, and they put out a new one every few months."

"That's a good thing, Mom. Do you like it?"

"I do. I need something to help me start the day right, more than just coffee. Though I need coffee, too," she said with a grin.

"Absolutely. Me, too."

Kim sat in silence and her mom quietly read for a few moments. Without a word, Evelyn put the book away.

"Mom, can I ask you a question?"

"Of course."

"I was thinking last night about you reading me that book when I was little. I really did love that. I just wondered, why didn't you read the rest of them to me? There were six more books in that series, and I know I asked you to. I can't remember what you said."

"Your father told you that you could read perfectly well on your own."

"I remember that. But I don't remember what you said."

"I don't think I ever said anything about it."

"Didn't you want to read to me, Mom? It seems like a silly thing now, but I have wondered about it many times."

113

Evelyn set her coffee cup down, then picked it up, then set it down again without drinking. She looked out at the lake, then back in the house, then out at the lake. "It's hard sometimes to look back," she said finally. "There are so many things I would do different."

"What do you mean, Mom? We had a great life."

"It was a good life. You're right."

The silence stretched out between them.

"Kim, I'm sorry I didn't read you those other books. I knew you wanted me to. When Roger said you should read them yourself, I just went along with it. I figured he was trying to protect me." She looked over at Kim, then looked back in the house, then out at the lake. "I never did very well in school, you know. I was never much of a student. And reading was the hardest for me. I did okay with numbers, but reading was hard work."

"Mom, you read just fine. You and Dad play Scrabble, for crying out loud. And you win!"

"Oh, I can read okay, silently. And Scrabble, that's mostly about figuring out the triple letter scores and that kind of thing. But reading that book aloud to you, it made me feel foolish. It brought back all that from being a girl in school and not reading well. Having the other kids... So when your dad said no, I went along with it, even though I knew you wanted me to keep on. I'm sorry, honey."

"Oh, Mom. It's okay. I just didn't know you felt that way. I loved having you read to me. Those are some of my best memories, Mom. My very best. I didn't know. Thank you for reading me that book, when it made you feel so uncomfortable."

"I wish I'd read you the others."

"Dad said I should read them on my own. So I did. I read them all, a couple times, and that was mostly because you helped me enjoy the first one so much."

Kim's mother grinned at her then, and quietly spoke, "You always were the smart one. I was always so proud of you. I still am."

They whiled away the day with small talk and a quick trip to the Chocolate Ox for dessert after lunch. They walked up the bicycle trail through Nisswa, admiring the swelling buds on the poplars and a few delicate bloodroots, their deep green leaves and fragile white blossoms emerging from the leaf mold along the trail right next to still-melting patches of snow. They strolled and chatted, just enjoying the time together. Part of Kim's mind detoured into the memory of picking one of those bloodroot flowers this time of year to see what she'd read about. The crimson juices flowed from the root where she'd broken it off, and the fragile white flower went dull and wilted within minutes of being picked. Something in her resonated with those beautiful, fragile flowers. She felt the weight of her grief. She felt the fragility of standing on her own at the helm of the foundation, missing Mac and trying to honor his memory as she made decisions. She felt the edge-of-the-knife uncertainty of her decision making regarding Brad, both on a personal level and professionally. By the time they returned to the car, Kim knew it was time to head for Duluth and back to her life there. Coming here had been a good choice, though. For a moment she smiled to herself as she wondered: What will I tell Brad, if anything?

About five in the evening, Kim packed up her things, hugged her parents, and set her mind on Duluth. As she was getting buckled into the car, though, her dad leaned in the window. "Kim, are you sure you don't want to be in that CEO slot?"

"I'm sure, Dad. I've thought a lot about it. And I even talked to Mac about it a couple times, before he died."

"Well, I've seen some leadership transitions, kiddo. And I want you to make sure they get you a damn good number one in that position. Don't settle for anything less than the right person, whoever it is. You're too smart, and too valuable to give your work to compensate for someone who doesn't belong in that kind of a position."

"Thanks, Dad. I get that. And I feel the same way. I want the right person in that spot."

"We just want the best for you."

"I know. Love you, Dad."

"Love you too, Kim. Drive safe."

Chapter Twenty-one

The following week Kim found herself at the office for many long hours each day. It felt like a relief, in a way. The foundation was disbursing a major grant to a group of charter schools in Michigan that incorporated wilderness ethics and adventure into their educational programs. Mac had been enthused about the opportunity to shape the way young people approached time in the wild, and Kim wanted to make sure this disbursement went without a hitch. It was also the first major event, aside from Mac's memorial service, in which she carried the visible responsibility to lead the foundation after Mac's death.

She was working past eight in the evening that Wednesday when her cell phone rang. It was Brad. She felt a twinge of guilt, realized in a flash that Misty would say she had no reason for guilt, and promptly answered the phone.

"Good evening, Brad."

"Hi there. Quick question for you. I hope I'm not calling too late."

"That's not really a question. But no, I'm actually still at work."

"That's dedication. If the board has any smarts at all, they'll put you in that CEO job."

"I already turned it down. A couple times."

"Yeah, that's what you said. So my question. I'm headed back into the Boundary Waters to get the rest of Mac's gear. Got any interest in going along? I need to get a permit and wanted to check with you before I booked a specific date. And if you'd rather not go back there, I'm happy to do it solo. Thought I'd give you the option."

Kim rolled this around for a second. She decided a little humor might be good. "A couple days in the Boundary Waters? That's an upgrade in the 'first date' department, Brad."

"Not everyone would see it as an upgrade. No tablecloths, no candlelight. But you have to admit, I tried with the whole concert-and-dinner thing. That was a classy first date idea."

Kim laughed, genuinely enjoying Brad's humor. "When are you thinking of going?"

"June, probably. Shouldn't be hard to get a permit, but I want to get it booked just in case. Snowbank is a popular entry point and it might just get booked up. Hoping to get up there before the mosquitoes get bad."

"That's smart. Wood ticks will be out in force by that time."

"Better ticks than mosquitoes."

"I have to agree."

"I assume weekends are easier for you to get away?"

"For this I could take time. The board would certainly understand. But yes, it would be a little simpler to do a weekend trip. Maybe leave at noon on a Friday and drive up to Ely, then get in the Boundary Waters early on Saturday?"

"Sounds good. How about that first weekend in June? If that doesn't work we could go the weekend before Memorial Day, maybe? That's pretty tight, only a couple weeks away."

"One second. Let me check." She pulled up the calendar on her phone and saw nothing that would prevent this kind of adventure on either date. "Looks like I can make June work."

"Great. We should coordinate gear. Do you want to get together that Thursday evening to pack?"

"Hold on… Nope. I have a meeting with the board that night. Can we do Wednesday instead?"

"I'm flexible. Wednesday is great for me. And I have most of my gear here, at the place I'm staying, if you want to just come here. If you're comfortable with that, I mean. There's plenty of room to work here, to get Duluth packs put together and stuff. I can load it all up and meet you someplace else, if you'd rather."

Kim smiled a little as she imagined what Misty would be saying right now. "Your place is fine. You want to text me the address?"

"Sure thing. Say about six that Wednesday?"

"Perfect. How about if I bring something quick for supper, then we can get the gear organized. Anything you don't like to eat? I'm thinking Chinese."

"I'm easy to please. Chinese sounds fantastic. Thanks for thinking of that."

"No problem."

"Great. I've got it all on the calendar. So how is the whole business with Mac's estate and leadership transition and all that going?"

"Slow. Just jumping through the legal hoops takes a long time. I'm sure that stuff won't be settled until sometime this fall. And the board is just starting to get moving with a search process. The initial stages of that are a self-assessment of the entire organization, and we'll probably bring in an outside consultant to help with that. Those things can take months. I'm just trying to focus on the day-to-day operations."

"I'm glad they have you, Kim. You seem like a steady hand for a situation like that."

"Thank you. How is your friend's business going? Is he still down in Tucson?"

Brad laughed. "Believe it or not, he's building a home in upstate New York, up in the Adirondacks. That's taking most of his energy these days. I don't quite understand why anyone needs three houses, but there it is. So I've got a couch to sleep on for a few more months, he says."

"Lucky for you. And it sounds like, lucky for him, to have you managing things."

"I try."

"I'd better finish up things here for the night, Brad. Good to talk to you. We'll be in touch."

"Sounds good. Have a good night, Kim."

She disconnected the call and sat for a moment, staring out at the lights of the harbor. Part of her wanted to cheer. Her stomach was doing little excited flips. But part of her thought she was a fool to go into the Boundary Waters with him. And then there were all those questions about logistics. Was Brad expecting to share tents? Sleeping bags? She could handle those things; she knew her limits. But even asking the questions inevitably complicated relationships.

Her phone buzzed. It was a text from Brad, simply "Good to talk to you," followed by a street address.

Her next call was to Misty.

"Hey, Kim. What's up?"

"Brad asked me out."

"You told me that. Like I said, he'd be a fool not to. And you had to go to your parents."

"And he called to ask me out again."

"Oh?"

"Yeah. He wants to go back to Disappointment Mountain and get the rest of Mac's stuff."

"Shit."

"Yes."

"So you said no, right?"

"I said yes."

"Shit."

"Yes."

"When is this happening? Please don't say this weekend."

"No, not until the first weekend in June. We're getting together the Wednesday before to pack stuff up. He texted me an address where he's staying. We're going to meet there to go through gear."

"Showing off, or what? 'Look at me, I don't live with my parents!' "

"Come on, Misty. No, that's where we're meeting to pack up our gear for the trip. Then Friday we'll head to Ely."

"So send me the address."

"Texting it to you now."

"Kim, this is a big step off the cliff in the first date department."

"That's what I thought at first. But then I thought, we've already been to the Boundary Waters together. And he behaved himself. Washed dishes and everything."

"Offered to wash dishes."

"You said it earned him points."

"Yeah, I guess I did. But this is different. This time I won't be along to hold him at gunpoint."

"That seemed a little over the top, honestly."

"Kim, I think your best bet is a nine millimeter. Probably a Glock. They're user friendly."

"What?"

"You need to get yourself a pistol and learn how to use it before you do this thing."

"How about I just carry a can of bear spray?"

"And then what? If he misbehaves, best case, he's on the ground writhing because you shot pepper spray in his eyes, and eventually he gets better. Are you back in civilization by that time? No. You're still packing up gear. You need to be able to take him out in a more permanent way."

"Ouch. Dating you would be a real bitch."

"Better believe it, baby. Why do you think I'm still single?"

"I've thought about the whole conceal and carry thing, but never seriously. Do you really think I should?"

"You're headed to a potential murder scene on a camping trip with suspect Numero Uno. My professional opinion is that you should consider packing some serious heat, sister."

"Can you walk me through the process?"

"Holy shit."

"What?"

"Kim, have you taken a look at that street address you sent me?"

"No, I just got it from Brad and sent it to you. Looks like it's north of town, out along the lake."

"Yeah. But this place? Wow."

"What?"

"I did the Google Earth thing with the address, then got the lot around it, then got on the street view. Some choice digs. Brad has nice friends if this is where they've got him sleeping."

"He said the guy is building his third house up in the Adirondacks somewhere."

"If this is his base, he can probably afford another house. This place has to go five thousand square feet. And the lot is enormous. Right on the lake. On the bluff overlooking fricking Superior. With a staircase going down to the cute little private beach."

"Nice."

"Say, Kim, could you just ask Brad when you have a chance if his friend the landlord is single?"

"Misty!"

"Sorry. Wow. So this is where you're packing up gear, huh?"

"I guess."

"To answer your question earlier before I got distracted by wretched excess, I can walk you through the process. You take a one-day class, do a little shooting at a range, apply for the government-issued permit, buy a pistol. That's all with my help, of course. And voila. It's a little frightening how easy the process is, but for someone like you that's a good thing."

"I'll do a little checking around, see if I can find a class."

"I know a guy."

"Of course you do."

"Former cop, teaches carry classes in Duluth. I'll call and make sure he gets you in. He's always booked because he's good and word gets out. You're free this weekend if he's got a class, right?"

"I will be."

"Good. Kimmy, this could be serious. Brad is probably a fine man, probably a really nice guy. In fact that's the way I'd bet if I had to place money right now. But I don't want you stuck in the backcountry when you find out I'm wrong."

"I get that, Misty. And that's part of why I'm calling you. You know how to juggle this stuff better than I do."

"I'm going to call my carry class guy. His name's Darren. Used to work with the BCA and before that he was a cop in St. Cloud or someplace. Good guy. I'll get back to you about the class."

"Thanks."

"Glad you called me. Let's stay in touch on this thing."

"I'd like that. Like I said, thanks."

"No problem."

Chapter Twenty-two

The next few weeks seemed to fly by, which was a bit of a relief for Kim. She had little time to think about possibilities. She sat through the conceal-and-carry class, paid the fees, participated in the range instruction using one of the instructor's pistols, applied for her permit, and was mildly surprised when the cogs of government cranked it out and it appeared in her mailbox within a week and a half. Misty took half a day and drove to Duluth and they went gun shopping. Kim did indeed opt for a Glock 9mm that seemed simple enough and fit her grip well. Under Misty's direction, she bought a membership at a local range and made time to go target practice three times in ten days. The Sunday before she was to pack gear with Brad, she drove up to Misty's place.

She pulled her Forrester into Misty's yard. A Ford Fairmont that had definitely seen better days blew in behind her in a cloud of dust. Kim coughed and squinted as the Fairmont rocked to a stop next to Misty's pickup. She vaguely recognized Misty's sister Jeanette. She was twenty years older than the last time Kim had seen her, but still strikingly like and unlike her little sister. Kim climbed out of her Forrester and was exchanging greetings with Jeanette just as Misty emerged from the front door of the house.

"Hey, Kim."

"Hi."

"Jeanette, Mom is sleeping on the couch. I'll be back in a couple hours."

Misty slammed in behind the wheel of the pickup and rolled down the window. "Let's go, Kim."

Kim grabbed her backpack that held her pistol, ammunition, ear protection, extra clip, and a bottle of water. She swung into the passenger seat of the pickup and before she had her door shut, Misty had the truck in gear and backing out. "Whoa, baby! What's eating you?"

"I'm pissed at Jeanette."

"Oh?"

"Yeah."

Silence.

"Because ... ?"

"Because I am. Leave it be."

"Fair enough." Kim looked out the window at the springtime woods speeding by. "Need a cigarette?"

"I gave them up. Cigarettes are stupid."

"Good call."

Silence.

"Where we headed?"

"Old quarry up the road a bit. It's a good place for the kind of shooting we need to do."

"So what did Jeanette do?"

"Leave it the fuck alone!"

"Okay. Sorry."

Silence. They turned off the gravel road into a narrow wheel track lined with trees and underbrush. After a couple hundred yards, Misty pulled the pickup to a halt. "We walk from here. Not too far. Bring your stuff."

Kim grabbed her backpack and followed Misty down a well-traveled trail through the trees. The path dropped down a steep hill. On Misty's advice, Kim had worn clothing she might be wearing in the Boundary Waters, or at least garments that were similar: hiking boots, poly underlayers, fleece over all, zip-off hiking pants with a belt made of nylon webbing. She could see rock faces rising up to her left and ahead of her, and she could guess that there might be a rock wall off to her right through the trees as well. This pit was probably a couple hundred yards across, and as far as Kim could tell, it was miles from anything. It did indeed look like an old quarry that the forest was beginning to reclaim. Judging by the age of the trees in the bottom of the quarry, it hadn't been used in forty or fifty years at least.

"Public land?"

"Used to be private. State forest these days. Shooting is technically legal. A couple of us set up a bit of a training facility here at one point back in the day. Still gets used now and then."

"Training facility? Are you going to go all X-Files on me and there's a big metal door opening into an old missile silo or something?"

Misty laughed. "Nothing quite so elaborate. Just a shooting course with some strategically placed targets on trees, as well as a few other odds and ends. Stop here and let's look at your setup."

They got Kim's holster and pistol in place, with Misty offering tips and insights about wearing a weapon, placement of extra clips, how to manage clothing for concealment and easy access. Kim felt like she was back in school after just a few minutes, but everything Misty said was valuable information, so she soaked it up as best she could. Kim's range time had helped her become comfortable with her weapon including safety, magazines, and all the operational details.

"Ear protection," Misty ordered. Kim pulled out her headphones and just before she put them on, Misty said, "Here's how this is going to work. I'm going to stay half a step behind you and we're going to walk through this course. Here and there you'll see a paper silhouette. I came out yesterday and set them up. Not all the silhouettes are for you to shoot at. You'll have to wait until I tell you, then do exactly what I say and react as quickly as you can."

"So just walk through and you'll tell me what to do?"

"Yeah. If I say 'threat' that means you shoot, right now. Shoot for the chest, and if you put a couple rounds in the chest, add one to the head for good measure. But remember this. Remember this. *Always* know where your muzzle is pointing. I'll put my hands on your shoulders if I need to steer you."

"Okay."

"Ready?"

"I think so."

"Let's go. It might get a little intense."

What the hell does that mean? Kim wondered. She started to walk forward on the obvious footpath, rounded a corner, and saw a paper silhouette tacked to a tree ten yards in front of her. Suddenly Misty nearly screamed behind her, right in her ear: "THREAT! THREAT!" Kim's heart was in her throat and she fumbled badly for a second trying to get her fleece and shirt out of the way of her pistol. It seemed like it took forever to get the pistol out, to get it directed toward the target, to take aim, to pull the trigger. The rush of adrenaline was overwhelming.

"Kim. Hold up. Steady."

Kim pointed her pistol toward the ground in front of her feet, removed her finger from the trigger, and finally turned her head. Misty's face was a foot away, right behind her shoulder. "It's okay, Kim. Breathe. And holster that thing."

With that Kim realized she had indeed stopped breathing for the last eternity or so. She took a deep breath and felt her shoulders sag. "I didn't know you were going to yell."

"That's part of the training. Got to figure out a way to get your adrenaline up."

"Oh. Damn. Oh. Okay. Okay. It worked. Shit."

"So. Keep breathing, baby. What did you notice about that?"

Kim laughed, a gasping sort of chuckle. "Took me forever to get the gun out."

"Okay. We can work on that. What else?"

"Um... I don't know how well I aimed."

"Let's take a look." They walked a few steps to the target and Kim could see the clear silhouette outline of a man intact, not a scratch or hole in his paper shape.

"I missed?"

"High and right."

Kim looked upward a full two feet and she saw, right at the edge of the paper, one small hole. "Just one, huh? And a clean miss? I know I shot twice."

"Take your clip out."

Kim obediently pulled out her pistol and ejected the clip that she had filled with nine bullets just before they started this exercise. Now three bullets were visible. "What?"

"Three, plus one in the chamber. It's a nine-shot clip. You shot five times."

Kim felt weak. "Five?"

"Kind of hard to keep track with the adrenaline."

"Misty, I..."

"You're fine, Kim. That's why training is important. You've never had to learn to do this before. It gets easier."

"Oh, God, I hope so."

"Clear that pistol and let's refill the clip as long as you have it out."

The next half hour was a blur of targets, shouts, and gunfire. On command Kim dropped to the dirt and fired from behind a tree, a rock, a bush. She shot one target and left another intact, wrestling through the split-second decisions. She learned to eject an empty clip without watching it fall to the ground and to insert her spare by feel, working the pistol's action to chamber another shell. Misty was always right behind her shoulder shouting instructions, putting hands on her shoulders to turn her or guide her, occasionally slowing things down to get Kim to change her stance, her grip, or her form. When they finished she felt spent, but far more capable than she'd been a short while before. After carefully making sure everything was properly, safely packed away, they climbed back into the pickup. Misty reached into a small cooler in the box and pulled out a couple sodas, handing one to Kim. "You earned it, baby," she smiled.

"Sure hope so. That's hard work."

"Yep. People think it's so easy to handle yourself in a shooting situation. They have no idea."

"I certainly didn't."

"And, remember this, you still don't. You've had a little training. You're far better off than you were an hour ago. But in that kind of a situation you have to be stronger mentally than you've had to be for just about anything else in your life. You can't let the crazy or the sad or the afraid get to you. You tough it out and do what you need to do."

"If you give in, you neither live nor win."

"What's that?"

"Something Brad said. You can't lose control in a situation like that. Though he was talking about being mentally tough to get through that blizzard."

"Same idea. Different context. And if it comes to a face-off, it's going to be the kind of intense that makes this all look like... well, like a training exercise."

"I hope it doesn't come to that."

"I hope it doesn't, too, baby. For your sake and for his. But if it does come to that, I hope you do absolutely everything you need to do, all the way through, and come out on top of it."

Kim took a deep breath. "Hard to think about."

"That's why training is so important. Part of it is training your body what to do, but part of it is helping your mind sneak up on the idea of what you might have to do someday. Your mind needs a chance to process it in advance."

"I can see that. I don't like the thoughts in my head after all that."

"We're designed to protect life. To preserve it."

"Yeah."

They sat in silence for a few minutes, staring out through the windshield into the trees.

"Jeanette set me up on a blind date."

"What? With who?"

"That's the thing. A guy from over in Cook who runs a bait shop. Mid-40's, thinning hair, checking his minnow traps every morning and selling refrigerated nightcrawlers and leeches by the dozen. Personality to match."

"Not some diamond in the rough, huh?"

"This guy couldn't make cubic zirconium on a good day."

"Ouch."

"That's why I'm pissed."

"I get it."

Misty sipped her soda. "But the hell of it is, Kimmy, I was thinking about settling. Thinking maybe running the waxworm concession is better than being meaningless and alone, you know?"

"Look, Misty, you're ..."

"Just–just shut up. I know what you're going to say, and I love you, and you're probably right to say it. But this life feels pretty damn meaningless most days, alright?"

"Oh, Misty, I'm sorry."

"No, this is my own dead end. That's why I'm so pissed. I'm not really mad at Jeanette. She's just a handy excuse. I'm pissed that I wasted the first few decades of my life and I've got no prospects of anything better. That's why I'm angry."

"I get it. Still, Jeanette should know better than to set you up with Mr. Bait."

Misty choked on her soda and started to laugh. "Darn right. Oh, baby, it hurts to blow soda pop up your nose!"

Now Kim was laughing as well, and pretty soon they were both roaring, leaning across the cab to put their heads together and wrap their arms around each other. The tears ran and they both wiped their eyes and dissolved into chuckles and then smiles. Kim reached across the cab and grabbed Misty's hand. "I have to say this, Misty, even though I know you know it. Taking care of your mom is far, far from meaningless. You've given up so much to be there for her and that's a beautiful thing, even if it's terribly frustrating."

"I know. At one level, I know. But you start to look at the balance sheet, at what you've accomplished, at what impact your life makes, and it's hard not to get angry."

"You remember our second summer at Wilderness, when the whole staff had to read that C.S. Lewis book?"

"Vaguely. *The Great Divorce,* wasn't it? I think I've still got that packed up in a box somewhere."

"I think about that story. The way our actions in this life looked so different, and the value of what we'd done, looked so different, in heaven. There was a woman in there who had been sort of the neighborhood caretaker, watching over kids and cats and dogs, the kind of person you wouldn't think twice about here, but in heaven she had parades and songs and praises. I think that's the kind of value of what you've been doing for your mom."

"Sure doesn't look like much on this side of things."

"Proof our perceptions are all screwed up."

"Maybe."

"That's one of the things I think about sometimes with the foundation. Most of my days I'm interacting with lawyers and financial officers and hedge funds. But every once in a while because it's a non-profit, because we get to give money to some really cool causes, I get to see things from a little bit different perspective. I get to see the world upside-down, once in a while. It's such a good reminder."

"You get to bet on David, instead of Goliath?"

"Sometimes, yes. But it's more than that. There's a real temptation just to buy David a sword and turn him into a giant. But the best days, the very best days, are when I get to walk down that slope a few steps with David, looking down to where Goliath is waiting, and whisper in his ear that courage matters, and that I believe in what he's doing, and then I get to hand him some really good rocks for that sling of his. That's the very best."

"You've thought some about this."

"Mac and I used to talk about it. And he actually liked that whole David and Goliath thing. That's a few years ago when Malcolm Gladwell wrote his book about that story and everybody was talking about it. Mac and I would have these conversations after giving a bunch of money away, or on days when the red tape and bureaucracy got to be too much to handle. It was one of the things he'd come back to again and again, like he needed to remind himself why he was doing what he was doing. The foundation is not David, he was clear, and we're certainly not Goliath. But we get to influence the fight."

"Well, that Glock is a pretty deadly slingshot. Seems like you're getting used to it. It fits you well, and you were getting pretty accurate by the time we finished up."

"I've been shooting some, and the accuracy is there. The hard thing today was the stress, the real-world feel of it all. Helpful to shoot in this kind of a setting."

"Real world is a different thing from the shooting range. I better head us back. Jeanette has a deadline." She started the pickup and found a space between a couple trees where she could turn around.

"Wednesday I'm packing gear with Brad, then we head for the Boundary Waters on Friday."

"I haven't forgotten. Call me before you go pack stuff, okay? And after."

"I will. But I don't think…"

"Better safe, baby. Way better to be safe."

"Yeah. Misty, you'll tell me if I'm being stupid, right?"

"You know I will."

"I could still call this thing off. Let Brad go by himself."

"Is that what you want to do?"

Kim considered for a moment. "No. I want to go back to that spot. I want to help get Mac's gear. I want to spend some time with Brad and see if I can figure him out a little."

"What do you want to figure out?"

"I guess it comes down to a simple question: Is Brad who he says he is?"

"How are you going to know?"

"It's like we've talked about so many times. Up there, you get to know a person for who they really are. The pretense goes away in a hurry."

"Is that true for you, too? Do you go back to being Wilderness Kim up there?"

"In some ways, I guess. There's a lot of what I do for work that isn't me. I can navigate the negotiations and the contracts. It's a learned skill. But it's not where I live."

"The Boundary Waters isn't where you live either."

"True. But there's a part of me that doesn't get much travel in daily life these days that comes out up there. I saw it when we were pulling those sleds in a couple months ago."

"You can certainly be a badass if you need to."

Kim laughed. "Maybe not the way I'd describe it, but yeah. So what if Brad doesn't like that?"

"Then he's an idiot. Kimmy, if there's anything that man doesn't like about you, he's a moron. You worried about that? You starting to get your heart in this thing?"

"I don't know. Maybe a little. I've spent enough time thinking about him that way now that I'd kind of like to try it out."

"Then try it out. You're a big girl."

"What if he's not safe?"

Misty gave her a withering glance and looked back to the road.

"What?"

"Two things. First, no man is ever safe. Not if he's worth having. You're so strong, you're going to need a strong man. That means he has to be at least potentially dangerous. But there's dangerous and there's dangerous. And two, safety and love aren't compatible. Love is a risk. Has to be."

Kim stared out the window at the trees flying by. "Love, huh?"

Misty shrugged. "Maybe not yet. Hopefully not yet. But you've got to be thinking ahead. Just don't go there too quickly."

"I'm in no rush. Believe me."

"And three …"

"You said two things."

"I thought of a third. Three: You are getting pretty scary yourself with that pistol. If he misbehaves, you just shoot his ass."

Kim snorted. "Oh, my god, Misty."

"So play it out. There's nothing wrong with just enjoying some good conversation or having some fun. How long has it been since you've been to the Boundary Waters, anyway?"

"About two months. You were there. You forgot already?"

"I mean in a canoe."

"Let's see. At least ten years. Maybe twelve."

"You looking forward to it?"

Kim considered. "I haven't thought much about it, but… yes. I am. When Brad offered me the option of not going with him, I really didn't want to say no. I wanted to be up there again. Not necessarily with him. I miss it. And..."

"What?"

"It's funny. I find myself sad that it's only for a couple days. I wish it was a longer trip."

"I get it. I've been back in a few times. Took a couple of my nieces on one-on-one trips four or five years ago. And each time I think, I live so close. Why don't I do this more often?"

"It's an amazing place."

130

Chapter Twenty-three

Wednesday evening, Kim stopped into her favorite Chinese buffet and selected enough of a variety to feed two hungry people, packaged it up, grabbed chopsticks and napkins, paid and was out the door in her car by five-thirty. It was a fifteen minute drive to the address Brad had given her, so she sat in the parking lot while she called Misty.

"You're headed there now, right?"

"Yeah. Just picked up Chinese."

"He's letting you buy dinner? He just lost all his points."

"I offered. Besides, this is the twenty-first century. Women are allowed to buy a meal."

"True. I was born a century too late."

"Yeah. Right. Maybe a century too early."

"Better believe it, baby. So you're headed there now, and you're going to call me on your way home, right? Don't forget."

"I'll call you."

"Okay. Have fun. But not too much fun."

"Thanks, Mom."

She grinned to herself when she got off the phone, remembering the long, late-night conversations she and Misty had shared in a cabin at the base camp or in a tent on some wilderness lake, talking about life and dreams. And, of course, guys. And Kim wondered again why Misty hadn't done anything with her writing. As she pulled onto I-35 heading northeast toward the Lake Superior shore, she resolved to ask about it sometime soon.

She had plugged the address into her phone, so she heard the directions in her car stereo and didn't have to focus too hard on navigation. She wove through the turns where I-35 came to an end and transitioned onto State Highway 61, which served as an arterial street headed northeast out of the city toward the North Shore. There it once again became a freeway. In a couple months this road would be cramped and crowded with boats, RV's, and all manner of cars with canoes strapped to their roofs, each driver chafing at the 35 mph speeds. She was able to appreciate the slow peace of springtime along Highway 61 through some of the oldest parts of Duluth, the massive lakeshore homes. They were mansions, really, most of which had belonged to some shipping baron or other in the past. They stood trim and lovely set back from the road behind stately gates and fences. Flowering crabs exploded in glorious bloom, pink and white, and the new-leafed trees were bright green. Here and there she caught a glimpse of the big lake beyond the homes, and by the time the highway left the city behind, she was dazzled by the view from the little rise where the speed limit jumped to sixty-five. The late afternoon sun glowed on the water. A couple of sailboats skimmed on the breeze a quarter mile or so out in the lake. She felt the rising anticipation of getting out of the city, getting away to the wilderness once again. Her winter trip with Misty (and Brad crashing the party) had been overshadowed by Mac's death and the grisly business of trying too literally to piece things together. Knowing a little better what she was facing, she was eager to be on a lake, paddle dipping in and out of the waves, feeling the solid weight of a pack along the portages, hearing loons call in the darkness.

    She had been following the highway as it climbed up the ridge. Highway 61 angled away from the lakeshore. Eventually it coursed a mile or more inland, away from the big homes along the shore, to provide enough space for the four-lane bypass to Two Harbors. After a few miles at sixty-five miles per hour, her phone directed her to turn off 61 toward the lake. She followed a series of winding turns until she was directed into a long, private road that climbed up the final low ridge that lay between the highway and the lake. As she turned into the drive her phone confidently declared, "Arrived." She knew she must be getting close to the lake again, but she was still in awe when she topped the ridge and saw Superior sparkling out before her like a massive blue jewel. She braked to a stop and just sat for a moment, soaking in the view. Finally she looked around and saw that the driveway curved left just ahead of her and descended another hundred yards to the northeast where it led toward a large garage on the right, toward the lake. To the left and high above, built on a massive outcrop of rock, stood a house that was all A-frame construction and enormous windows facing the lake. Kim was used to seeing large homes along this lakeshore, but this one was massive even by North Shore standards. An expansive deck stretched across the front of the house with steps leading down to the concrete pad. She drove in front of the four-stall garage which was attached on the far end to some sort of shop or storage building or something, Kim assumed. She pulled in front of one of the stalls, not quite sure where to park. But then, if the owner was in New York, she only had to worry about inconveniencing Brad.

As she got out of the car and reached for the bag containing supper, she heard Brad's voice from above. He leaned over the railing on the deck and called down. "Do you need a hand?"

"No, I've got it," she called back. "Unless you want me to bring my gear in now, too."

"Nope. We'll eat first, like you said, then pack down there in the shop. Come on up!"

She crossed the wide concrete pad and climbed a flight of stone steps that led up to the deck. She'd planned and hosted enough large events for the foundation to see at a glance that you could host a party for a hundred guests on this deck without ever going in the house.

"Nice little place you've got here," she finally said when she reached the top.

Brad laughed. "It's a little much for my taste," he opined. "But it keeps the rain off." As he led the way across the deck toward the double glass doors, he added, "I'm thankful I don't have to pay the property taxes. Let's eat inside, and I can show you around a bit. Can I carry that?"

"No way. This is my ticket in."

Brad laughed again. "You're welcome with or without the food. But I'm glad you brought it. I haven't had Chinese in a long time, and I'm starving." He turned and led the way through the doors. Kim followed.

They walked into a great room that rose thirty feet or more to a massive center beam. The cathedral A-frame created a dizzying sense of height when Kim looked up. Across the great room, she looked up to a second and third story where balconies provided a way to stand ten or twenty feet above the floor of the room where she now stood. What a view, she thought, to wake up in those bedrooms, walk out on an indoor balcony in the middle of winter and peer out the glass walls at Lake Superior.

"I imagine the views of the lake from that upper balcony are incredible."

"That's Todd's master bedroom. And yes, the view from up there is pretty cool. But this place is full of amazing views." They took ten or fifteen minutes to wander through the house. There was a well-equipped office on the main floor toward the back, a kitchen full of stainless steel fixtures and counters and appliances over a ceramic tile floor, not to mention the views from the guest bedroom on the second floor and the truly breathtaking view from the third floor balcony, looking out at the lake. What Kim had not noticed, and what Brad said was a little tricky to see from the ground level, if you didn't know what you were looking for, was a railed catwalk that led over the great room out to a sort of crow's nest right in the peak of the windows. The nest itself was a relatively small space, maybe eight by ten feet, with a tiny desk on one side and a couple adequate chairs on the other. Walking across the catwalk was dizzying, like a balance beam two dozen feet above the living room, though quite safe with the railings. Sitting in the crow's nest made Kim think what it would be like to have such a retreat. "With a view like this, even I could be a poet," she murmured.

Brad looked away from the lake. "Do you write poetry?"

"If I get to hang out here, I will," she quipped. He grinned, but his eyes remained curious.

"Todd says this is his problem solving spot," he offered.

"I can see why. Talk about perspective."

"We can sit for a while, or we can head back down and get something to eat."

"Just one question. You live here, at least for the moment. Do you spend much time up here?"

"Honestly? No."

"Why not?"

"I'll explain later."

Now it was Kim's turn to wonder about her host, and she watched Brad's face for a few seconds, but he wasn't giving anything away. Finally she asked, "Still starving?"

"Absolutely."

"Let's go eat."

They retreated back across the catwalk, down the stairs, and retrieved Kim's bag of victuals. "Did you bring drinks?" Brad asked.

"I assumed we'd get by on water. Good practice for the Boundary Waters."

"True. But we're not there yet. It's a warm enough evening. On second thought, why don't we set up outside, on that small table at the edge of the deck. I'll be right there."

Kim let herself back out the glass doors and began to set out containers of fried rice, General Tso's Chicken, sweet and sour pork, eggrolls, and all the rest on the table. She set chopsticks and two fortune cookies in the center. Brad emerged with plates, napkins, a container of soy sauce in one hand and two green bottles in the other. "Tsing Tao beer," he explained. "Just seems right with Chinese."

They dove into the meal, laughing about the challenges of eating with chopsticks and commenting on the delight of a meal neither of them had to prepare. "Since you cooked, I'll volunteer to take care of dishes," Brad offered.

Kim laughed. "You offered to do dishes back in March, in the Boundary Waters."

"So I did. You turned me down. And you're bringing that up why?"

"Misty was impressed that you offered."

"I'm a little nervous that you and Misty were talking about such a thing."

"Don't be. It was a good conversation."

"So Misty approves of me, huh?"

"I didn't go that far. I said she was impressed that you offered to do dishes."

"Hmm. Might have to keep working to earn Misty's approval."

"She can be pretty tough."

"I got that impression."

They commented on the quality of the food, which was excellent, and cleaned up everything except the last of the fried rice. "Open your fortune cookie," Kim commanded. "And read it out loud."

"Oh? What if it's intensely personal?"

"All the better. House rules."

"Not your house."

"Not yours either, for that matter. But I bought supper, so you have to read your fortune cookie out loud."

Brad laboriously cracked the fortune cookie and withdrew the tiny slip of paper. "Let's see … your lucky numbers are six, eight …"

"Not that side. The other side. Come on!"

Hamming it up a bit, he turned the paper over. He read it first to himself, and frowned.

"What does it say?"

"It says, 'A man of integrity is valuable to find.'"

Kim peered at him. "And are you a man of integrity, Brad?"

He looked her in the eyes. "I try to be."

Suddenly the conversation had plunged into deep water. Brad, ever sensitive to the social atmosphere, broke the tension. "Your turn. Read it out loud."

Kim grinned. "I don't have to. I bought, remember? House rules."

"Oh, no, fair lady. Fair is fair. You read yours out loud like I did."

"Alright, alright. Let's see ... 'You will soon have an unexpected adventure.' Well, I hope that's positive."

"Could be."

"Gives me a little case of the butterflies to read that and think I'm headed to the Boundary Waters with some guy."

"Am I some guy?"

"I don't know you very well."

"But I'm not just some guy, right?"

"No, Brad, you're not just some guy."

"Good. Then let's go pack up some camping gear." He got up and gathered dishes, and she stood to help him, thinking about how easily he slid them both out from under difficult topics. Was that just a skill he learned growing up in a nice Minnesota household? Or was he really that smooth, that careful about intentionally manipulating the emotional tone of the conversation?

Oh, the questions.

Chapter Twenty-four

Brad helped her get her gear out of the back of her car and brought everything into the garage. Stepping through the door, Kim quickly realized that there was more to this than just a "garage," however. Yes, there were a couple very nice cars off to the right in clean but more-or-less traditional garage stalls. But as they walked in, the view to the left looked more like a high-end repair shop, complete with cupboards, countertops, floor-to-ceiling cabinets, and a carpeted area with a few comfortable chairs. What would have been the first garage stall was empty except for a Souris River kevlar canoe on sawhorses. Brad pointed to his own gear piled neatly near the front of this space. "I have been collecting my things there. I figure this area gives us plenty of room to organize. Let's set your stuff here. Is this all of it?"

"I've got a couple things in the car that I don't think we'll need, but we can grab them if we decide we do. Probably duplicates a lot of your gear, I'm guessing."

"Okay. We can start with this."

"Brad, can I ask–where is your space here? I'm assuming you stay up in the house?"

He laughed. "No. I actually live right through that door." He pointed to a door just beyond the carpeted area that led into what Kim had assumed earlier must be a shop of some kind.

"Can I see?"

"Please. I'd love to show you." He set her bags down, went to the door and held it open for her. "Entre vous, madame." Kim stepped through the door and gasped. She stood, it seemed, at the top of a cliff. A few feet from her toes the ground dropped away and she stood staring out at a fifty foot drop down to Lake Superior below her. The entire wall to her right was glass, floor to ceiling, wall to wall. She stood for a very long time, breathless with this incredible view: the waves breaking and crashing just below her feet, gulls wheeling and soaring in the updrafts from the cliff, cedars and pines and birches growing up out of the cracks and crags to the left and right, a stairway leading down off to her left, until at its foot a small rocky beach received the constant pounding of the waves. And out in front, her eyes were drawn to the view across the massive water toward the Wisconsin shore, lovely in soft light as the sun descended toward the horizon behind her. Far out in the lake, a freighter made its slow way east. Nearer, a couple fishing boats and a sailboat danced on the waves. But dominating the view, the gibbous moon, three or four days short of full, hung in the sky above the dim line of the far shore. Kim stood, letting the incredible beauty of this view, completely unexpected, soak into her heart and her mind.

"Glorious," she finally breathed. She tore her eyes away, finally, and looked behind her. The room she had just entered was a living room, more or less, but carefully arranged so that the view out this window-wall could be enjoyed from either of the chairs or the couch. While the room was not large, it was big enough, and simple enough. Two doors in the wall opposite the window led, she assumed, to the rest of what had suddenly been revealed as a delightful apartment. She turned slowly back to Brad, who still stood in the doorway. "This is your space?"

He grinned. "That view is why I don't feel the need to go up in the crow's nest very often. It's sort of like a mother-in-law apartment, but Todd's not married. He said he built it either for long-term contractors coming in to work on projects, or for someone like me who is on site long-term to be a caretaker."

"You said you were sleeping on his couch," she accused.

He pointed to the couch. "I sleep there a lot of nights. Can't tear myself away from this view to go back into my bedroom."

"I can't believe I felt sorry for you, shacking up at a friend's house."

"The suffering isn't too bad. It's been a good place for me, that's for sure."

Kim just shook her head and looked out at Superior for a few moments more. As the evening deepened, the moon grew brighter and brighter, and she began to see its reflection across the waves.

"Want to enjoy the view for a few minutes more? Or are you ready to get to work?"

Still looking at the lake, she murmured, "I think I'm ready to get to work. With that moonrise, I'm guessing it's not going to get any easier to tear myself away from this." With a sigh, she turned toward the garage to find him watching her, smiling.

"I'm glad you got to see it like that, Kim. It's always an incredible view, but that's pretty spectacular."

"Wow. Just wow."

Soon they were lost in the details of packing gear. For the most part, Brad's things were newer, and he provided most of the necessary items. She had her own favorites, of course, and they soon had worked together to create a very serviceable equipment pack.

"We need to define a couple things," Brad said.

"What are you thinking?"

"Well, I'm perfectly happy toting two tents just for the sake of propriety. But if you're okay with it, my four-man would have plenty of room for both of us."

Kim considered. She'd known, of course, that they would have to figure this out.

"I appreciate you bringing it up, Brad. Knowing we were making this trip together, I've done some thinking about what exactly is comfortable for me."

"And?"

"Just for the sake of clarity, I'm fine with sharing a tent. As long as the tent is all that is getting shared."

"Well, that's a relief."

"A relief?"

"Yes. As attractive as you are, Kim, and as much as I enjoy your company, I like knowing that just because I'm not 'some guy' doesn't earn me those kind of privileges. I was going to suggest exactly that solution. One tent, but pretty careful, clear boundaries beyond that. Also, on a different note, I thought about simply planning to use Mac's tent once we got in there, but I don't think it's smart to plan on that in case something has gotten into his gear."

"That's settled, then. Do you have mosquito spray?"

"I thought the hope was to get there ahead of the mosquitos."

"Want to bet your sanity on that? Let's bring some DEET. I saw a mosquito in my yard yesterday."

"Good idea."

An hour and a half later, they had discussed and debated every item to be included. Kim knew a few tricks from all her trips years ago, and Brad found himself learning from some of her stories. Finally one carefully packed Duluth bag sat in the middle of the garage floor along with paddles and life vests. They each planned to bring a personal pack as well. Kim stood up and stretched, groaning. "If packing gets me sore, I desperately need this trip. Got to get out of the office for a while and get my muscles working."

"We'll work the kinks out of your back, for sure. But it's a pretty short trip."

"I know. I was telling Misty I kind of wish it was longer. It's been a long time since I was in the Boundary Waters for any length of time. I miss it."

They made arrangements for meeting up on Friday, and Kim offered to book a couple rooms in Ely for that night so they could get an early start on Saturday morning.

"Thanks for bringing supper."

"You're welcome. Glad you liked it. Brad?"

"Yeah?"

"Don't take this wrong. I'm glad we got sleeping boundaries settled. But can I check out the view from your living room one more time?"

He grinned. "Of course."

They walked into the apartment and Kim found her breath completely taken away once again. The moon was higher now, and the landscape and the lake were dark, so the glow of the moon streamed across the water like a spotlight headed straight for her. Brad stood a comfortable step away. For a brief second Kim thought how natural it would be for him to wrap his arms around her. Did she want that? The moonlight reflected blue off the cliffs and the trees and the beach. She stood for a few moments just soaking it in, then turned to Brad. "I'm excited for this weekend, Brad. Thanks for asking me to come along."

"You're welcome. I'm glad you agreed to come." He walked her out to her Subaru and opened the door for her. "See you Friday."

"See you then."

Chapter Twenty-five

Just before she reached the highway, Kim dialed Misty's number. The phone didn't even ring and Misty picked up. "Kim?"

"Yeah. Whoa. That was fast."

"Everything go okay?"

"Yeah. Yeah, Misty, it was fine. You sound stressed."

"Oh, shit. Kim, you have no idea. This is why I've never had kids. For the last half hour I've been pacing the floor thinking through everything that could have happened. You sure you're alright?"

"I'm great. It was a nice evening. We had dinner and got all the gear packed and everything."

"Good. That's good. That's a relief."

"Misty–breathe, for goodness sake."

"Just a little anxiety going here."

"You were worried?"

"Yeah. I guess."

"Misty, this isn't like you."

"Oh, guess what. Tonight it is."

"Honestly, you were just worried about me and Brad?"

"I was worried he was a creep and lured you out to that swanky remote lake house. I was about ready to drive down and check up on you."

"It's not even that late. You sure that's all it is?"

"I think so. I don't know. Yeah. I'm just worried. Had myself convinced he's a jerk and he's going to hurt you."

"He was a perfect gentleman."

"You didn't tell him about your pistol, did you?"

"No. But Misty…"

"Good. Okay, I'm starting to breathe better. You're headed home now?"

"No, I've changed my mind. I'm turning around and heading back to Brad's place for a night of wild sex."

"What? Son of a bitch!"

"I'm headed home. Misty, I'm headed home. I'm fine, Brad's fine. You're fine. Deep breath, baby. I'm meeting him Friday and we're headed up to the Boundary Waters for the weekend. Just like we planned."

"I don't know how parents of teenagers do it. Mom has been laughing at me all night. This sucks."

Kim laughed. "I'm with your mom. Let your blood pressure down. I'm going home to go to bed. Alone. Get some rest."

"Okay. I'll try."
"Misty?"
"Yeah."
"Thanks for caring so much."
"Whew. Better believe it, baby."

Chapter Twenty-six

Friday at exactly 3:30 pm, Kim drove onto the concrete slab between the massive house and the four car garage. She pulled up in front of Brad's apartment. A light drizzle had been falling all morning giving Lake Superior a dark and brooding look, but the rain had stopped about noon. The skies were starting to break up into ragged tatters of clouds and fleeting patches of blue. Brad's pickup was parked outside on the slab, canoe securely strapped to a rack that fit in his pickup box leaving plenty of room for Duluth packs and paddles underneath the canoe. They loaded Kim's things, pulled her Forrester into the empty garage stall, and closed up the buildings. A few minutes before 4 pm, they were on the road, pulling onto Highway 61 and headed northeast for Two Harbors. From there they would leave the lakeshore and head northward to Ely. They talked about the weather, both having noted that the forecast was for clearing this evening and then excellent weather the next couple of days. Kim offered details of the rooms she'd reserved and Brad talked about the mechanics of reserving the permit–a process that had changed significantly since Kim spent any time in a canoe.

"It's all online now," he explained. "You just go to their website and choose the entry point you're looking for, and it tells you how many permits are left for that entry point on that day."

"I don't imagine we have a lot of competition this early, do we?"

"Snowbank Lake is our entry point, and I think that had something like twenty permits each day. Two or three of them were taken when I booked this, so I'm guessing it will be pretty quiet."

"That's the nice thing about off-peak Boundary Waters."

"Yeah. It's a different experience when it's full of people. I've only seen it those few days last August when it was busy. Compared to that, the silence day after day in the fall and winter was pretty amazing."

"You spent a lot of time talking with Mac, though."

"True. But even so, even if we were talking a couple hours a day at most, it feels different when the rest of your days are full of solitude."

"Full of solitude. Isn't that an oxymoron?"

Brad chuckled. "Not at all. The solitude gets to be like something that fills everything. Fills the night sky, and the trees, and the water, and the space between your heartbeats."

"Why, Brad. You must have been spending time in the crow's nest. I do believe you're a poet."

"Not really."

"A philosopher, then."

He laughed. "Honestly, I'm not sure what I am anymore. It goes in waves. Some days I feel like I'm healing up from everything, figuring out who I am, and then the next day I'm depressed and half-crazy. I stew about what I did that made my life fall apart, and what I should have done different. Some days I have answers and some days I don't have a clue."

"You have anyone to talk to about those things?" As the words streamed out of her mouth, Kim realized this might be offensive, but Brad didn't seem to mind.

"A little. I do some counseling on and off, when I have things I need to talk about. Last week I ran to the Cities and made a point of scheduling lunch with Pastor Bob."

"How was that?"

"Good. Time with Bob is always good. I told him about you, about this lightning trip this weekend."

"Did he have any helpful insights?"

"He asked about me healing up. Said he can see I'm more comfortable in my own skin than I used to be. Well, what he actually said is that I don't look like death warmed over anymore. I look like I'm doing pretty well."

"You do seem like you can stand on your own two feet."

Brad took a long pull from his water bottle, then replaced it deliberately into the cup holder. "Is there any option? I mean, really? I know I could have a nervous breakdown, get hospitalized, all that. I've taken a long look into that abyss a couple times. But if you fall apart, it takes a hell of a long time to put yourself back together again. I think it's better just not to fall apart."

Kim stared out the window, watching the buildings of Two Harbors sliding by. "So what happens for people who can't keep it all together?"

"I know there are lots of people who fall apart. And sometimes they need other people to carry them for a while. I saw that on the farm growing up. One family has a tragedy, and all the other farmers come together to get their crops harvested. Things like that. Or the way everybody in that community showed up with a hotdish or a pan of bars when there was a death in the family. It was a way of carrying each other. Sometimes you need to fall apart, and sometimes you need other people to carry you. But in my situation, after the divorce, I mean, I don't know that I had anyone who would have stepped up to carry me. I would have been in a psych ward. And sometimes that's necessary. But for whatever reason I was able to keep myself mostly together."

"I have to admit, that first conversation we had, I had my doubts."

"What?"

"Your thing about stop lights."

"That was just pure science. I told you, I timed them."

"Aaaand that's why I thought maybe you were a little ... "

"Crazy?"

"Sure."

"So what do you think now?"

"You seem like a solid guy, Brad. You seem like a guy with both feet on the ground. You seem like a decent man who is trying to live a rough patch of life well."

"Thank you."

"I mean it. That's what you look like to me. But I think that's the way most of us want to come across. In our own minds, we're all the good guys."

"Is there anything wrong with seeing ourselves that way?"

Kim stared out the window for a few seconds, considering, and Brad gave her a moment to think. "It just seems like if we were all as good as we think we are, I wouldn't be working for a foundation that tries so hard to do a little good. Looking around from where I sit, it's a screwed up world with massive needs."

"So where do the needs come from?"

"People make mistakes. More than that. Maybe it's easier to see when you get up to thirty thousand feet and look at bigger trends."

"Meaning?"

"Meaning it makes more sense if you look at scale. Call it the law of unintended consequences. You know a few years ago how everyone was so fed up about those Asian beetles that swarmed so thick in late September?"

"Yeah. I remember standing on the south side of my house with a shop-vac trying to get them before they got inside. Phew."

"Right. Well, those beetles were imported to eat aphids, the way I read it. Somebody thought it was a brilliant way to get rid of an aphid infestation. They never figured those beetles would reproduce like mad and create all kinds of problems. Same thing with the carp in the Mississippi River. Somebody figured carp was a great food fish so they imported a bunch of them, now they're taking over, driving out the native species. Unintended consequences."

"How does that impact the foundation's work?"

"Neither of those examples do, not directly. But I look at the things we've donated money to. We pay for clean water wells in impoverished areas, or charter schools that are desperately trying to connect kids with the outdoors, or dozens of other things. So many of the problems are just the negative consequences of someone's good idea."

"The whole charter school thing. Play that one out for me."

"Someone comes up with a personal sized computer, and the technology just keeps getting easier and easier to use. Miniaturization, all that. Everybody gets a computer in their home, and then it's a laptop, and then it's on your phone. For the last thirty or forty years, kids are learning from day one that they should be on computers. Technology is a good thing, right? Think of how much good it's done for us. But the kids. They're not out playing in the creeks or climbing trees or riding bikes. They're playing a video game about riding bikes instead. So we get more obese kids. We get health problems. We get kids who've never climbed a tree, never picked up a frog or a crayfish or paddled a canoe or caught a fish. Computers are great things, and kids need to know how to use them at some point. But now we've got a need for innovative programs in schools to put a few kids back in touch with the outdoors again."

"I see what you mean. Unintended consequences."

"Exactly. And we're a couple generations into that move now, so it's not just the kids. It's the parents. The parents are on their screens all the time and don't think about taking their kids outdoors either."

"Guess I was lucky to grow up playing in the creek. Even then, it seemed like I was losing out because the town kids were watching MTV and out on the farm we didn't have cable. Just the three network channels."

"Technology is a good thing, but we don't know how to set limits on it."

"So we see ourselves as the good guys and don't know the damage we're doing."

"We all see ourselves as the good guys, but we try to find the easiest, cheapest ways to solve our problems. So we cause new problems that we don't intend. But we still see ourselves as the heroes."

"Here's a question. Do you think we honestly believe that we're the good guys–so we're lying to ourselves–or do we know we are making things worse, but we can't stand to be honest with others so we just lie a little bit to everyone else?"

"Some of each, I guess. I think most of us really want to see ourselves as good people. We see our intentions, which are usually good, while everyone else sees the actual consequences of what we do."

Brad chuckled. "Yeah. I spent a lot of time resenting Lauren and how hard it was to be married to her. It was satisfying in a way to be hurting so badly."

"Satisfying?"

"Kind of. Maybe that's the wrong word. She left me, you know? I could be righteous and see myself as the victim."

"Ah."

"It was an unpleasant moment when I started to realize how much I could have done different to try to make the marriage work. I wanted to think at first it was all her problem, but when I lived with that for a while, I had to realize I was a big part of what went wrong, too." Brad's off-the-cuff confession hung in the air for a moment.

Kim finally smiled at the awkward silence. "Well, that's a personal perspective on it. Didn't mean to go there."

"I know you didn't. I did. I need to see things like that. I need to be honest about who I am and how I screw things up. Otherwise I'm just going to be the same rat on the same hamster wheel. And I don't want that."

"After all you've been through, do you really feel like you're in danger of making the same mistakes?"

"Absolutely. I could very easily fall back into the same patterns if I stop paying attention. That's what I've learned more than anything, I guess. To pay attention."

"Where did you pick that up?"

"Mostly from Mac. Bob some, too, but mostly Mac. No surprise. His biggest lesson was, don't breeze through the wilderness screwing yourself and everyone else up. Pay attention to what you're doing, and do it well."

They both sat in silence with that thought for a few seconds, then Brad spoke. "Now that I think about it, I learned something similar as a kid watching my parents on the farm. It seemed like such a limited world at that time, and I dreamed of getting away from it. But looking back I see that they were so intentional about things. They were paying attention."

Thinking about Mac, Kim was quiet for a few miles. The silence was a comfortable thing that stretched between them as she watched pine trees and cattail swamps and stands of poplar flowing by outside her window.

"Can I ask a question, Brad?"

"I don't know, Kim. I'm not comfortable sharing personal information. So as long as it's nothing that really digs into tough things, I guess that's okay."

Kim gave him a withering look, and he grinned a boyish grin at her. "Sarcasm. It's just one of the many services I offer." She shook her head and smiled and looked out the window, then turned back to him.

"Why is this trip important to you? Is there more than just getting Mac's gear because you promised that you would? What are you hoping for?"

Brad gazed through the windshield and pondered for a few moments.

"A few things, I guess. I'm not sure what's most important to me. Yes, the obvious reason is I promised Mac I would take care of cleaning up his gear. But you're right, there's more to it than that." He slowed to deal with an old station wagon that was doing about forty in a fifty-five zone. He followed the old car on the two lane highway until they crested a hill and he could see a mile or so ahead, and smoothly accelerated around the slower car. Back in his own lane, he continued. "One thing I'm excited about, to be brutally honest, is getting to know you a little better." He glanced across at her. She met his gaze but didn't speak, so he continued. "And probably down in my gut somewhere, I'm still not at peace with Mac's death. What happened up there was rough, and I want to make sure I'm processing it well. So partly I guess it's a grief thing."

Kim digested this. "That last one, that's certainly true for me as well," she said finally. "I've got grief to process, and when you invited me to come along, I jumped at that chance. I know I've got more work to do in that way."

"It's hard work. It takes time."

"Time, yes. And I've never been good at grieving. I don't know. Do you ever get good at grieving? I don't think I want to get good at that."

"Grief is hard. I've spent more time than I ever expected this last year grieving."

"I've lost my grandparents, but as far as close personal relationships, Mac is by far the roughest death I've had to deal with. Your parents are both gone, right?"

"Yeah. Mom died suddenly about fifteen years ago, and Dad lasted a couple more years, but it's eight years ago now we buried him. So I've been through those. But in a way, you expect at some point to lose your parents. I think both Lauren leaving me and Mac's death hit me harder. Or at least differently."

"I can see that. You expect a marriage to last a lifetime, right?"

"Till death do us part. That's what I figured, even if things weren't great. Or even very good."

"And Mac... Honestly, Brad, I've spent a lot of time imagining what that must have been like for you, but I can't really get my mind around it."

Brad stared at the highway for a while. "It was hard. Harder than I know how to tell, probably." Silence. "A lot harder."

Five miles passed. Brad chuckled, and one corner of Kim's mouth turned up. "What?" she asked.

"I'm trying to decide what I think about the fact that you never listed this hot date with me being your main motivation for coming along on this trip."

She laughed aloud. "We kind of got derailed from my list of motivations. But I was getting to that one."

"Really?"

Pause. Think about what you want to say next, Kim. Deep breath. "Honestly, I'm enjoying getting to know you, too, Brad. Most of the time I'm focused on work, on the foundation. And if it wasn't that this was about Mac and so indirectly about the foundation, I probably wouldn't be going. I think sometimes I get too nose-to-the-grindstone. But I'm enjoying getting to know you as well. Back when I worked those summers in the Boundary Waters, we always used to say if you wanted to know who someone was deep down, go wilderness camping with them. It takes off all the surface layers and lets you see what's underneath."

"No pressure."

"Lots of pressure. That's what's best about it."

"I think I should be flattered. Or terrified."

She smiled at him, a genuine smile that gave external evidence of a warmth she had been relishing deep inside. "I don't know yet for certain. But I suspect that you are a genuine, authentic man, Brad Swenson. That is, you seem to be the same guy in a lot of different situations. The Brad who was standing in your friend's gorgeous house, the Brad who is driving up the highway toward Ely. They seem to be the same guy. Call it consistency. And I suspect that is the same guy you're going to be carrying a canoe on a portage or waking up on the ground with a sore back. As long as I've been watching, you've been the same person. Consistent. You might be surprised how rare that is."

Brad looked across the cab at her, and he was not smiling. His blue eyes were intense, fixed on her; even when he glanced back at the road every few seconds they immediately returned and homed in on her face. "Thank you. Thank you. That means a lot, Kim."

"You're welcome."

Chapter Twenty-seven

They rolled into Ely hungry for supper, but decided to take care of their permit and check into the hotel first. They drove through town and started out the road eastward that led toward the Boundary Waters entry points. Just east of town they turned into the Forest Service station. The new-looking building was large, airy, and filled with colorful displays of the natural wonders of the north country. No other canoers were present. The twenty-something woman behind the counter checked their permit. She asked if they needed any maps, and played the obligatory orientation video on a little screen at the end of the counter. She dutifully reviewed the information included in the video, checking off boxes on the back of the permit as Brad or Kim gave the accurate answers.

"Any issues with bears this spring?" Kim asked.

"No, it's been pretty quiet. Not many people going in yet. A few fishermen Memorial Day weekend, of course, but pretty slow other than that."

Next they drove back into town and checked into their hotel. Key cards and bags and all the necessities taken care of, they debated a few dining options and landed at the Insula. "Misty and I ate here before heading into the woods in March. It was pretty good."

"Tell me about your friendship with Misty. Seems like you guys are pretty close."

Kim considered. "Honestly, before I got in touch with her after Mac's death, we hadn't talked in a decade." They walked into the restaurant, got a booth, and perused the menus. Once they'd ordered, Brad brought the conversation back on track.

"Really? You hadn't talked with Misty in ten years?"

"Yeah. My fault, I guess. Nose to the grindstone again. Misty is a little rough around the edges, but she's an amazing person. Talented. Strong. The summers we worked together at Wilderness, she was my favorite camping partner. We just clicked somehow."

"So what was that like, working there?"

"We were mostly guides, which is a really glamorous way of saying we kept groups of high school kids from doing stupid stuff in the backcountry. We cooked and cleaned for them, and we maintained gear."

"Good college job, huh?"

"Pay wasn't great, but it was pretty cool to be up here for months each summer."

"Did you and Misty escape back to civilization on the weekends?"

"Sometimes. You know, you get to missing Dairy Queen at that age. We'd run into Grand Marais and get a Blizzard and then drive up to her family's place, which is pretty rural. Misty still lives there. Takes care of her mom. Her family was all noise and conversation and people coming and going. I grew up in the calm, structured suburbs."

"Did her family drive you a little crazy?"

"No, honestly. I loved the chaos, the people, the relationships. It was harder for Misty. At that age I think we were all embarrassed by our own families. But she could see I loved it, and we went there a dozen times over three years."

"What did you do on weekends when you didn't go there?"

Kim laughed. "Mostly we went camping. As deep and far into the woods as we could. Snag an unused permit and throw packs in the canoe and paddle far and fast. A couple times we went up into the Quetico–the Canada side of the border–and explored a little bit. But mostly we just paddled around the U.S. side."

"You must have loved it to guide all week and then paddle in on your own time."

"I did. We did. Misty was a great camping partner, like I said. We did this thing once..."

"What?"

"It's a long time ago."

"C'mon, Kim, I hear a good story being squelched here."

Kim laughed. "Some of the guides on the Gunflint Trail had this challenge they'd do. Mostly the macho male guides, you know? The idea was to go from the end of the Gunflint by canoe to Ely and back in 24 hours."

"That seems impossible."

"Oh, it's possible. But there were some requirements. Anyone could say they'd done it, so the unwritten rule on the trail was that you had to have someone document when you left, paddle to the Moose Lake landing east of Ely, hitchhike into town, mail a postcard back to your base on the Gunflint, and buy an ice cream cone at the DQ in Ely and save the receipt. Then you have to paddle back to your starting point on the Gunflint and have somebody document the time you got back."

"Now it really seems complicated. All that in twenty-four hours?"

"Exactly. All that."

"So you paddle all night?"

"Usually the way they would do things is to leave about sunset on a night with a full moon and paddle the border lakes, so you'd get to Ely sometime in the morning the next day. Then you'd have to get back before the time you left the evening before. By the time you're done, you've probably been awake for about forty hours."

"Gear?"

"You're not camping or fishing on a trip like that. We took a little day pack full of granola bars and a tiny first aid kit, a knife and some matches just in case."

"So you and Misty actually did this."

"We did. I'd be curious if we still hold the record."

"Record? How long did it take you?"

"Twenty hours."

"Holy cow. How did you do that?"

"Misty checked the weather forecast and came to me all excited one Friday. We'd both been guiding that week, and our groups came back into base camp about noon Friday. Two in the afternoon or so she woke me up from a nap. She was all excited and said that the next day we were supposed to have a strong west wind. It was almost a full moon, and the weather was supposed to be clear. Perfect conditions, she said. Perfect for what, I asked. Perfect to set a record for the twenty-four hour challenge, she said. I rolled over and meant to go back to sleep, but she convinced me to get up. And we did it."

"Playing the wind and the moon like that?"

"That was a big part of it. We left a couple hours after sunset, paddled in the moonlight all night up Saganaga and southwest on the border chain. That's fast canoeing, short portages. We came into the Moose Lake landing early in the morning, and it just happened we found an outfitter who had dropped off some paddlers and was headed back to Ely. So we hitched a ride, talked to him about what we were doing, and he dropped us at Dairy Queen. We got our cones and a receipt, bought a postcard at the drugstore and mailed it at the post office. That same outfitter had said he was headed back to Moose to pick up another group at eleven, and we hitched a ride back, so we didn't have to waste much time hitchhiking. But the big deal was that by that time of the day, the wind was coming up. The outfitter was a little worried about us paddling back in it. There were whitecaps out on the lakes. The group he was picking up was there at the landing, huddled and cold in the wind, and they looked at us like we were crazy to be launching into that stuff. But we were young and stupid and we just laughed."

Brad just shook his head, entranced by the story.

"We paddled like mad all afternoon. If you're going with the wind and get your speed just right, you can surf on those waves, especially on the long lakes where the wind has a lot of room to build a swell. We surfed a lot of the way back, with the waves just pushing a little bit to give us that extra edge. It's still a lot of work. You have to paddle like crazy, and you have to keep your canoe tracking with the waves. And if you ever have to change directions, then you really have to fight the wind and the water. But we were headed east-northeast almost that whole way, and the wind was out of the west-southwest. We did it, and we figured that the wind took a couple hours off our time. We pulled into base camp about suppertime. Nobody would believe that we had actually been to Ely until we showed them our DQ receipts and then a couple days later the postcard arrived, and they had to believe it."

"You must have been exhausted."

Kim smiled, remembering. "We were so high on adrenaline I don't think we got to sleep that night until close to sunrise. Then we both slept all the next day."

"No doubt." Brad shook his head. "The two of you must have made a terrifying pair."

"Not really. At that point it was our third year working together. We knew each other. We'd camped and paddled together a ton. We'd sit up into the night talking about everything under the sun. We just worked really well together, and we knew exactly what the other was capable of, what was too much." She stared at her plate for a few seconds. "It was a pretty incredible partnership."

Brad frowned. "That's amazing." Long pause. "I think deep down, without ever thinking about it, that's what I expected marriage to be."

"How do you mean?"

"I figured it would be that kind of incredible partnership. I like that phrase. I figured when Lauren and I got married that we'd come to know each other's strengths and weaknesses and limitations, and we'd work so well together we'd just conquer the world."

"Not quite how it happened."

"Sad thing is, I don't think we ever tried. We just assumed the partnership would be there. We didn't have any dragons to slay or anything. We were just building the suburban American dream, and it's not because we thought that was the right thing to do. Just what we drifted into. I don't think our marriage ever had a mission beyond just existing. So each of us started drifting toward our own goals rather than working together."

"That's sad, but I suspect lots of marriages could tell that story."

"Yeah. How many marriages have a sense of their shared goals, of where they're headed? Not many, I'd guess. I wonder sometimes if I get the chance again, if I'd be able to build that kind of partnership."

"Better do a good job of defining your mission. And screening potential partners."

Brad grinned. "So tell me your theories about taking potential boyfriends wilderness camping to see if they're worth the investment."

Kim's eyes sparkled just a bit and she dipped a french fry in ketchup to consider her answer. "I think we just lived it those years so many times, we sort of assumed it was a good way to do things."

"You checked out a lot of potential boyfriends?"

"No. A couple, maybe. No, what we did was we took groups of high school kids out in the wilderness over and over again, and each week you'd see the surface layers of those campers get stripped away and you'd find what people were really made of."

"What were you looking for?"

"We didn't go looking for it, not at first, but it was so obvious week after week. Get a couple days of rain and watch a girl who's vain about her hair go into a meltdown. Watch the kid who twists his ankle on a portage deal with being weaker than he wants to be for a few days and you'll see what's under the surface. Watch a group of kids who are used to getting pretty much what they want, and suddenly they have to paddle or portage to get anywhere. They find out they can't read their maps very well. Not to mention that they don't have the option of going to the mall or watching a movie to tune out. You see what's under the surface."

"Same story for the guides?"

"Yes, but the bar is higher. We'd all signed on for the wilderness experience, and we knew more or less what we were in for. But the leadership part of it, the relationship part of it is what ground the guides down."

"How so?"

"By the middle of the season, you know who can handle a group of campers with some relational conflict going on. Some guides can take a group of novice campers on a challenging route. Others had better just go out to a base camp on Seagull and do day trips for the week. You know when you get that adult chaperone that comes with the kids and wants to be in charge of everything, which guides can handle that and which can't. That's maybe more challenging than the physical demands of the backcountry."

"I can see that. Adversity, I suppose, whatever shape it takes."

"Adversity. That was part of Mac's vocabulary."

"Yeah. We talked about that a fair amount."

"Did he ever give you his 'suffering desolation' speech?"

Brad laughed. "We talked a lot about suffering desolation."

Kim shook her head. "The first time he gave me that speech I thought he was certifiable. Of course, I'd only been working for him about a week at that point. He went off on a tangent about how most of the troubles in our society these days were because we were unwilling to suffer desolation. You read the gospels and Jesus was always seeking out desolate places. For a while I honestly had him pegged for some kind of fundamentalist Bible thumper."

"Mac?!"

She laughed. "It didn't last long. But he was so convinced that we needed to seek out desolate places. He'd rant about how Disneyland was the worst place to go if you needed personal renewal. Desolation is good for the soul."

Brad chimed in, "'The average American is unwilling to suffer desolation, and so all they can do is settle for entertainment.'" He raised his beer glass. "To Mac, and suffering desolation."

Kim toasted with him, and as she did a sadness welled up in her. She thought about Mac's overwhelming personality, his strong opinions and his absolute dedication to his work. "I miss that man," she said quietly.

"Me, too. You talked about how he was so much more open with me those days in the Boundary Waters. That's true. But I find myself jealous of you and the years you had to work alongside him. I think there's a lot more he could have taught me."

"Yes. But I think you have a sense how much frustration I experienced working with him. Mac was so closed off most of the time. He'd just fume and keep to himself, or he'd bluster and gripe and pontificate and make everybody keep their distance. So it isn't like I enjoyed years of deep conversation with him. I picked up a lot of things here and there, but it was sparse."

"You told me once that you were content in the second chair at the foundation. It's been a while since you said that, and I assume the board has started their search process. Are you still thinking you don't want that lead spot?"

Kim watched his face for a moment, thrown back by his question into her ongoing debate about Mac's last wishes. Behind her eyes her brain was suddenly whirling with Mac's recommended future for Brad in the foundation. Her thoughts touched on the more personal aspects of all that as well. "I've spent a lot of hours lying awake at night wondering about that."

"And?"

"I'm still convinced I make a great second. I don't want the lead role. But I want someone in the top spot I can work with, someone who can build that kind of partnership so my gifts are making a difference to the foundation."

"Back to the idea of partnership, huh?"

"Very much so. It's not hard to be second in command if you feel that sense of partnership. Even if the leader makes a decision you disagree with, you know you're not being taken for granted or dismissed out of hand."

"So you don't need to be right all the time, but you do need to be valued?"

Kim considered. "Something like that. I know I'm not right all the time. But my voice needs to be heard, and considered. Maybe 'valued' carries that sense."

"More than anything, I think that's what wore on me in corporate middle management. It seemed like anyone could do the job I was doing. My little cog in the corporate wheel had no chance of changing the corporation, for good or for bad."

"That's got to be frustrating."

"It was."

They lingered over dinner, indulging in decaf and dessert. A little after eight o'clock they agreed it was a good idea to get an early start the next morning. Kim paid for dinner, on the foundation's dime. They walked the three blocks to the hotel. At Kim's door, Brad asked, "What time do you think? Meet you in the lobby at five? The sun's up about then."

"Five it is. We should be paddling across Snowbank right into the sun. Bring your sunglasses, Brad."

"Good idea. Good night, Kim."

"Good night."

As she readied herself for sleep and eventually crawled under the hotel blankets, Kim couldn't shake a little bit of uneasiness about the next couple days. What would this trip be like? What would she learn about Brad? Dinner was nice. She enjoyed how transparent he was about things that were important to him, uncertainties he had. And she could tell he was genuinely interested in her. He asked good questions and listened well.

What was not to like?

Her last considered action before bed was to check on her pistol. Her mind was like a pendulum when she remembered it, sitting in a nondescript brown pouch in the bottom of her daypack, a full clip in the magazine and a spare in its separate pocket in the pouch. She took it out, checked on it, replaced it in the bottom of the pack, set the pack by the door. On second thought, she set the daypack next to her bed within easy reach. Misty had made sure she was comfortable with the pistol. She could load it, fire it, field strip it, clean it, reload it, all the necessaries. Part of Kim's brain just thought it was needless weight, a foolish suspicion to be carried into the wilderness. Excess baggage. It weighed on her mind for the minutes it took her to fall asleep, and that night she dreamed uncomfortable dreams.

Chapter Twenty-eight

She woke in the dark and glanced at the oversized numbers of the digital hotel clock. 4:05. Her alarm would go off in five minutes. She found her phone and turned off the alarm, and with a tiny thrill remembered that in a couple hours, that phone would become nothing more than a camera. No cell tower reached into the Boundary Waters, thank goodness. Her mind came fully awake as she thought with great anticipation of the day to come. Loading gear into the canoe, checking its trim front to back and side to side, grabbing a paddle and launching into the clear waters of Snowbank Lake. For the first time in too many years, she would be carrying Duluth packs and a canoe on portage trails, selecting a campsite, setting up a tent. Her trip in March with Misty (and Brad, sort of) didn't count as a Boundary Waters trip in her mind. That had been a lightning run built on the necessity of Mac's death. In a way, the same could be said of this trip. All the same she was excited, excited to be on the water in a canoe. She was excited to be back in the wilderness, even for a couple nights.

And what would it be like, camping with Brad? She wasn't too worried. He was, as she had said, very consistent. It would be different if she hadn't seen him winter camping. She had heard his detailed descriptions of how he'd coped with the wilderness in the past. He was capable, she was sure. Part of her relaxed back into that fact, realizing that some of the big questions about respect and capability were settled in her mind. There were other questions to be settled. She wasn't sure how she felt, for example, about the question of attraction. Even so, she felt a great deal more attracted to Brad now than she had when she first met him. No hurry.

He knocked lightly on her door right at 5 am, and she grabbed her bags and followed him to the elevator. Brad had pointed out a 24-hour gas station / convenience store the evening before, and they stopped there for coffee and breakfast. The sun was just clearing the treeline when they drove east out of Ely, headed for Snowbank Lake. "Glad you told me to bring my sunglasses," Brad mumbled.

"Bet it will be worse on the water, at least the first leg across Snowbank," she responded. "Paddling east into the morning sun. But it's a great day for canoeing. How'd you sleep?"

"First night in a new place is always hard. But for all that, it wasn't bad. You?"

"Fairly well. I have to say, I'm just excited to be canoeing into the backcountry again."

"Miss it?"

"Yeah. I didn't realize how much. Why haven't I done more of this, Brad? It's not like Duluth is a long ways from the Boundary Waters."

"Guess you grew up, huh?"

"Lots of grown ups go to the Boundary Waters."

"Yeah, but you grew into the whole work ethic thing. Like you said, nose to the grindstone. Be responsible."

"I suppose. I'm glad to be getting out here today, though. I think it's going to be a great day." It was about sixty degrees, and the high was forecast to be in the low seventies–a perfect Boundary Waters day. The lakes were still cool, of course, so it might feel cooler on the water. Jacket weather. But the sun was potent and promised to provide the needed warmth. Something in Kim was irrepressible this morning.

They drove through the brilliant sun as it filtered through birch, poplar, pine and fir. They followed the lazy curves of the two-lane road up and down hills, past lakes and cabins and resorts. Finally they found the signs for the boat landing at Snowbank Lake, and Brad pulled in and found a parking space near the lake. Snowbank was a big lake, three miles and more across each way, but the landing perched on a peninsula that stuck up from the south end of the lake. So their target, a portage into Disappointment Lake, was only about a mile and a half to the east. A light breeze out of the southwest promised to make their crossing even easier. They unstrapped the canoe from its frame, and Kim climbed up in the pickup box to guide the canoe off the rack while Brad backed it away and positioned it over his head. While he carried the canoe over to the boat ramp Kim grabbed their big Duluth pack, her daypack, and Brad's small day pack. She had debated whether to carry her pistol in her jacket pocket, but it seemed safer and less likely to be discovered in the bottom of her daypack. What would Misty suggest?

She swung the big pack on her shoulders, took a daypack in each hand and followed Brad. One more trip and they had paddles and life vests, and Brad locked up the pickup. He glanced around the vacant parking lot. Two other cars sat near the far end of the lot, but no one else was visible. He said, "Just so you know, there's a magnetic key box inside the front bumper with a spare ignition key in it. If something was to happen to me."

Kim considered this. "Okay. I suppose in theory that's possible, but it's not going to happen. We're going to have a great trip. I can tell."

"I think so too, but I just wanted you to know. In case."

They lifted the canoe into the water parallel to the shore and set the packs into it. "One of the things I thought about when I couldn't sleep last night," Brad grinned, "is that I've never paddled with another person before. So do you have a preference, front or back?"

"I've done a lot of both," Kim laughed, "but not for a very long time. So how about you take the stern and I'll sit up front for now? We can always switch off if we want to."

"Works for me. I figure that will make a difference how we load the packs, since I must outweigh you by…"

"Careful, buddy."

"… a considerable amount. So what do you think–the Duluth pack behind you, and the daypacks in front of me?"

"Let's try it and see. Should be okay that way. If need be we can shift the daypacks around."

They loaded the packs and Kim stepped carefully into the bow seat. Brad stood in the shallow water and held the canoe steady. Once Kim was in place he shook water from his shoes and stepped carefully into the stern. "How's it feel?" he asked.

"I'm good, I think. Let's give it a try. The lake is pretty smooth. If it's not perfect we can change after the portage."

Brad reversed his paddle, turning it blade upward and using the handle to dig into the gravel along the boat ramp and push them out into deeper water. A few strokes and they were facing east, into the sun, feeling the breeze on the backs of their necks. "The way we did things back when," Kim said, "if you've got two solid paddlers the one in the front sets a pace, and the one in the back takes care of the steering. You let me know if you want me to paddle faster or slower, or if you need me to switch sides. Otherwise I'll just leave the steering to you."

"Sounds like a lot of responsibility. But I think we can handle it."

Soon they were gliding across the lake, the gentle lift and drop of shallow swells keeping them aware of the water, and they both fell into an easy rhythm. They paddled strongly, but unhurried. Kim found her arms, shoulders, and upper body remembering subtleties and techniques from years ago. Brad seemed capable of steering, and kept their bow pinpointed on the destination east and just a little bit north across the lake.

"Oh, my God, how I have missed this!"

"So this is going okay, as first dates go?"

Kim laughed out loud. "I'll let you know. But I'm definitely enjoying the process. I'm glad you invited me."

"Good."

They paddled for a few moments without speaking, then Brad commented, "You know, I'm pleased with this canoe. I bought this model because they said it was big enough to use as a touring canoe for two people for a week or so, but you could also reverse it. Take out that thwart just behind your seat and use it as a solo canoe. If you load it right, it works great solo, and I put a lot of miles on it that way. Then I wrecked it. Had a guy rebuild the kevlar shell for me. Thought about buying a different canoe, but stuck with this one. I had no idea how it would work with two people. It's not the fastest canoe on the lake, but it seems to be functioning pretty well."

"It's a joy to have quality equipment. Yeah, I think you made a good investment."

Chapter Twenty-nine

It took most of an hour to cross Snowbank. They crossed a large open stretch of water and navigated past a couple islands, checking the maps and comparing what they were seeing on shore. They entered the bay shown on the map and looked toward the trees at its end. They didn't have to look for long; the portage landing was obvious, a broad gravel area well-trampled over the years by hundreds of canoers entering the Boundary Waters through Snowbank Lake. They pulled up on the beach, and Brad stepped out into the shallow water.

"I'm impressed," Kim complimented him.

"With what?"

"You don't grind the bow of your canoe up onto the beach. You step out into the water. You get your feet wet to save the canoe."

"Pays to take care of the equipment that is going to take care of you. That was one of the things Mac emphasized, but I'd had it drilled into me already by both Pastor Bob and the guys at BTO. Just makes sense when you think about it. You're not going to keep your feet dry up here anyway."

"True," she smiled as she stepped into the shallow water. "You want to take the Duluth pack or the canoe?"

"You have a preference?"

Kim looked sheepish. "Mind if I carry the canoe? I haven't portaged a canoe in a long, long time."

"Be my guest."

She slung her daypack over her shoulders and Brad pulled the Duluth bag out of the canoe and toted it up on the beach. Then he lifted the bow and steadied the canoe as she settled in under it, the canoe perched above her upside-down. Kim rested the portage pads on her shoulders. "Can you get the rest of our stuff?"

Brad looked around at their gear. "Shouldn't be a problem. See you on the other end." She moved a few feet up the trail into the forest while Brad gathered his daypack and their paddles and lifted the Duluth pack to his shoulders. She walked up the trail, balancing the long canoe, and Brad was out of sight behind her. Kim could only see the trail in front of her feet and a few yards to either side. This was a fairly long portage, a hundred and forty rods, so almost half a mile. At first the kevlar canoe felt like nothing at all on her shoulders. The ground rose gently before her. The portage was wide and well-traveled, without muddy pools or boulders to slow her down. By the time she topped the low ridge between the two lakes and started her gentle descent down to Disappointment Lake, though, Kim could feel the ache in her shoulders. She had to be cautious about her footing so as not to stumble as her legs and core and arms all began to feel the onset of fatigue. It had been a long time indeed, she grimaced. Of course, back in the day she'd have been ashamed to have someone help her get a canoe up on her shoulders. Especially a kevlar canoe!

She found herself playing the same mental games she remembered from years before, counting steps, estimating distances, trying to imagine how far she'd come and how far she had yet to go. She reminded herself to pay attention and enjoy the process. Even the little bit of the forest she could see from under the canoe was lovely: ferns thick on the slopes, low ground filled with Labrador tea and blueberry plants, stately pine trunks rising up from the moss to reach for the sun, lichens covering boulders alongside the trail. She could smell the Boundary Waters, too. It was a rich combination of boreal forest, warming air, and damp shoes. Finally she saw blue water through the trees ahead and she came down a long last slope. She walked right out into the lake a few steps. She carefully flipped the canoe over her right shoulder and gently lowered it to the water. Setting her daypack in the bow in front of her seat, she pulled out a canteen. Before she'd finished quenching her thirst, Brad came strolling down the trail. She helped him offload the Duluth pack directly into the canoe. They stowed their gear and were paddling out into the bright waters of Disappointment in less than a minute.

"Odd name for a lake, huh?"

"Don't tell me you haven't played the map game."

"What do you mean?"

"Sitting up in your tent with your flashlight, or killing a half hour in the afternoon just looking at your map reading weird names for all the lakes. Across the border in the Quetico they get even more bizarre. Negligee Lake? Really? And the "Man" chain–This Man Lake. That Man Lake. Other Man Lake. There are so many lakes up here they had to get pretty creative with the names. I don't know what the story is, but you can almost imagine that 'Disappointment' makes sense."

"Ever camped here before?"

"No. I paddled through a couple times, but never stayed here. It's a pretty lake."

"It is that."

They paddled east into the lake, navigating around a couple small islands and veering north. The southwest breeze was coming up a little, just enough to cause riffles across the bright water and tousle their hair. The sun climbed higher in a brilliant sky, and Kim tried to open her eyes wider to soak up the texture of the pines along the lakeshore, climbing toward Disappointment Mountain to the northeast. A loon popped up out of the water fifty yards ahead of them, surveyed them for a moment, and dove cleanly under the water again.

Kim had her map folded so she could see the entirety of the lake represented. She had positioned the map in the bottom of the canoe next to her feet. She glanced down to see the red dots indicating designated campsites, then compared that with what she could see ahead of her. They passed a campsite on an island to their left, and she could see one ahead a few hundred yards on the west shore of the lake. She knew Brad had his map similarly positioned, and without looking back she called, "Where do you want to camp?"

"I was wondering about those two sites on the east shore. See them, where the hiking trail along the east shore comes close? That way we could hike up the hill and not have to paddle to a different landing spot."

"Sounds good. We just need to go around this big island ahead of us and see if they're taken." It was such a contrast, she reflected, paddling with someone who was competent with maps, canoes, packs, and portages. Her years guiding newbies taught her to expect that she'd be correcting people, teaching them how to navigate the wilderness well in every detail. But this was a lot more like paddling with Misty, though she and Brad didn't have that same kind of synergy. At least not yet, she smiled to herself. It was a joy just to paddle, to have that job of being in the front of the canoe and providing power to propel them forward without having to worry about steering. She loved paddling in the back of the canoe as well, but she hated trying to correct someone else's incompetence. After the first two or three minutes in the canoe that morning, she hadn't even thought about Brad's steering. Trust, she thought. It is nice to be able to trust that he knows what he's doing. And in tandem with that trust, she realized that her respect for Brad was growing.

Ever since she first heard his story, she'd respected him. He wasn't willing to be a victim. Not in getting stranded in the Boundary Waters, maybe not even in his divorce. He recognized his own mistakes and wanted to correct them if he could. He wasn't arrogant. He wasn't boasting about his own capabilities or his own prowess. He seemed to want to take her desires into account. And that was nice. In her work she was constantly dealing with people who wanted something from her, who treated her like she could provide access to the foundation's dollars. That was part of the job. But it was a joy to have Brad treat her like an equal, not just using her for his own goals.

They rounded the east side of the island. Straight ahead, Kim could see the first campsite. It looked empty. A large open area of rock protruded out into the lake, and behind that pines covered the higher ground. One giant pine towered just to the left of the rock slab, right along the lakeshore. Years of choosing campsites rattled around Kim's mind. "Looks like a decent site. Exposed to the south, and that rock will make a good place to cook or dry things out if we need to. Shade back in the trees for a tent. But we should check the tent pad and the latrine just to make sure."

"Is that a landing to the left?"

"Looks like it."

Brad guided the canoe into the shallow water at the foot of the tall pine. Kim's attention was focused on the rocks, looking for a place to step out without slipping or falling into deep water. Brad interrupted her thoughts. "Look up."

She looked up at the tall pine and realized with a start what she was looking at. A weathered rope was tied around the trunk of the tree and led up to a branch about fifteen feet above the ground. From the branch the rope dropped four or five feet and ended abruptly. At the end of the rope hung the faded shreds of a backpack–just the shoulder straps and a patch of fabric.

She laughed wryly. "Looks like someone's had bear trouble."

"A bear did that?"

"I've heard of mother bears sending their cubs up trees to jump out onto a pack that's been hung like that, breaking the rope. Or in this case, tearing the straps off the pack and riding it to the ground."

"Bear cubs?"

"Could have been an adult, too. I just like the image of mom sending the kids up the tree grocery shopping."

Brad laughed grimly. "So we need to think about problem bears. Want to look for a different site?"

Kim considered a moment. "If there's a problem bear around here, it's going to be ranging all over this lake, and probably a few others around. We're not going to find a spot that is out of the bear's reach."

"An island site? There are a couple on this lake."

"They're fantastic swimmers."

Kim looked back down at the rocks and found a reasonable place to exit the canoe. Once she was on shore, she steadied the bow while Brad climbed out.

"What do you think? I've been to the Boundary Waters at the peak of the berry season, when the bears had plenty of food, and in the middle of winter, when they were hibernating. I don't have a ton of experience dealing with them when they're hungry."

"Let's check out the campsite anyway. This still might be an okay spot. Bears aren't usually an issue. Most people never see them."

They pulled the canoe carefully up to rest on the rocks so it wouldn't drift away in the breeze, and Brad followed Kim up onto the granite slab. A trail opened out into the trees to the north, and she led that direction a few yards until they came upon an open spot the size of a small room. "Tent site," she said matter-of-factly. "Looks okay. Fairly flat, no big rocks. Let's go check out the latrine." The trail went onward, and another fifty steps back they found a standard issue Forest Service fiberglass latrine. Kim peered down into the dim interior. "No candy bars, no discarded food."

"What do you think?"

"If this is where we want to be on the lake, I'd say this site is fine. I have to say, I like the idea of that rock out there as a place to sit in the evening watching the sunset."

"Sounds good to me."

They returned to the canoe and unloaded packs. It was early enough in the day that they were in no hurry, so they worked together on the tent, then checked out the fire grate and talked about where to do their cooking. A large flat boulder provided a great place to put a stove, to do dishes, and the like. "Luxury accommodations for the Boundary Waters," Kim observed.

"Lunch?"

"Yeah. I could eat."

They brought out plastic bags of jerky, trail mix, and cheese, and Brad retrieved their water bottles from the canoe. They sat in the midday sun for a few minutes, enjoying the warmth on well-used muscles. They chewed jerky and savored M&M's in the trail mix. Kim watched a pair of loons hunting past their campsite.

"How's it feel to be back out here?" Brad asked between bites.

"Good. It feels really good. It has been way too long. Portaging, paddling, navigating, all of it. I have missed this."

"You want to hike up and get Mac's stuff this afternoon, or leave it for tomorrow?"

"Do you think we can get it all in one trip?"

"I think so. We'll be loaded coming back down. At least two full Duluth packs. Tent, sleeping bag, winter gear, stove, cook kit, a few other things. Assuming it's all intact."

Kim sealed up the plastic bag of trail mix and set it aside. She pulled the pony tail out of her hair and shook her head. Her brown hair fell just over her shoulders and she laid back on the rock in the warm sunshine. "A solid type-A person like myself should be ashamed to suggest this, but what would you think of just relaxing for a bit, maybe exploring the lake for a while, and then cooking supper? Then we could hit it early tomorrow morning? That way if we had to make two trips tomorrow, we could, but we could figure on getting it all at once."

"Sounds good to me." Brad laid back in the sun as well, and sighed deeply. "Oh, this rock feels good on my shoulders. We didn't paddle that far, but it takes a little while to get those muscles toned for canoeing."

"A lot different from driving a desk."

"You're in good shape for a desk jockey."

"I try. It's a struggle, that's for sure. And I'm sorry, but going to the gym is a poor substitute for this kind of life."

"Amen."

"So what do you do to keep in shape, Brad? Looking at you, you must get a fair amount of exercise."

"There's some stuff at Todd's place. He's got a weight room and treadmill in his basement I use once in a while, but that's not really my thing. I split firewood by hand sometimes. Walk up and down the stairs to the beach a couple times a day. Haven't brought myself to swim in Superior yet. It's still too cold for that. But there are some trails on the property that connect up to the bike trail along Highway 61, too, and I run a little bit."

Kim sat up and surveyed the placid lake. The loons had moved on, but she could see an eagle or an osprey circling a quarter mile or so southwest. "For me it's mostly just the gym. I do a little hiking in the summers. I try to get out snowshoeing in the winters if the snow is decent. But mostly the gym." She sighed. "I need to make this kind of trip a priority."

"I have a hunch we'll both be feeling sore muscles by the end of the day tomorrow."

They relaxed there for another ten minutes until Kim abruptly sat up. "We're going to get sunburned if we stay here like this much longer. Where did you pack that sunscreen?"

"I think it's in your daypack. Here, I can get it."

Kim jumped up, mindful of her pistol in the bottom of her pack and Misty's warnings. They seemed foolish in this calm moment, but she didn't want Brad to find the pistol and have that awkward conversation just now. She stepped past Brad and picked up her daypack, rummaged through until she found the sunscreen, and started smearing it on exposed cheeks, neck, arms, and legs. "Want some?"

"Sure."

She tossed the tube to Brad and he began to replicate her applications.

They policed up their campsite in preparation for canoeing around the lake. Rather than stash the food pack somewhere a troublesome bear might find it, they just took the small bag along in the canoe with their daypacks and water bottles. They launched the canoe and pushed out into the clear water. The bottom dropped rapidly away beyond sight. "If you'll hold us more or less in one place, I'll refill our water bottles," Kim offered. Brad paddled lazily while she set up the water filter and pumped the fifty or so strokes it took to refill each of their bottles.

They spent an hour paddling through the inlets of Disappointment Lake. As they approached the north end, Kim asked, "Did you ever get up to that waterfall off Cattyman Lake?"

Brad hesitated. "No. I was going to do that the next day, when Mac..." He paused.

Kim plowed onward, realizing this was a painful topic for both of them. "I always heard it's a pretty falls, but I never got there. Want to make a day trip?"

They pulled the maps out and talked about distances and portages. "You really are a type-A person. If you want to, I say let's do it," Brad finally said.

169

Chapter Thirty

It was a fun way to travel, different from paddling earlier in the day. The afternoon was getting warm, almost hot. They paddled through a series of small lakes with short portages between. On each portage Kim would grab the daypacks and paddles. Brad hoisted the canoe up on his shoulders, and they were off. At the far end he'd wade into the water, though one landing was so muddy he had to be pretty careful, and she'd deposit the bags. She'd hand him his paddle, and they were on the water in seconds. Down in the narrow curve of the channel that led to Cattyman, the breeze failed and they could feel the sweat soaking their clothes. "It's hot." Kim commented. "I didn't expect this. I'm sweating out my clothes."

They arrived at the far side of Cattyman and beached their canoe at the head of the portage trail, which descended into the dark forest. The roar of the falls somewhere off to the left filled their ears. Eventually they found the side trail off the portage and clambered down to a beautiful pool. The falls, about ten feet high, cascaded down over a rocky drop and thundered into the pool at its upper end. The bottom of the pool fell away in a series of rocky rapids down to the lake below. They stood and admired it for a few minutes. After her initial joy in seeing the waterfall, Kim found herself enjoying watching Brad, seeing him soak in this beautiful place.

"What are you thinking?"

"I was just wondering what it would have looked like in the winter, if I had gotten here. Bet it would have been a whole different kind of spectacular."

"Probably right."

As Kim watched, Brad's face changed slightly, taking on a determined but mischievous look. He turned from the falls to face her. "Well, you ready?"

"Ready for what?"

"You were complaining about getting all sweaty. Ready to do laundry?"

Kim laughed. "Oh, no. I brought a change of clothes."

"Yeah, but how can you pass up this opportunity?" Without another word, Brad was down the bank, working his way along the pool's shore until, fully clothed, he stood at the edge of the roaring waterfall. "Come on, Kim!" he shouted, holding out a hand to her.

She laughed again, but feeling a rare wildness she followed his pathway and approached Brad and the waterfall. She nearly slipped on a submerged rock and by reflex, reached out and took his outstretched hand. He held on to it and grinned at her.

"This is going to feel great."

One step and Brad was in the full force of the cold, cold water. It poured over his head, immediately soaking his clothes and his entire body. He whooped and gasped, but he took a step farther into the torrent and pulled Kim along with him. She could feel the mist against her face, had been feeling it more and more with each step closer to the falls, but that was nothing compared to stepping into the cascade itself. It was like having frozen hammers thrown down on top of her skull one after another. The force of the cold water was exhilarating and exhausting. It took her breath away and made her fill her lungs completely. She whooped and screamed, then threw her head back so the water cascaded over her forehead and down her face. How was Brad, right in the midst of the falls, standing this? She endured this as long as she could, sputtered and blew. She leaned her head and shoulders out of the torrent. "Enough! Come on!" She pulled Brad's hand and drew him outward, away from the center of the falls and back toward the shoreline. They were both absolutely soaked, shaking, chilled, panting as though they'd run miles, laughing and gasping. She held on to his hand and led him back up to the bank where they'd left their daypacks. When she let him go, she turned to him and she could feel the exuberance in her face. Grinning, she shouted, "That was a terrible idea!"

Brad grinned back at her, lips going a little blue. "I'm wet!"

She shook her head, still smiling, and picked up her daypack. "You'll dry. Let's get back out into the sun. I'm cold. So are you."

They climbed, dripping, back up the steep trail to the canoe and the little patch of sunshine in the clearing where the portage met Cattyman Lake. Slowly, slowly the sun began to warm them from the outside in. They laughed and chattered and breathed the warm air deep into their lungs. Kim thought how absolutely afire she felt. Nothing in her life in Duluth felt like this. Nothing brought her so vibrantly aware as what she was feeling now. All the years since she had last been in this wilderness fell away as her mind raced. The giddiness overtook her with a kind of euphoria she'd rarely known in these last few years. She could see the same exhilaration mirrored in Brad's eyes, his broad smile. She watched as he held his chin to the sky and let the sun bathe his face, closing his eyes against the brightness but soaking in the warmth, arms out to catch that much more sunlight. On the spur of the moment she turned to him and wrapped her arms around his chest in a full, damp hug. She felt her own surprise mirrored in the jolt of his body just a bit, but he quickly wrapped his arms around her as well. It was simply a hug, but in that moment Kim thought how rarely anyone touched her, and how rarely she reached out to touch anyone. The feeling of Brad's body against hers fit with the sunlight, the waterfall, the forests marching away down the reedy shoreline.

"Thank you," she spoke quietly against his jawbone.

"For what?" Brad pushed her back a little, placing his hands on her shoulders so he could get a look at her face. "For what?"

She met his even, Scandinavian eyes and considered. "For bringing me here. Thank you for suggesting this."

"The waterfall?"

"Yes. And this entire trip. For getting me back out into this beautiful, vibrant country."

For just a second he pulled her back against him. "You're welcome." A second, a second and a half he held her there, then released her and stepped back, smiling. "You're so welcome. Thank you for coming along. And we need to start paddling back."

Loading and launching the canoe was becoming old hat, and within seconds they were back on the small lake, paddling toward the next portage. The skill of moving the canoe cleanly across the lakes filled Kim with a deep sense of satisfied joy. The euphoria of the waterfall had been replaced with a rock solid sense of contentment. In spite of her soggy clothes and wet hair, she breathed deeply. She soaked in the brilliant sunlight on the water, the smell of the pines, the clear, linear call of the white-throated sparrows, the filigree of waterbugs skating along the surface of the lake, the graceful arc of a loon's neck as it dove under the water. A part of her was so content here. It didn't feel like home, not exactly, but that was the closest she could come to naming the deep peace in her heart and mind. The bow of the canoe cut through the water just in front of her knees and the dragonflies hovered over the lily pads. She heard the repetitive, reassuring swish of Brad's paddle behind her, and with each stroke she could feel the canoe surge forward.

Chapter Thirty-one

The sun was just touching the trees on the western horizon when they paddled into their campsite. They were tired, mostly dry, and ravenously hungry. They busied themselves with food preparation and squaring away the campsite for the coming night.

"It's amazing how much better food tastes up here," Brad observed as he finished the last morsels from his plate and set it down beside him. They had elected to eat out on the rock by the water, and they had a great view of the last shreds of the sunset. A few stars appeared high overhead.

"If you worked your body that hard every day, your food would probably always taste this good."

"Probably. But there's something about being out here that makes it better."

"You won't get an argument from me."

They sat in silence for a few minutes, watching the sky go from indigo to black above their heads. "These June days are so long. It's almost eleven already, I'll bet."

"Yeah. And it will be bright out just after five a.m. Not going to get any more sleep than we need. Hopefully we can sleep in a little with the tent set back in the trees like that."

They stashed the food pack across the channel on an island, paddling across by headlamp and picking a spot that looked hard to reach. With bear activity close by, they were more than a little concerned about food and smells. Back at camp, they did a careful job of washing up their dishes. Kim spread the pots and pans out on their Duluth pack to dry. "Hopefully if a bear decides to tear into this pack, the dishes falling on the rocks will scare it off."

"Let's hope."

They navigated the awkwardness of getting ready for bed. By the time Brad finished a once-over of their campsite in the dark, Kim was tucked into her sleeping bag. The ecstasy of the day was gone, replaced by fatigue and sore muscles. She was deeply grateful she could sleep for at least a few hours. Brad crawled in with a minimum of bumping around.

"I suspect we'll be at least this sore tomorrow night," he groaned.

"No doubt. What time do you usually wake up?"

"I'm not a crazy early riser. Maybe six or six-thirty most mornings. How about you?"

"Weekdays my alarm goes off at five. Weekends usually six-thirty or seven."

"Is this a weekend?"

"I didn't bring my alarm clock."

"That's a relief."

"I vote we sleep until we wake up."

No response. Kim listened for a few seconds before she realized Brad was already asleep. Within a matter of minutes, she was unconscious as well.

Each of them opted to work through the stiffness they felt the next morning without resorting to any medications. They ate a substantial breakfast and cleaned up carefully. They discussed exactly what to bring in their day packs, and stashed the food pack back on the island.

"Ready?" Brad asked as he surveyed the camp one last time.

"I think so. We should have what we need."

They took a trail that disappeared east into the timber along the lakeshore. It connected with the hiking trail after a few yards and they turned north.

"Where did you camp last winter? Weren't you on this site?"

"No, I camped on the north side of this peninsula, closer to where the trail goes up the hill. I just walked a few yards across the bay on the ice, then up the trail. This is almost a half mile farther. Only trouble is the slope there makes the first twenty or thirty yards off the lake a challenge."

"Makes sense."

They walked on in silence for half an hour until the trail forked. "We want the right hand, uphill," Brad said.

"I remember. But it looks a lot different than it did a couple months ago. Forest Service crews haven't been out to cut these trees, either. I imagine they're busy clearing downed trees on portages first. Hiking trails usually don't see much traffic until later in the summer anyway."

They worked around the big fallen pine that had slowed Kim and Misty down in March. After that the trail was mostly clear all the way up. Occasionally Kim recognized a spot on the trail from being there only a couple months before, but the absence of snow had radically changed the appearance of everything they could see. She commented on that difference to Brad.

"I noticed that, too. I walked this trail so many times back and forth coming up to see Mac, but it looks completely different now. Snowmelt sure changes things."

It didn't take long to reach the crest of the hill, and Kim recognized the dog-hair poplars off to the right. They passed those, and proceeded to the mature pines a little farther east. Brad led to the right, downhill toward the opening they could see through the trees ahead. The air was still cool under the big trees, but when they emerged into the clearing they could feel the power of the June sun as it climbed into the late morning sky.

"The swamp has a lot of water standing in it," Brad commented as they looked around. "We'll have to try to stay up on the higher ground and circle around to Mac's cache."

"I wonder if anything bothered his bones after we buried them in the snow."

Brad considered. "Hard to say. No real reason for the wolves to come back and dig them up. I suspect they stayed pretty much where we put them. It's going to be wet that far out now, though."

"No reason for us to be disturbing Mac's bones now. We just need to get his gear."

"Well, let's see if we can pick out a trail that keeps our feet dry."

They managed to avoid mud and only a couple times had to circle up into the trees to find firmer ground as they circled to the right. It occurred to Kim that carrying a pack back this way could be more challenging.

Eventually they arrived at the southwest corner of the clearing where Mac's tent had stood. His gear remained on the raised platform, covered with a tarp and tied down. Brad surveyed the scene. "I have to say I'm glad nothing got into his stuff," he said. "At least we don't have to try to collect all the shreds of something a bear tore up."

"What's the best way to get his gear down?"

"I think I can get it. It was easier to get stuff up there with four feet of snow on the ground."

After a few failed attempts, Brad resorted to a long pole which he used to push the tarp covered bundles off the platform and down to the ground. Two large Duluth packs held most of the gear, and these fell to earth with heavy thuds and the sound of breaking twigs. Beyond that was just the tarp itself and some cords that had held everything together on the platform. Brad started to busy himself checking packs and straps, folding the tarp, and coiling up the cords. Kim looked around, remembering what the scene had been like when she and Misty found Mac's bones scattered on the bloody snow.

Brad paused, watching her face. "Kim. You okay?"

She looked away from the vision in her mind and back to Brad, shook her head, and said, "Just remembering Mac's bones scattered all over here."

"Yeah. I know. I've been trying not to think about it."

She looked at his face. "That's fine, Brad. Really. But I think I need to take a minute."

"Take all the time you need. No rush."

She gazed east at the swamp, trying to pick out the exact spot, close at hand, where they had buried Mac's bones in the snow. It looked so different. She could see the scar of the rifle bullet on the pine tree next to where Mac's tent had stood, the way Brad had described the scene. She could see the cache and Mac's gear lying on the ground where it had fallen. For a moment she tried to picture Mac's face and she couldn't. She couldn't remember what he looked like. She tried to picture him in the office, standing by the window looking out at the harbor, and suddenly, recalling that specific scene, she could see him.

Brad was eyeing her. "Take your time, Kim. Seriously. This is hard stuff."

She shuddered for just a moment, trying to shake the stress and grief that threatened to overwhelm her. "I'll be okay. I think I need a bathroom stop anyway. The coffee from this morning is working its way through me."

"Okay. Whatever you need."

Kim looked away from the lowlands, up toward the summit of Disappointment Mountain. "I'll just head up in the trees a ways."

"I think I'll go through these packs. Maybe there's stuff that could be packed better. Or there might be stuff we don't need to bring out."

Brad knelt and started unstrapping the Duluth packs. Kim picked her way through brush and over logs up the slope, away from Mac's bones, away from wolves tearing Mac apart, away from the man who had been there when Mac's life ended.

Chapter Thirty-two

The shade in the trees felt good, and she climbed quite a ways up the slope. It helped to have some separation from the memories, from the place where Mac's bones lay in the mud. She set about the business of urinating, leaning back against the white bark of a poplar trunk. She loved the pale poplar trees, and she tried to take some comfort in the quiet whisper of the leaves overhead. The light green leaves gave the sunlight an odd cast as it filtered down into this part of the forest. As she was zipping back up, she was struck by the white bark and how even a couple fallen poplar trunks stood out in the relatively dim light under the trees. Her eyes had become accustomed to the dim light, and she noted the different shades of pale bark against the dark background of fallen leaves and duff. Closer at hand, just a few feet from her daypack, there was a white rock that had a different tone than the —

As if in a dream, Kim took two steps toward the rock. It was rounded and had indentations, almost like…

It was a skull. A human skull. Mac's skull? Had to be. She slowly leaned over and picked it up from where it had been laying, partly covered with dead leaves. There was no lower jaw, but the skull was intact. It wasn't shiny and polished like a biology display. Bits of discoloration, fragments of tissue, clung to it. A few places rodents had gnawed the bone.

She looked back downhill for a moment. A wolf, she thought. A wolf must have carried it here. She started to picture that scene, but quickly turned her mind away from exactly how Mac's skin and muscle would have been stripped from the bones. She thought of Misty's comments about all the skull could tell them. She tried to take comfort in knowing, now, that at least the skull wasn't the key to some strange twist on Mac's ending. She believed Brad's story. She had come to know him, and even started to trust him.

She could not tear her eyes away from the bullet hole through the back of the skull. She imagined Mac pulling the trigger, imagined him so desperate to end his life, imagined that tiny piece of lead speeding through his brain, through his skull, and stopping in the trunk of that big pine.

Then she saw another track—the track of another bullet. It had to be another bullet. What else could do that? This was not a hole like the other; it was a crease, a groove where a bullet had torn a furrow along one side of the skull, roughly where the right ear would be. Through the irregularities of the side of the skull, a clear pathway showed where something had grazed the side of Mac's head. She tried to imagine what this meant. This bullet–it had to be a bullet–probably wouldn't have killed him. Destroyed his ear, torn the side of his head, maybe his face, terribly. He would have bled. A lot. It might have knocked him unconscious. The shock of the bullet's passage might have done terrible brain damage. Or maybe he had remained conscious, bleeding, suffering.

With a jolt, she realized the more immediate meaning of this second bullet track.

Brad lied.

Instantly Kim felt the shift deep in her gut. All the trust, all the affection, all the respect that had been growing in her was gone. It evaporated on the track of the second bullet. Whatever happened to Mac, Brad had lied. Nothing in his story allowed for two shots. Emotion flooded her stomach like acid. Pain at being lied to. Grief for Mac, all over again. Anger, furious anger, at Brad. She wanted to run back down the slope and confront Brad with this evidence. But then what? He was physically stronger than she. He didn't know about her pistol, but what if he had weapons along she knew nothing about? Could she shoot him if she had to? Anger began to give way to fear. If Brad had lied about Mac's death, he needed to cover things up. Was that why they had come back here? Was the entire business of retrieving Mac's gear just an excuse? Why invite her along?

Kim's mind raced with questions. Brad's story of his encounters with Mac, the envelope he delivered to her, Mac's documents and his instructions, and above all, this damned skull with the mark of two bullets. All of it suddenly became a crazy jumble of fear and uncertainty.

With a jolt, Kim realized she couldn't go back down the hill. She couldn't go back to Brad. She had to get away, had to take this skull, this evidence, and get out of the Boundary Waters. Brad would have to face justice. Tell the truth. Confess to whatever he had done. He would have to stop lying. Her mind raced. She desperately wished Misty was here. What to do next?

She listened a moment. No sound of Brad. She was far enough away from the swamp that he might be making quite a bit of noise and she wouldn't hear. But if she didn't come back he would be looking for her. Especially if he had lied about just coming up here to get Mac's gear. She knelt in the dead leaves on the forest floor and opened her daypack. She reached into the bottom and pulled out her pistol. She felt the weight of it heavy in her hand. She tucked it back into its case, reassured. Then she carefully set Mac's skull into her pack and zipped it up.

She listened again. Nothing.

Quietly, as quietly as she could, she started to climb farther up the hill, away from the clearing, away from Brad. She tried to angle southwest, toward their campsite, but the sun was high enough it was hard to tell just which direction that was. Her heart was racing. Panic kept rising up in her throat and she kept choking it back down. She was nearly frantic, consumed with the desire to get far enough away from Brad that even if he started looking for her, he would not find her.

She climbed toward the top of the hill, always trying to get farther and farther away from Brad, from Mac's campsite, from that swamp, that place of death. She began to run as she gained distance, breaking through brush and dodging trees. Branches thrashed her arms. She came out in an opening where she could see Disappointment Lake through the trees, and it gave her a sense of direction. She ran southwest, down the hill now, down and down, trying to control her speed and the amount of noise she made. Too late she realized that Brad might be able to track her. Was he skilled that way? She couldn't remember. What would Brad be able to do? She felt the pack on her back rise and fall with each step, and she was keenly aware of the two weights in her pack. Her pistol and its deadly responsibility stuck into her back. Mac's skull hammered up and down between her shoulders as she ran. Her breath came in ragged gasps. A few hundred yards down the slope she stopped, leaning against a tall pine trying to catch her breath. Her arms and hands were torn and bloodied from running through branches.

Chapter Thirty-three

She heard Brad's voice inside her head, saying, "When things go bad, you have to get mean, plumb mad-dog mean. If you give in, you neither live nor win." She forced herself to stop and breathe. Finally she started to work her way down hill, picking a path between the trees, doing her best to walk without breaking into a run, without crashing through branches. She tried to be quiet. She choked back on the panic. Vomit tried to rise in her throat. She let the anger in, let it spread through her chest like fire, but she never let it have control of her mind. She needed her mind. The anger heated her lungs and her heart. She'd gladly have torn Brad's throat out given the chance, but she kept her mind cool and clear.

She almost ran off the cliff before she saw the drop in front of her. The trees grew right up to the edge of a fifteen-foot precipice on the side of the hill where a granite outcrop had refused to erode. She grabbed a pine branch and held herself back from falling over the edge, teetering out into open space and then pulling herself back, praying without words that the branch would hold and she wouldn't fall. She teetered for an agonizing second. Then she was back on both feet, pulling herself back into the cover of the trees. She stopped again, forced herself to stop. Breathe. Think.

She needed to get to their campsite. Would Brad be there before her? No. Probably not. She'd need to have her pistol ready in case, but she didn't think he'd beat her back to camp. There would be precious moments of uncertainty for him when he'd wonder what had happened to her. He'd think she'd simply gotten lost. Then if he followed, he'd have to go back to the north and east to catch the hiking trail. Once he was on the trail he could run faster than she could, and he'd make up time. But for the moment, she was confident that she was winning this terrible race.

Taking care to step back from the precipice, she skirted the granite outcrop until she could climb her way down. The advantage of that particular misadventure was that she'd had a clear view of the lake again. Somehow she'd turned too far south, and now she worked her way a little farther west.

Eventually she came down into flatter ground where the trees grew thicker. Her progress was slow here, and she was terrified that Brad was gaining ground. She wove her way through branches, struggled through tangled deadfalls, crawled under storm-downed trees and over fallen logs. This part of the journey seemed to last forever, until finally she could glimpse the glittering blue surface of the lake ahead of her. Suddenly, without warning, she stepped out onto the hiking trail. For a second or two she was completely disoriented. Which way should she turn? Think, Kim, think.

She finally realized she needed to turn left, to the south, and she sped down the trail. In a muddy stretch she saw their boot prints from that morning, just a few hours before. As she jogged she caught out of the corner of her eye a bear track superimposed on one of the boot prints. She passed a distinctive boulder she remembered from the morning, and then she came to the trail that branched off to their campsite. She turned abruptly to follow this trail. A sense of caution flooded over her and she slowed down, moving quietly up the trail. She caught a glimpse of the fabric of the tent through the trees. She could hear something moving on the rock off to the left, but the view was screened by too much brush.

Kim rounded a corner in the trail, easing along almost silently. The gear pack. A black bear was tugging at it, dragging it bit by bit across the rock, stopping to try to open the flaps or tear through the heavy fabric. For the moment the bear hadn't seen her. She took a stealthy step back, screening herself behind a tree. Slowly, she eased her daypack off her shoulders, lowered it to the ground, and knelt next to it. She painstakingly worked the zipper open, glancing up toward the equipment pack over and over. She could still hear the bear working at the pack's fabric.

Keeping her eyes up, focused toward the noise coming from the campsite she reached into the pack, sliding her hand past the skull, down to the very bottom. She found her pistol in its case and pulled it up into the daylight. She pulled the handgun out and worked the action to chamber a bullet. The action slid back into place with a loud *click*, and she stood up and took a step forward. The bear was staring her direction now, alert. Would it run away? Or maybe toward her? She knew that most of the time black bears were timid, but she also knew that this was a bear used to people, used to finding what it wanted in packs and tents. She stepped forward, keeping the muzzle of her pistol pointed generally toward the bear.

"Hey!"

"Get out of here!"

"You need to leave! Go on!"

The bear simply stood and watched her, one front paw resting on the equipment pack. Kim took one more step forward. "Get out of here!"

The bear didn't move.

Now what?

She didn't want to make noise, didn't want to fire. What would Brad do if he heard a gunshot? Was he already on the trail, approaching the campsite? Had he heard her shouting?

At that moment the bear removed its paw from the pack and took a step toward her.

"No! That's enough! You back off NOW!" The bear stood still, watching her. It didn't seem aggressive, just alert, but she knew that could change. The bear took another step toward her.

That was too much. Kim aimed toward a patch of trees behind the bear, well over its head, and fired. The gunshot seemed obscenely loud on the quiet lake. The bear flinched and turned away, then looked back at her.

"That's right. Go on!" She fired once more into the trees. The bear suddenly wheeled away and ran off toward the trees, off to Kim's right. Her ears rang. She knew it might not run very far. She held on to her pistol and surveyed the campsite. The equipment pack was torn, but not badly. Since there was no food in that pack, she assumed the bear was simply used to finding good things in packs and started tearing it up out of habit and hopefulness.

Should she take the tent down, tidy up the equipment pack? Her training never to leave a mess behind ran deep.

No. Nothing mattered but getting the skull back to Misty, forcing Brad to deal with his lies. What if he came back to face the bear? That was his problem.

She untied the canoe, found her life jacket and her paddle, all the while glancing back toward the trees and holding the pistol in one hand. After a moment's thought she sprinted to the equipment pack and opened it, dug around until she found the water purifier pump, and stashed that in her daypack next to the skull. She left the equipment pack open, Brad's life vest laying on the ground next to it. She remembered Brad talking about using this canoe for solo paddling, and she looked at it carefully. She could see how the canoe could be modified for one person to paddle sitting facing backward in the front seat. That seat was closer to the centerline and would help balance the canoe for a solo paddler. She debated for a second whether to take time to change things around, and realized that unless she had perfect winds it would be impossible for her to paddle the canoe across the lake with its bow sticking far up in the air.

Eventually she went back to the equipment pack and found a multi-tool with a screwdriver, removed the thwart just behind the front seat of the canoe, and left the thwart on the rock next to the equipment pack. Every few seconds she glanced up from her work, afraid both of the bear returning and of Brad appearing on the trail. She lifted the canoe to the edge of the water. It would still need weight in the front. She stashed her daypack far in the front, but then realized she'd need more. She cast about until she found a rock as big as Mac's skull, and she pried it up out of the shallow water and set it gently in the bottom of the canoe.

When she sat in the front seat, facing backward, with the heavy stone in what had become the bow, it all balanced the canoe nicely and she was ready to paddle solo. Kim scanned the treeline. She considered the open equipment pack, the tree where the shredded pack straps still hung like a strange ornament from that length of rope. No sign of the bear. No sign of Brad. She pushed out into the calm lake.

For just a moment she thought of the food pack, still stashed among the rocks on the island. Should she take it? She didn't feel hungry in the least, but that was probably just adrenalin. There were granola bars in her day pack; they would be enough. Most of their lunch had been in Brad's pack. She needed to get out, to get across the portage and into Snowbank and back to a telephone. She thrust the canoe strongly out into the lake and began to paddle southwest.

Chapter Thirty-four

"Hello."

"Misty, it's Kim."

"Hey, Kimmy! Aren't you supposed to be..."

"Shut up for a second. Sorry. Just shut up and hear me out."

Silence on the other end.

"Okay. I found Mac's skull. I found it when I was away from Brad and I left. I paddled out by myself. I'm back at the resort on Snowbank. There was a... no, that doesn't matter. But you need to see the skull, Misty. And I think when I get off the phone with you I need to call the police."

Silence.

"Kimmy?"

"Yeah."

"Take a deep breath. Slow down, baby. Are you safe right now?"

"Yeah. I think so. Yeah."

"Okay. Deep breath."

Silence.

"Now. Tell me about finding the skull."

"I went into the trees to take a leak and I found it. It was up the hill from where Mac had been camped."

"Kimmy, what is it about the skull that makes you want to call the police?"

"There are... well, I'm pretty sure there are two bullet wounds."

"Two?"

"Yeah. One through the back of the skull like I expected, but there's another trench torn along the side of the skull. Maybe I'm wrong but it looks like a bullet wound to me. How could there be two bullet holes, Misty? Brad lied, right? His story doesn't make any sense if there are two bullet holes."

"Shit. Yeah. Something's fishy, and it has to start with Brad. Are you just stuck there at Snowbank waiting for the police?"

"Yeah. No. I don't know. I could take Brad's truck, I guess."

"You have his keys?"

"He told me there's a spare in the bumper in case something happens to him."

"Huh. Okay. Kimmy, I need to get someone to come stay with Mom, and it might take me a bit. Do you want to go to the police in Ely?"

"I guess. I don't know. I don't know what to do, Misty."

"Take it easy. Are you okay otherwise?"

"Um... my knee is messed up. I slipped on a rock on the portage and fell pretty hard. Bruised up and limping, but I'm okay."

"Oh, baby. You keep it together. Okay. We need to get some distance between you and Brad right now. So take your stuff–especially that skull–and meet me in Ely at the police station. No, let's meet at the Forest Service station. We'll call in the cops if we need to. I can be there in about an hour and a half, I think. You just wait for me there, okay?"

"Okay."

"Kim, you just take it easy, now. You've been scared and you've been hurt and you're nervous about Brad. And you're carrying your dead boss' skull around with you. You've got a lot going on, so take your time. Deep breaths. Where is Mac's skull now?"

"Right here. In my backpack."

"Good, so it's not just out in the open. Good. Keep it in your backpack. Still got your pistol?"

"Yeah. I shot it twice."

"At Brad?"

"No, at a bear that was in camp. Well, to scare it off."

"Oh, my. Oh, my. Deep breaths, Kimmy. You're out of the woods. Make sure you're okay to drive. Take your time, find that key, get to the Forest Service station just east of Ely. I'll see you there in a little while. From there your cell will work, too, and you can call me if you need to."

"Okay. Thanks, Misty."

"See you soon."

Kim hung up the land line to find Roger, the resort owner, standing a few feet away, holding a cup of coffee. He set it on the counter in front of her, next to the phone.

"I heard most of it," he said calmly. "What can I do to help?"

Kim sipped the coffee, grateful for something she could do that didn't require thought. A second sip, and she set the cup down. "Thanks. I need to leave my... the canoe here. It belongs to the guy I paddled in with. Brad. Swenson. I imagine he'll walk out. Probably take the hiking trail."

"Swenson? That guy that got snowed in off the Gunflint last fall?"

185

"Yeah. That's him."

They both pondered this for a second while Kim took another sip of the coffee. It was hot, and good, and reassuring.

"What did you decide about calling the police?"

"I'll meet my friend Misty first. She used to be a cop."

"Okay. So you'll leave the canoe here. I can just put it on the rack next to the others. And you'll take his truck back to town? Where is the truck now?"

"It's at the public landing. Just south of here."

"I can have you there in just a couple minutes."

"I really appreciate that."

"If Mr. Swenson is hiking out, he will likely come out on the road at the Lake One landing. That's three miles from here."

"We were camped on the east side of Disappointment. How long would it take him to hike out?"

The outfitter considered. "It's probably six, seven miles from the Lake One landing to where you were. I'd guess there's spots where that trail is still blocked with blowdowns. So figure it will take him most of a day to hike out?"

Kim considered. "I don't know what he'll do. He'll likely come back to camp and see the canoe gone. If he decides right then and there to hike out, he could be getting to Lake One in just a few hours."

"You left a tent and gear there, at the campsite?"

"Yes. Everything except what I needed to paddle out."

"So he might stay overnight. Or pack up the gear and hike partway out, then camp."

"Hard to say, I guess. I wish I knew what he's going to do."

"It's suppertime now. How about I fix you a sandwich and you can get back to town and meet up with your friend? And we can clean up that elbow."

"Elbow?" Kim reached her left hand around to her right elbow, found a ragged tear in the sleeve of her shirt and the whole area was sticky.

"Your shirt is torn and you've bled some. Looks like it's mostly stopped."

"I had no idea. Did I bleed on your counter? I'm so sorry."

Roger laughed. "You've got bigger things to worry about. And my counter is designed to wipe down pretty easy."

He fetched a first aid kit and some wet paper towels. Kim rolled up her torn sleeve and cleaned the scrape. "Must have done this when I fell on the portage," she mused. "I was so worried about my knee. Worried I wouldn't be able to walk on it."

"I noticed you were limping. Hold still now." Roger applied a large bandage to Kim's elbow. "That's a tough spot to reach yourself. This should hold. It's one of those flexible ones, with the tabs on the corners, designed to hold on joints and stuff."

"Thank you. You're very kind."

"I've been in tight spots before. Other people helped me out. Just paying it forward. Do you need anything for that knee? Got an ace bandage back here. Not sure I can do better than that. Maybe some Icy / Hot around here somewhere."

"No, I think it will be fine. Just need to take it easy."

Roger cleaned up the first aid supplies and stepped into the back room while Kim rolled her sleeve back down and pondered how best to proceed. She realized that the Forest Service station would probably be closed by the time she and Misty met there. And while she'd seen Forest Service personnel carrying firearms, she didn't think they were trained to apprehend murderers. If that's indeed what Brad was.

Roger emerged with a styrofoam to-go box and a can of soda. "Want to eat here, or take it with you? You're welcome to stay as long as you need to."

"Thank you so much. No, I'd better get back to town in case Misty gets there earlier."

"What do you want me to do if Brad shows up here looking for his truck?"

Kim pondered a moment. "I guess you can tell him the truth. Just don't tell him about the skull I found."

"I'm not asking. It's not my business. But is there more I need to know about this guy?"

"I wish I knew. I'm sorry. Thanks so much for all your help, Roger."

"No problem. Let's get you down to the boat landing and Mr. Swenson's truck."

Roger drove her the short distance to the boat landing and pulled up right alongside Brad's truck. She climbed out of Roger's minivan and ducked under the end of the wide homemade canoe rack on the top, limped around to the front of the truck, and felt inside the bumper to find Brad's spare key. Once she had that in hand she started to breathe a little easier.

"Make sure it starts. I'll wait to see before I take off."

"Thanks." Kim climbed into the driver's seat, adjusted the seat forward a few inches, and cranked the truck to life. Roger waved and pulled out; she followed him out of the parking lot, then turned onto the winding paved road that led back to Ely.

Chapter Thirty-five

She sat for a full hour before Misty pulled in, and by the end of it Kim was questioning everything she'd seen, everything she'd experienced. She almost pulled the skull out to examine it again, but forced herself to sit and relax in the Forest Service parking lot. It was a lovely evening with a light breeze out of the west rustling leaves and the sun angling toward the horizon in all its glory.

When Misty's pickup finally wheeled into the lot, Kim bolted out of the cab of Brad's truck to stand and wait for her friend. Misty piled out and enfolded Kim in a hug. "Oh, baby. You okay?"

"I think so. Calming down a little."

"Sorry it took so long. Anything new?"

"I'm just going half crazy. That's about all."

"Oh, Kimmy. Climb in here. Let's sit for a minute and think this through." Kim grabbed her daypack and the keys to Brad's truck out of the ignition and climbed into the passenger seat of Misty's pickup.

"Let me see that skull," Misty demanded. Kim opened her pack and handed it over. Misty took a minute or more to look hard at the various markings on the skull. "You're right," she said finally, "there are definitely two bullets involved here. There's some damage on the far side of the skull that's probably just rodents gnawing on it, but this track along the right ear is definitely made by a bullet."

"So what does that mean? I guess we know enough to know that Brad lied about how Mac died."

"Yeah. That's certain. But what the real story is, we don't really know. I don't think Mac could have fired both these bullets. Whether he fired one and Brad the other, or Brad both of them ... that's hard to say."

They both sat quiet for a few moments, considering. Finally Kim spoke. "Brad will get back to our campsite. I'm sure he's done that by now. He'll find me gone with the canoe. My guess is that he'll hike out on the trail that comes out at Lake One. That's not certain, but it would be the easiest way to get out of the woods."

"Have you seen anything in Brad that makes you think he would run away?"

"What do you mean?"

"Let's say just for the moment that Brad realizes you've found the skull, that you know he lied. Would he head for Canada? Try to avoid you?"

"I don't know. He hasn't said or done anything that makes me think he'd take off. He kept joking about this trip being such a great first date. I don't think he expected me to find this."

"Probably not. But he lied, and anyone who tells a lie worries about what happens if they get caught. So what I'm wondering is if he'll come back to face the music or if he'll run to try to protect himself."

"I don't know."

"Have you thought anymore about going to the police?"

"Yeah, I've thought about it a lot. And there's something that just doesn't feel right about it. Do we know Brad is a murderer? Not really. We can say pretty confidently he is a liar."

"Lying about how somebody dies is pretty serious."

"I know."

"If you could play this out any way you wanted, Kim, what would you want?"

Kim considered. "I guess I'd want to have a conversation with Brad, with guarantees he couldn't run off and he'd have to deal with the consequences of his actions, whatever that means."

Now it was Misty's turn to think about things. "I am pretty certain we can make that happen," she said after some time. "Might involve holding the bastard at gunpoint for a while."

After a heavy sigh, Kim murmured, "And all that is assuming he hikes out, that he comes off the trail at the Lake One landing, that we can find him." She looked out into the moonlight. "Do you think he'd hike in the dark? It's a pretty bright night."

"Maybe. We could go sit at the landing and wait for him just in case."

They talked again through the timeline of the day: when Kim had left Brad in the clearing, how long it had taken her to hike back to camp, to paddle out. "If Brad realized you'd left and moved as fast as he could to get out, he could be arriving at the landing anytime now. We'd better get out there."

They drove in silence. The full moon rose above the tops of the pines along the highway, and the strobe effect of the moonlight shining into her lap hypnotized Kim. She was so tired. They rounded a gentle curve and suddenly Misty hit the brakes hard. The panic-inducing sound of screeching tires filled the night. Kim lurched forward against the seatbelt. Out the windshield she saw a massive form. Big. Black. One wide dark eye. Then it was gone, lurching out of the roadway. They skidded past a few feet away. Misty regained control and brought her pickup to a stop.

"Shit!"

"Moose?"

"Yeah. Wow."

"You okay, Misty?"

"I'm fine. Heart's racing like a jackhammer."

"Me too."

"Good thing I was only doing about forty."

"Yeah. Good thing he kept walking. I don't think you missed him by five feet."

"I thought we were going to hit him for sure. Damn, girl, that was close."

Slowly Misty crept the pickup forward again, easing up to twenty, then thirty miles per hour. "I know we're just crawling along here, but I'm nervous."

"This is plenty fast for me. Curves and hills don't help."

"You said it."

"Probably just a few miles to go anyway."

"Yeah. Watch the signs."

Two or three miles later Kim said, "There. Sign on the right that says Lake One Landing." Misty followed the turnoff and drove into a parking lot large enough for forty or fifty cars. Four cars, all unoccupied, peppered the lot. A boat landing lay off to their right, and at the far end of the lot the headlights illuminated a sign saying "Kekakabic Hiking Trail" with an arrow pointing straight ahead into the forest. Beyond the sign, a well-worn hiking trail disappeared off into the darkness.

"Where do we set up, do you think?" Kim wondered.

"If he's going to come walking up that trail, I'd say let's park over there so we can watch the opening without having to crane our necks. We might be here all night, so I'd say we should stay in the pickup cab. We can take turns sleeping and watching."

"Not sure I'll be able to sleep."

"We'll play that one by ear, I think. But we will need to make some plans of what we want to do if he shows up."

Misty drove the pickup over toward the northernmost tip of the lot and backed it into a parking space that more or less faced the trailhead. The full moon soared high above the trees now, and the light shone through the windshield. "We'll have to keep the lights off. I'm going to rig the dome light so it doesn't come on if we get out." She pulled the cover off the dome light over their heads and pulled the tiny light bulb out, dropping it in the ashtray for later.

"You have a flashlight? I left mine in the equipment pack, I think. Or maybe in the tent."

"Yeah, I've got a pretty bright one right here. We'll want that if he shows up in the dark."

Silence stretched between them.

"So what was it like, camping with Brad? Before the skull, I mean."

Kim thought hard. She'd been so consumed with the skull and what it meant she hadn't really processed their trip in.

"Maybe that's the weird thing about this, Misty. It was really good. I was having a great time. It was probably the most fun I've had since you and I used to do this kind of thing."

"You need to get out more."

"Funny."

"No, I'm serious. You bought into that big job in Duluth, and that's great. But every time I turn around you're telling me how much you love this wilderness. And baby, I saw that way back when. You were so alive out here, so badass. When we were working together in those days I honestly didn't think there was anything you couldn't do."

"That's exactly what I thought about you."

Misty chuckled quietly. "Didn't tell you, but a couple years ago I ran into Larry."

"Larry? Like camp director Larry?"

"Yeah. It was at a funeral, and I guess the guy who died had been a big supporter of the camp. I just knew him from community stuff, had no idea he was tied to the camp. But there was Larry at the funeral. We got to talk a little bit."

"Where's he at now?"

"Moved to another camp. Someplace south, down by the Cities I think."

"Huh. Haven't thought about him in a long time."

"Yeah. I was pretty surprised. But he was full of stories of you and me."

"Really?"

"Yeah. All kinds of stories about how there was no job too big for the two of us, no group we couldn't handle. Said he'd never had another pair of counselors like us."

"No way."

"I laughed, but he was all serious. Wanted to know what you're up to. I knew a little about the foundation, and he didn't seem surprised by any of that."

Kim slowly digested this, watching the parking lot in the moonlight, part of her mind focused on keeping an eye out for Brad. Out of the corner of her eye she saw Misty's hand go to her face for a second, heard a deep intake of breath.

"What else?"

Misty shook her head and wiped her other cheek. "He said... he asked about my family, and I told him a little about taking care of Mom. She was just starting to need watching back then. He remembered a lot about my family. More than I expected. Then he said that he was always impressed with the way I cared for people, the way I protected people."

"That's absolutely truth, Misty. Look at what you're doing right now."

"This? This is just a good excuse to get out of the house. And maybe take out my aggression smacking your boyfriend around a little bit."

They both chuckled, and silence bloomed like moonlight in the pickup cab. "You know, up until I found that skull, I was ready to start calling him my boyfriend. I don't know. Do women in their thirties have boyfriends? I guess so. But I really, really enjoyed canoeing with him."

"Tell me more about that."

"You know how you can tell a lot about a person by how it is to paddle with them? He was in the back of the canoe all day, and I didn't worry once about his steering. I set a rhythm and he didn't complain, didn't make a fuss about anything. We paddled all over Disappointment and watched loons and then we day tripped up to the falls by Ashigan."

"That's a pretty falls. I took my niece there on that trip I told you about."

"We got there and we were hot and sweaty. It was actually hot out. He just walked along the pool and into the falls. And he convinced me to join him."

"So now you're showering together?"

"Shut up. He made the trip fun. And he made the waterfall an adventure. I never felt pressured or awkward."

"You're never awkward, Kim."

"You know what I mean. You and me, we keep a pretty good facade, but there are situations that just make you feel like you want to crawl out of your skin. I have never felt that with Brad. Not even sharing a tent. It's like he went out of his way to make sure I didn't feel weird about it."

Misty took a deep breath, then let it out. "That's one of the reasons I was okay with holding off on calling the cops. I know you respect this guy. And you're smart about stuff like that."

"Is that why I'm still single?"

"You're still single because there are way too many substandard men in the world, and you're smart enough not to settle."

"But I think about that. Even with Brad, in that first conversation we had, I was totally ready to blow him off. I had half a dozen reasons."

"Has he changed since then?"

Kim considered. "Kind of. When we first talked, he was pretty beat up. He was still dealing with a lot of the fallout from his divorce. He had just come out of the woods after Mac's death, and whatever happened there was still hanging over his head. He was hurting pretty bad, I think."

"And what have you seen since?"

"It's like he found his feet again. He's solid. Calm. 'Strong' sounds like a cliche. Or maybe a deodorant commercial. But there's some of that as well. He hasn't told me a lot of it, but I think he has done a lot of healing up."

"That's interesting. I worked with a police psychologist a couple times who used to say that pathological personalities don't heal. They find ways to numb, or they find ways to use their pain to do damage to others, but they won't allow themselves to really heal."

"Hm. I'm no expert, but it sure looks to me like he's really done some healing."

They sat in silence for a few minutes, and Kim yawned hugely. Misty smiled at her. "Why don't you see if you can get comfortable and fall asleep? I'm wide awake for a while yet. I'll wake you if I start dozing off."

Chapter Thirty-six

It was about six in the morning and the sun was filtering through the trees to the east when Kim stirred awake. She looked across the cab to find Misty sitting upright, gazing out into the treeline across the parking lot, wide awake. "You haven't slept at all?"

"No. You were pretty tired, I think."

"Guess so. I've had a few short nights in a row, and lots of paddling and hiking. I still feel like I could sleep another eight hours."

"Wish you could, baby, but we've got company. I think this is your boyfriend."

Kim felt the adrenaline surge as her heart started to beat faster. She looked at the trailhead and saw Brad with just a daypack on his back walking up the trail. "Just like we talked about?"

"Just like we talked about. Let him get another thirty yards, so he's well into the parking lot." They watched him walking quickly past the trailhead sign and onto the paved lot. To Kim he looked tired, but not wary. "Let's go."

They opened the pickup doors and climbed out to either side simultaneously. Brad was walking about fifty yards ahead of them and he looked over at the sound of the doors. Misty raised her pistol and called sharply, "Brad! Stop right there!"

Brad did indeed stop and looked more carefully at them. "Kim, is that you? Oh, thank God! Are you okay?" Kim didn't answer, and he looked from her to Misty, and Misty's handgun, and back to Kim. "What's going on?" To Kim's eyes, though, it looked like he deflated a little bit.

Misty took charge. "Brad, we need to talk to you. We have some questions, and you need to answer them. First I want you to slide your pack off and put it on the ground. Then take your jacket off and put it next to the pack." Brad did both of these things, and Misty kept her pistol fixed on him, though Kim noticed she hadn't put her finger on the trigger. Kim's mind flashed back to the training Misty had led her through. In the midst of this craziness, in some tiny way it was comforting to see in such a tangible way that Misty hadn't lost her head.

"Okay, Brad, that's good. Now step back toward the boat landing a few feet. Three steps. Good." Without a word, Kim walked forward toward the pack and jacket Brad had set down on the ground.

Misty took two steps to her left so she could keep a clear shot at Brad without Kim getting in the line of fire. Kim watched Brad's face and he watched her, wordless, as she took his daypack and jacket, then walked backwards to the pickup. Once she reached the truck she opened the passenger door, set jacket and pack on the seat, and quickly went through each one.

"No weapons here," she called to Misty.

Misty's eyes never left Brad. "Okay, Brad, you're doing great. Now I want you to raise your shirt above your beltline, then slowly turn around so I can see you don't have a pistol in your belt." Brad complied. He raised his untucked overshirt and t-shirt so his belly was exposed, and slowly turned completely around.

"Good. Now you're going to raise your arms so they're straight out and hold them there. Stay standing just like that. Kim is going to do one more check for weapons, then I think we're ready to talk." As they'd agreed, Kim walked around to the lake side of Brad, crouched down and patted Brad's ankles up to his knees, checked his hips, and patted down the back of his shoulders, then the front. Brad kept his eyes focused on Misty and his expression stayed neutral. Kim finished the basic pat down Misty had talked her through the night before, then circled well away from Brad and returned to the pickup.

"Okay, Brad. Thanks for cooperating. Now I'd like you to walk over here and climb into the pickup box." Brad looked at Kim, then back at Misty, then started walking toward the pickup. When he got there, the tailgate was already down and the pickup box was empty. Brad climbed up and looked back at Misty.

"Where do you want me?"

"We'll have you sit on the bed of the truck box. Kim's going to hand you a roll of tape and I want you to tape your ankles four times around, one over the other."

"Really?"

"Brad, Kim likes you. And I want to believe you're a nice guy. But if we turn out to be wrong, I want this to slow you down enough that I can put three or four rounds into you before you get the tape off your ankles. It's simple. I'm hoping we can have a conversation and nobody gets shot, alright?"

"Sounds good to me." Brad sat down, and Kim reached into the pickup cab for the roll of duct tape Misty had brought along. She handed it to Brad over the side of the pickup box while Misty stood well back, pistol never leaving Brad's chest. Brad carefully ran four loops of tape around his ankles, and the sound of him ripping the tape was loud in the still morning.

The way Misty had parked, a picnic table rested about ten feet behind the open tailgate of the pickup. She positioned herself sitting on top of the table with her feet on the bench. Kim stood to one side of the table. Kim fought to choke down the powerful surge of emotions that threatened every second to rise up in her: love for Misty and the deep trust between them; fatigue and an overwhelming desire to put her head down and go back to sleep; a sharp, poignant sense of loss as she thought about Mac and what he had meant to her; a strange, interrupted kind of affection for Brad that was strictly on hold; confusion and anger about the skull and all it represented. All this and more stirred in her.

To ratchet up the intensity, she felt the weight of her pistol resting in her jacket pocket. "You won't show this at all unless things go really bad," Misty had said. "It's just a backup gun. If Brad attacks, you bring it out and you shoot to kill, just like training at the quarry that time. Otherwise, even if he runs, that gun stays in your pocket. I'm hoping we won't see that gun." Kim found herself praying that Misty's hope would be granted.

"Brad, we have to ask you some hard questions, and we want to hear everything you have to say in answer. But we also know this is a public landing, and for the moment we don't want to create a scene. So if other people come driving up, or if they drop off canoes or whatever, we'll pause our conversation. If people come up to talk to us, Kim will deal with that. You don't talk to anyone. Do you understand?"

"I understand."

Kim had expected more emotion from Brad. She was laser-focused on her responsibilities as she and Misty had agreed earlier, but in the back of her mind she wondered if he'd run, or explode, or weep, or argue. This cooperative silence seemed odd to her.

Misty continued. "So, Brad, let's chat a bit. Any idea why all this is happening?"

Brad leaned back against the cab of the pickup and folded his hands in his lap. He looked, thought Kim, like a man relaxing in his living room. "Yesterday we were on Disappointment Mountain when Kim disappeared. She said she needed to go to the bathroom, and I didn't think anything more of it. Kim, when you didn't come back after about twenty minutes or a half hour, I got worried and started looking for you. I didn't find you, didn't find any sign of you. I worried that you had hurt yourself, run into that rogue bear. Had a breakdown, I don't know. Had a stroke or something. I was crisscrossing the woods where I'd last seen you when I heard two shots from the direction of our campsite. I figured that was you, though I didn't know if you had a gun along. Of course at that point I thought of the bear."

Kim kept silent, as agreed. Misty spoke again. "What did you do then?"

"I worked my way back down to Mac's camp where I'd been organizing his gear when Kim went off into the woods. I grabbed my own stuff but left Mac's things there. I knew I needed to get down to our camp in case Kim needed help."

"So you went back to the trail?" Misty had told Kim she might ask a lot of questions about details just to get Brad in the habit of talking, even if the details didn't matter.

"I did. I worked basically back the same way we'd come. I thought about cutting across country but figured the trail would be faster." He looked at Kim. "I assume you went southwest down the side of the mountain?"

Kim kept silent, and Misty answered. "She did. So you left Mac's gear there and took the hiking trail back to the west, over the crest of the hill. Were you running?"

"Yes. Most of the time. I didn't want to roll an ankle or anything, so I was pretty careful. But I was worried about what had happened to Kim. I had to assume at that point that the gunshots back at our campsite were hers, or someone trying to hurt her, and that meant she was in some kind of trouble."

"How long after the gunshots would you say you arrived at the camp?"

Brad thought about it. "Probably two hours? Not much more than that. I don't think."

Just about the time I was getting to the resort on Snowbank, Kim thought.

"What did you find when you got back to camp?"

Though Misty was leading the conversation, Brad looked at Kim and spoke to her. "Something, I assume that bear, had been into our equipment pack and torn things up pretty bad. Gear was scattered all over the rocks." Kim looked at Misty, but Misty's attention was completely focused on Brad. "I found the thwart from my canoe laying next to the torn-up pack, so I assumed you had solo paddled out. The tent was still up, sleeping bags still in it. I looked around a bit and figured something happened to scare you. I didn't think a bear would freak you out, especially if you had a pistol. I wondered if maybe someone else had fired those two shots. Got pretty nervous for a while. But there was no blood, no sign that you were hurt, so I breathed a little easier. And everything else, especially that thwart, made it look like you were paddling out solo."

"What next? What did you do?"

"I figured whatever was happening, my first priority was to find Kim and make sure she was okay. So I went through my daypack and restocked it with things I thought I could use from the scattered equipment pack. I couldn't find the water filter, but I wasn't worried about that. I figured you maybe took that, Kim. There really wasn't much I could use there. I tried to gather it together and clean up the mess but I realized I was wasting time, so I just refilled my water bottle from the lake and started hiking back."

"Did you try to recover the food pack?"

"I thought about it, but no. I'd have had to swim to the island and that seemed foolish. I had a few snacks in my daypack and figured that would be enough to get me out to civilization."

"What time of day was it when you left the campsite?"

"The sun was still above the horizon. I suppose it was an hour or a little more before sunset."

"How long did you walk?"

"I walked until dark, maybe three miles or so, then used my flashlight. I didn't have very good batteries, but pretty soon the moon was high enough I could see. Not sure of the exact timeline on all that. Hard to tell time in the dark."

"You walked in the moonlight?"

"Yeah. Had to take it kind of slow, but I made some progress. Kim, I was pretty worried about you. I had no idea if you were okay or not."

Kim stirred as if to speak, but Misty glared at her, and Kim bit down on what she was going to say.

"You kept walking all night?"

"Until the moon went down below the trees and it got so dark that walking was dangerous. I'd used up my flashlight batteries by that time. I leaned up against a tree for a while and slept some. When I woke up it was just starting to get light, and I could see well enough to walk again. I walked an hour, I suppose, until I got here, to the landing, and you guys were waiting. And here we are. I've been thinking since I walked out and saw you both. I have a guess what's going on."

"Oh?"

"Kim, did you find Mac's skull?"

They had talked about this question and what to do if Brad asked it. Kim didn't take her eyes from Brad's face, did her best not to show any reaction. Misty stirred.

"Why does that come to mind right now?"

"If you found that skull, Kim, you know I didn't tell you the whole story about Mac's death. I have to believe that would freak you out. That could explain you heading back to camp and solo paddling out."

Kim did her best to remain outwardly impassive. Misty continued. "Brad, this is important. I want you to tell us the story of Mac's death. The whole story. Kim knows your version of it and I heard the recording she made of your conversation. And we were all three together up in the snow on Disappointment Mountain. So now you're going to tell us the real story. No protecting yourself, or Mac, or anyone else. Just the facts."

Chapter Thirty-seven

"Going to be cold tonight."

"It's winter in Minnesota, Mac. It's cold every night."

"You hear the wolves last night? They were howling off to the southeast."

"No. Missed that. Must have been asleep already."

"Probably more like early morning. A while before daylight."

Brad got up and added a few more sticks to the fire they'd been tending all day. It had dwindled to little more than coals, and he began to build it back up again.

Mac lifted his nose to the winter air like a dog sniffing the breeze. "You can feel the temperature dropping. Sun's still two hours from setting and it's getting cold already. Going to be a rough one tonight. Bring a hot water bottle to bed with you."

"I do that every night."

Mac grunted, and they sat in silence for several minutes, watching the flames consume the dead wood.

"Swenson, I have not been entirely forthright with you."

Brad said nothing.

"I'm afraid this might be my last wilderness trip. My last time in this beautiful, desolate place."

"Why would you say that?"

Mac shifted, re-wrapping the sleeping bag around his body. "Ever see 'The Shootist'?"

"John Wayne, right? With that kid. Opi. Ron Howard. Isn't that the one where John Wayne's character is dying?"

"That's it. Jimmy Stewart plays the sawbones doctor who tells him, 'You have a cancer.' John Wayne ends up arranging a shootout so the bad guys coming to town kill him. Makes a guy think hard. Exit strategies."

"Get to the point, Mac."

"I had that conversation with my doc about five months ago. Did all the double-checking, all the second opinions."

Three crows flew up from the south and landed in the tall pines along the south side of the clearing. They chattered between themselves, and the men listened for a moment to their conversation.

"Pancreatic cancer. Advanced. They said they could get aggressive with it, do all the chemo and surgery and everything, but chances were about ninety-five out of a hundred that it wouldn't do a damn bit of good."

"Damn. I'm sorry, Mac. They give you a time frame?"

"Back then, they said less than a year. Maybe all the chemo and such would add a couple months. Miserable months."

"I'm sorry, Mac."

"To hell with sorry. I've had a damn good run, most of it on my own terms."

Two more crows joined the first three. The small branches at the very tops of the pines swayed under their weight.

"I can feel it. I've been feeling it a little at a time for months now, but lately I can feel the weakness. My body is fighting this hellacious interloper. Bit by bit, the cancer is winning."

The crows took flight, circling the clearing and then heading north out of sight. Brad watched them go, wondering what to say, what not to say. He kept silent.

"Tennyson put it into the mouth of Ulysses: 'Life piled on life were all too little, and of one to me little remains.' I wasn't sure it was a good idea, coming up here this winter. I laid these supplies out last fall thinking if I could still make it, this would likely be my last trip."

"Why didn't you say anything about this when we spent all that time together last fall?"

Mac glared at him across the snow. "Damnation. I was trying to soak it in myself. Didn't have a clue how to process it. Truth be told, I was mostly still in denial at that point. It's a hard thing figuring out you're not immortal."

Brad thought back to those days. The odd first meeting, the feisty conversations, days of silence, and Mac's grudging eagerness to travel together.

"You showing up last fall surprised me. I've always kept to myself, kept myself apart in this desolate place. You know that. But I think right about the time you showed up I was starting to let the cancer in. I was starting to look hard at my own death."

"Not an easy thing."

"Every man dies alone. That's by definition. But the walk to the gallows... Well, most of us like a little company along the way. You showing up was enough to make me disbelieve in coincidence."

"How's that?"

"Call it mercy. Or grace. A help in time of trouble."

"You didn't strike me as weak and needy."

Mac laughed then, long and quietly. "I suppose not. A man does his level best to project the illusion of sufficiency and potency.

Over time that projection just becomes a habit and we start to believe our own press. Eventually, though, there comes a point when the facades start to crumble under the weight of our illusions."

The silence stretched out between them. Chickadees broke the cold air with their odd buzzing call from the trees behind. Shadows began to lengthen across the snow. Brad added fuel to the fire.

"You hungry, Mac? Want me to fix some thing?"

"No. I don't get hungry much anymore. Food just goes to feed the tumor anyway. Maybe some tea."

Brad set a pot of snow on to melt, then boil. The crackling of burning wood, the hiss of melting snow connecting with the hot metal of the pot, the popping of the lid expanding in the heat were all comforting sounds.

When the tea was ready, Mac took a sip and seemed to wrap his hands and entire body around the insulated mug. "Swenson, I need to ask a favor."

"Of course."

"Nobody gets any guarantees. But it is no surprise that lately I have a newfound sense of my own fragility and the unpredictability of life. In my research I've heard too many stories of people thinking they have months to live and then dropping unexpectedly. Life is uncertain. Stipulated. If something should happen to me, I need something from you."

"Okay."

"In my tent there's an envelope. Big manila envelope. It's sealed, and I'd prefer it stay that way. It's got an address on the front and a name. Kim Norby is my executive assistant at the McPherson Foundation in Duluth. I'd like you to hand deliver the envelope to her."

"You'll take it there yourself."

"I'm covering contingencies here. *If* something should happen to me. Are you not listening?"

"I'm listening. You're saying just in case something happens to you, I'll deliver the envelope."

Mac sighed and sipped his tea. Brad thought how last November Mac would have been muttering imprecations under his breath about the idiocy of the populace in general and Brad in particular, but now he was silent. Maybe it was just the thunderbolt of the news of this cancer, but to Brad's eye it looked now like it took most of Mac's strength to sip his tea. He looked somehow defeated, drooping.

"Kim's a strong woman. She's been my right hand for a long time now. Incredibly capable. Smart as whiplash. Are you willing to help her through the transition if she needs anything?"

"Doesn't sound like she needs much from a guy like me."

"You're a good man in a storm, Swenson. She might need some help."

"I'll do what I can. But…"

Mac cut him short. "Contingencies, Swenson. Contingencies. We're just covering a few what-ifs that keep me from sleeping at night."

"Yes. I get it. Deliver the envelope and be available if Ms. Norby needs help."

"Settled. I'll rest more peacefully tonight."

"Mac, if you want, I could move my tent up here. Might be nice to have someone a little closer."

"Damn it to hell. I told you, I'm looking for a neighbor. Stop offering to be a nursemaid. This is why I didn't tell you about my ever-so-fragile condition in the first place. And if you start to hover, I swear I will pull that rifle back out and shoot you myself."

"Okay, okay. I get it. I'll keep my camp set up down on the lake."

"In fact, I think tomorrow is going to be one of those clear, cold days where you can practically touch the sky. Have you ever seen the waterfall up by Ashigan, north of here?"

"No. Didn't know there was a waterfall."

"You should make a day trip tomorrow. It's a hefty hike, but if you're not toting gear it ought to be a good one day excursion. That waterfall is worth seeing any time of year, but when it's frozen, it's pure art."

"You sure? I could come back up in the morning like usual."

"The whole point of my suggesting such a diversion is to get you out from underfoot. Not to mention giving me a little space to hear myself think. I tell you I've got cancer, and suddenly the air gets all thick and emotional between us. Give it a day off, and I'll see you the day after tomorrow. Let things get a little bit back to normal."

Brad looked westward to gauge the sun's position. "I should probably head back down if I'm not going to hike in the dark. Mac, if you change your mind and you want me to relocate back up here, just say so. I'd gladly move camp."

Mac glared at him.

"Or, I could just go sleep back down by the lake, then."

"You know Yeats? A great pillar of the Irish literary establishment. He wrote a line that you ought to live by. 'I will arise and go now.' You push my tolerances, Swenson, and for the first time in a long time it's starting to feel crowded up here."

Brad chuckled and shook his head. "Well, we wouldn't want you to feel cramped. I'll get out of your hair, Mac." He stood and began gathering his few things and strapping on his snowshoes. "And I won't even bother checking on you tomorrow. I'll just go see that spectacular waterfall." Mac didn't respond as Brad took a few steps away across the shadows of the trees that now reached halfway across the clearing. Finally Mac coughed, then coughed again, and spoke.

"Swenson. You're a good man. And though being an insufferable ass myself I have little basis for judgment, you're a good friend as well. I'm self-centered and arrogant, but I'm not so blind I can't see the gifts I've been given."

Brad stood still a moment, studiously examining the tops of the pine trees above the camp. Finally he brought his gaze down to Mac's face. "Good night, Mac. Rest well." He walked off into the fading sunlight.

He was careful not to look over his shoulder as he traversed the clearing. The lengthening shadows gave a purple cast to the snow. He could feel each breath, the cold air going down his windpipe into his lungs and chilling him, each exhalation re-warming those same tissues. It was beginning to be cold enough that he could feel the chill in his teeth, even with his lips closed. Would Mac stay warm enough tonight with just a cup of tea in him? Maybe. The man was quite capable of taking care of himself, of course.

Once he reached the treeline, Brad walked ten or twelve more steps into the deep shadows, then turned. He could see Mac up against the snow under the trees, still seated in the same position. It looked, though Brad couldn't be sure, like he was still watching Brad leave. With a sigh, he turned back up the hill and climbed until he came out on the trail and turned westward toward Disappointment Lake and his camp.

Chapter Thirty-eight

Five months earlier on a brilliant October day Mac had sat in a small clinic that served as a satellite of the Mayo Health system. "It's not the kind of news I like giving my patients."

Mac glared. "Dr. Pinzler, I've known you since you were a snot-nosed little boy, so I'll speak plainly. I don't really care how uncomfortable this makes you. Comes with the job. You signed up for this. So tell me."

Dr. Ron Pinzler was in his early forties and well respected by his colleagues. He had a passion for research but still saw a limited number of patients. Mac was one of those few. They shared old family connections and a passion for making the world a better place. None of that made the doctor's present task any easier.

"I'm afraid I agree with the other doctors you've talked to. I wish I could tell you something different."

"So it's cancer. Pancreatic cancer."

"Yes."

Mac kept himself under rigid control. He'd known it. Those upper abdominal pains, a little too much fatigue just to blame on encroaching old age, and a host of other symptoms all pointed the same direction. When he'd gone in for some routine tests and got the initial diagnosis, he'd called Ron Pinzler's cell phone immediately. "Need a second opinion," was all he'd said.

"I know you guys don't like timelines and predictions. But what can I expect. Shooting straight."

Dr. Pinzler took a deep breath. "You can hope for six fairly good months," he began. "After that you'll increasingly want to take measures to deal with the pain. Comfort will become more important than capability."

Mac nodded. "Anything else I need to know?"

"We have some excellent specialists in this clinic. They are always exploring new trials for this kind of thing. There's a lot of energy going into pancreatic cancer these days." He paused. "And as far as lifestyle choices and treatments, I can give you the number of our... "

Mac stood abruptly. "Thanks, Ron. I appreciate you seeing me. I imagine I can find the resources I need closer to home."

"Would you like me to ask around? If I find anything promising I can let you know."

Mac opened the door of the tiny exam room. "Greet your parents for me, would you?" He walked down the hall toward the red letters of the "EXIT" sign. How ironic, he thought. A foretaste of the feast to come.

He was in his office the next day by 6 am. Be damned if he was going to stop living. He tried to focus on what needed to be done but his mind kept stalling. He wrestled to get his brain around the awareness of his own oncoming death.

He didn't fear the going, whatever that would be. He didn't fear the newness, or the oblivion, or whatever lay ahead. In Mac's mind the jury was still out on the afterlife. He'd know, or not, soon enough. It was hard to shed the religious rigors of being raised an Irish Catholic. But try as he might, Mac had always feared pain. Most of his bluster and severity was a running battle with his internal terror at the prospect. That included pain of all kinds. Though anyone who knew him would laugh to hear it, his was a sensitive soul, and he'd always known it. His walls were about self-protection. Over the years he had learned to face into discomfort, to turn toward it rather than away. He'd forced himself to this as a discipline. It had become his rigid code.

That was so much of what these wilderness trips were about. You had to make a friend of desolation. Not terror, this was not an *Apocalypse Now* thing. But desolation. You had to learn to go into the empty places, the desolate places. It was there you found your strength. It was there you learned to measure yourself against your need. And there you faced your fears.

He'd learned to gaze into economic fears and fear of conflict, fear of alienating people. It had made him a good financial manager, unflinchingly able to make good executive decisions while still realizing that his decisions affected real people. The one fear he had never been able to get past was the fear of emotional vulnerability, the fear of revealing his heart. In that way the taciturn emotional culture of northern Minnesota fit him like a glove, and when that wasn't enough he resorted to bluster. People backed away when you transgressed the unwritten rules of Minnesota Nice.

Physical pain was another arena he'd never gotten good at. Dig into the decisions he was pondering, and that's what it was all about. Minor physical pain sooner to avoid debilitating, morphine-managed pain later. The prospect of the short-term, self-imposed physical pain made his stomach do somersaults, made the acid rise in his throat. His aversion to physical suffering was a large part of what drove him into the wilderness time and again. Out there he could force himself to do the uncomfortable thing, to push his body another time across the portage, to paddle until his shoulders ached, to sleep hard on the rocky ground. This going into desolation had become a key part of his identity. And much needed for his own sake. He gazed out the fourth floor window of his office at the Duluth harbor, but his mind was a hundred miles away.

"What?"

"I've got the paperwork from the charter school group." Kim stood in front of him holding a thick folder.

What about Kim? He allowed his thoughts to transgress into the personal for just a moment. She had been invaluable to him these last years. What did he owe her? He wondered about her at times. Was she happy?

What a damn fool question. Who was really happy for more than a few minutes at a time?

"Mac?"

Mac realized he had been lost in his own mind again. Kim stood waiting for his response. "That's fine. Just leave it here and I'll take a look." He paused, uncomfortable, then added, "Thanks."

Kim set the folder on Mac's desk and turned to leave his office. He knew he would be a poorer man without her looming so large in the background, taking care of details and freeing him for more public roles.

How to structure the next few months in regard to Kim?

Chapter Thirty-nine

Mac watched Swenson disappear into the trees across the clearing. He pulled out the weatherproof notebook and opened to the note he had nearly completed the night before.

What would Swenson do with all this? Was this the right choice for him, and for the foundation? Was Brad indeed Mac's Telemachus, "to whom I leave the sceptre and the isle"? That remained to be seen. But it seemed like a fair gamble.

And Kim, again. Kim might think he had lost his mind. No. He knew her better than that. She'd take him seriously and then decide for herself. He trusted her to do that. But in spite of herself, she'd be hurt. She didn't like feeling excluded, and he had kept her far out of this process. She might need to lean on Brad.

Back to business. He looked over the note again. One sheet in the precise handwriting that always looked clear to him, but seemed to mystify other people. He read, then reread.

He tried to muster grief for the people he knew would be horrified at this choice. Up in this desolate country he always felt such a distance from them all. Physical distance, yes, but even more he felt the freedom of an emotional distance, a weightlessness that separated him from the mass of humanity, from the transactions and the decisions and the little bits of affection that dripped back and forth in people's words. That last was always a foreign language to him anyway. He sighed. Relief, he guessed, to be done with it all. At the bottom of the sigh, though, his stomach flipped. He choked on the fear, turned his mind away from the future to contemplate the lengthening shadows. Tennyson had it right. All too true.

Swenson must be halfway down the hill by now. He would help, if necessary. Mac had sized the man up pretty thoroughly these last months, and he was confident of his assessment. Swenson was a man who would do what needed to be done. He came from steadfast farm people who knew how to pay the price for life. What exactly that looked like on this evening in particular remained to be seen, but the waiting was winding down now. Just a few more uncertain moments.

Chapter Forty

Pancreatic cancer. Brad didn't know much about it, but he'd known a few people so afflicted, coworkers or friends of friends, and he realized it was a desperate diagnosis. Mac wasn't the kind of person to go without good information. No doubt he'd done a thorough job of investigating the possibilities, challenging his doctors, seeking out the best experts.

With a start Brad found himself wondering. Who does Mac have to rely on? Who are his caretakers when he's back in Duluth? Who does he belong to, and who belongs to him? The foundation he'd talked about. There must be people there who cared for Mac, and vice versa.

Slowly he started turning those questions back on himself. Since Lauren's note, who did he really belong to? Since the end of his old job, who were his caretakers, and who depended on him? It was a desperate, lonely feeling. As he crested the hill and started the long descent toward the lake, he let the loneliness wash over him. Mac's parting words hung like treasures at the front of his mind. Friendship was such a fragile thing, and this particular friendship had crept up while he wasn't paying attention. He replayed in his mind the final encounter between Jeremiah Johnson and Bearclaw Chris Lapp in the movie, and he remembered how the tone of their relationship had changed by that time. Instead of wise mentor and greenhorn they were now equals, respecting and valuing each other. Maybe that was a good model for his friendship with Mac.

What an odd thing to say. A friendship with Mac.

The sound of the rifle shot vibrated through the forest as though it was bouncing hard off the frozen tree trunks. No question that it came from Mac's camp. Brad stopped in the trail and considered what it might mean.

"Oh, God." He turned back uphill and started double-timing it up the trail. Was Mac shooting at wolves? Maybe. But the pit of Brad's stomach felt tied in knots, and every step brought his sledge-hammer heart up into his throat. He dreaded what he would find when he got to the camp. He wracked his memory for any indication that Mac might hurt himself. He was surprised to realize how little Mac spoke of the future, and how much of the conversation had been about those "contingencies."

Brad broke from the trees, jogging on the trail packed with so many journeys back and forth. Shadows lay heavy under the trees and he couldn't see much across the clearing. The frigid air was searing the inside of his trachea. He knew he couldn't keep gasping for breath much longer without doing himself some serious damage in the cold.

Across the clearing he could see in the twilight a couple bundles next to the big pine by Mac's tent. That had to be–yes, Mac's sleeping bag, off to one side. Brad ran on his snowshoes again, covering the last hundred yards in a few heartbeats that seemed to take forever. Mac himself lay next to the tree. The right side of his head was covered in blood, and blood was congealing from a long gash that started halfway back on Mac's right cheek, tore his ear in half, and left a bloody trench behind the ear almost to the back of the skull. Red flecks left a pattern in the snow behind Mac. Blood soaked the snow next to his head. Mac's rifle lay next to him, dropped into the snow.

It seemed clear to Brad what had happened. Mac sat against the big pine and tried to shoot himself. He must have flinched at the last instant. It seemed the most natural reflex in the world to Brad to avoid putting a bullet in one's own body. He reached across Mac's neck and checked for a pulse. To his surprise, he felt the strong pounding of the blood in the artery. He'd thought Mac must be dead, but apparently he was just unconscious.

What now?

Mac's eyes flew open wide, staring about in panic. He opened his mouth and began to gasp. Brad could hear a gurgle in his breath. Mac's right arm flew up and his hand clutched like a claw at Brad's shoulder. His left side didn't move, but the right arm was quite strong, and he seized a fistful of Brad's parka. The panicked eyes found Brad's face, and Mac began to keen, to wail. It was a terrible, unearthly sound, and it set Brad to the edge of panic as well.

"Ba - ba - ba - " Mac tried again and again, but couldn't get words out.

"Mac. Take it easy. Mac. You're going to be okay." What a stupid thing to say, Brad. He's far from okay. "I've got you."

"Hof."

"Hof."

"Easy. Calm down. I've got you. We're going to get through this."

Mac seemed to slow down just a bit, then. His eyes were slightly less like those of a wild animal in pain. "Hep. Meh."

"I'll help you, Mac. I've got you. Where is your first aid kit?" Brad looked back toward the tent. "Is it in the tent?" He reached inside a pocket and grabbed the bandana he always carried in the wilderness. "I'm going to put this against the wound here, Mac. I want to stop the bleeding." He folded the bandana into a long rectangle and gently laid it against the trench that had ripped the side of Mac's head apart. "Easy. I'm just going to hold this here."

Mac's right hand released his parka. It came up and firmly grasped Brad's forearm. "No." Mac's lips and tongue still struggled to form words, but the shock was giving way to a little more coherent speech.

"No? Mac, I need to stop the bleeding. This will help for now, and then I'll get some gauze out of your first aid kit."

"No."

"What do you want, Mac?"

"Hep me."

"I'm trying to help you, Mac. You need to trust me."

"Do. I do. Trush you."

Mac took a deep breath, and Brad watched his eyes close and reopen. They were full of tears now that leaked out the sides and fell down into the snow on one side, and into the bandana on the other. "So. Scaed."

"Scared? You're scared? Me, too, Mac. But we got this."

"Fnish it."

Brad searched Mac's face. "Finish it?"

"Need. Hep. Cant do it. A'one. Fukd it up. Bad. See?"

Brad began to weep then. He couldn't keep the tears from leaking out of his eyes and dropping on Mac's arm, on his coat.

"Need hep. Scaed to puh a triggeh." Mac groaned. "Jerk. Bad."

"Mac, why did you do this? Why?"

"You unnastan."

Brad tried to think of something intelligent to say, but found nothing. From Mac's perspective, he knew, this desperate action made perfect sense.

Mac's eyes closed, and he shuddered. "Code. Gettin code."

"Let's help you sit up. Here." Brad got his arms under Mac's shoulders and lifted him so he could rest against the tree trunk. Once Mac was propped up there, Brad looked at his face. "Can you sit like that for a second? I'm going to grab your sleeping bag." He got the heavy bag, unzipped it, and tried to pack it around Mac's legs and torso. "Is that any better?"

"No. F'nish it."

Brad shook his head. "I can't do that, Mac."

212

"Don' wanna freeze. Gonna freeze. T'night. Wanna be. Over."
"I can't."
"F'nish th' pain. Wanna be done. Wi' th' pain. Fast."
A sob convulsed from Brad's throat. "Mac. You said it. You're my friend. I can't put that rifle in your face and pull the trigger."
Mac seemed to consider. He squeezed his right hand open and closed, grabbed Brad's arm again and squeezed. "S'okay. You holda barreh. I pullah triggeh. My lef' han' i' no good. Can' movet."
Brad's mind raced, looking for a way out of this. "Are you sure? Mac, I think we can get you patched up, get the bleeding stopped. And I'm sure we can keep you warm enough tonight. I'll build a big fire, and stay here with you. We can get you out of here. I'll put you on a sled and take you out, get you to a hospital."
Mac's words were getting clearer, though it took him immense effort to form each one. "Ben to a hos'tal. Then what? Oh, Mac, we'come back ta canceh."
Brad looked at the rifle laying on the ground a few feet away, considering it like a poison snake.
"F'nish it. Please. Brad." These last two words were crystal clear, and that somehow tripped the balances. Brad checked to see that Mac was sitting upright, then scooted across the snow to the rifle. Pointing it carefully away from himself and Mac (as he had been rigorously trained as a boy on the farm) he worked the bolt to eject the spent shell casing, and levered a fresh cartridge into the chamber. He turned back to Mac whose eyes were watching the whole process.
"You ready?"
"Moh' than ready."
Time slowed to a crawl and Brad felt like he was moving in a dream. He set the butt of the rifle between Mac's knees, checked to make sure the safety was off, and fighting every bit of conscience, training, and reflex he possessed, he lowered the barrel down just in front of Mac's face. Mac's eyes never left Brad's.
"Thank you. You ah good friend."
Brad began to shake, holding the barrel in place with his left hand. His ungloved hands were freezing. He looked down to find Mac's right hand groping, and gently guided it to the stock, then the trigger guard, then to the trigger. He brought his own right hand up to help steady the barrel that shook from his shivering. Both hands on the barrel, checking its position, he looked back at Mac's face. Mac's eyes were no longer panicky. He looked steadily at Brad. If he was concerned at all about the rifle barrel inches from his face, it didn't show..

"Afteh. In ma ches' pocket. A note fo' you."

"In your chest pocket. Okay. And I'll take the manila envelope. To Kim."

"Good." Mac's eyes looked beyond Brad, focusing up at the darkening sky. "Stars comin' out." He looked back at Brad's face, then closed his eyes. "You come far, Pilgrim." He smiled.

The roar of the rifle, the lightning flash of the muzzle in the dark, the painful jerking of the barrel in his hands, the intense ringing in Brad's ears overwhelmed his senses for a moment. When he focused again on Mac, there was a small bloody hole just next to his nose where the bullet had gone in, and a little blood spattered on the tree just behind his head. This new wound looked far less gory than the first botched shot down the side of Mac's head. The pounding of his own heart thundered in his ears. He tried to stop shaking.

Brad felt the heat of the barrel in his hands. He removed Mac's right hand from the trigger and carefully put the gun aside. He checked the artery in Mac's neck again, felt a fluttery pulse beat a few times and then nothing. As gently as he could, he lay Mac's body down on the snow next to the tree. Brad knelt and placed his right hand gently on Mac's cheek. Words unbidden came to mind then, echoing from the depths of the hundreds of times he'd heard them as a child, and as an adult. He spoke aloud, as if hoping someone could hear: "The Lord bless you and keep you. The Lord make His face shine on you and be gracious to you. The Lord lift up His countenance upon you and give you peace." He paused then, thinking of Mac's Irish Catholic background, realizing Mac probably wouldn't object to this. With his finger he traced a cross on Mac's forehead and completed the words, "In the Name of the Father, and of the Son, and of the Holy Spirit. Amen."

Epilogue

Kim won't quit pushing me this direction, so I suppose I might as well give in. It was probably a mistake to show her that story back when.

That's not really honest. I wanted someone to read it, and she was about the only person I trusted. I was an insecure kid in those days. Now I'm an insecure adult. Well, a few more miles on the odometer doesn't change the basic character. She's still about the only person I trust to talk about writing. That hasn't changed much. Some of that stuff is just so personal. Hard to share it. After she read that story back when, I was so embarrassed. She gushed about it. She kept bringing it up. Like once every decade or something. Just wouldn't let it rest. Ha.

What would it take, to write? It's not like it was back when we were kids. Back then it was like I was desperate to get my soul out on paper. Now it seems like if I write, it ought to matter. To be honest, that pressure has pretty much kept me paralyzed.

Kim asked me about it again a month ago, and pushed until I agreed to think about it. I told her I'd start keeping a journal for a while, at least to get back into putting words on paper. That can't hurt. Much. I read somewhere that a journal is where you do all the bad writing you have to get out of the way so you can write well. Maybe.

She's starting to come to peace with Mac's death. It took her a long time, like months, to forgive Brad. I don't quite get that. What was to forgive? The man was caught in an impossible situation. Kim's an idealist. I guess she wanted Brad to come up with some miraculous way of healing Mac and hauling him out of the woods. Not really, but deep down I wonder if that's what she longs for. We haven't talked about it much, but when it comes up she's had a lot of hurt to process.

So I think she's finally forgiven Brad. Well, obviously. Though with Kim it's hard to tell sometimes. She didn't even talk to him for three months. Chilly silence between the two of them. On her end, at least. Came up here every other weekend for a while, and we did a couple short paddles into the Boundary Waters during the summer. It's been so good for me to spend time with her. That hard shell that has become reflex with almost everyone has melted a little bit with her. I've needed that.

We hiked up Disappointment Mountain one more time, but just once. Had a good cry up there. And it seems like that was enough for her, at least for the moment. It was the next week, she said, that she finally called Brad.

Crazy. Called him out of the blue after all that time and what does she say? Brad, you're a son of a bitch. Brad, I have questions. Brad, I'm so angry at you. Brad, I have issues.

Nope. Kim being Kim, she calls him up and tells him about this fall festival at the same winery he asked her out to last spring. That poor man. He didn't know which way to jump, I'm sure. But give the guy some credit, he rolled with it and went out with her. Kim didn't say a lot about their conversation, but she did say they had a good time.

So now it's November, and they're officially a couple. Been on half a dozen dates that I've heard about. Kim talked about bringing him along up here next time she comes. I would be glad to see him. I don't know where he stands with everything that happened with Mac, but I want to tell him I get it. Spent enough years as a cop that I get hard situations. And that was a hard situation for sure. When he talked us through that scenario, things fell into place for me. I think it took Kim a little longer. Well, a lot longer. I could see right off why Kim had felt so uncertain around him. Usually that girl is solid as granite, but she couldn't make up her mind about him. I think she really wanted to like him, but she could feel something was a little off. Makes total sense now. Brad couldn't exactly come out with that whole story, could he? So all that happened around Mac's death hung like a dark cloud in the background of all their interactions. Duct tape and gunpoint dragged it out of him, finally. Damn. What a day that was.

When he told us the truth, I thought Kim would explode. Or collapse. One or the other. But she's got some steel in her. She didn't even flinch. Scared me a little to watch her go stone cold like that. Especially knowing she had a loaded piece in her pocket.

After he finished, we all three talked for a bit. Not on an emotional level, but deciding what to do with all of it.

I've gone back to that decision a lot lately. Did we do the right thing? It wasn't quite a pact of silence, but close. We just agreed that the world wouldn't be well served by trotting out the full story of Mac's death. The 'backcountry accident' plays a lot better in most circles. So at this point, Brad, Kim, and I are the only ones who know. And I'm not talking.

But there are other things to talk about. I wonder if Kim is going to talk to the board about Mac's plans for Brad. Mac figured that Brad should succeed him in the executive slot. But only if Kim thought it was a good idea. I asked her about that, and all she said was, "Gotta figure this out first." I asked, "You mean the romantic thing?" She just nodded. The two of them will need some time for that, I'm sure. I wonder if she has even told him about Mac's plans. I doubt it. That would skew everything, and Kim's a better poker player than that. Especially for stakes this high.

This journaling is hard work. The words just flow, but I have to keep fighting the temptation to go back and edit for effect. Get the language just right. Eliminate fragments. Correct punctuation.

If I'm going to try writing again, I need some help jump-starting the process. So I've been digging into some old friends. Was digging through some T.S. Eliot the other day and ran across a fragment that just sounds like Mac. Wonder if the old guy ever read it. I'll have to ask Brad if they ever talked about it. Probably. It's from "Four Quartets," just a few lines:

Old men ought to be explorers
Here or there does not matter
We must be still and still moving
Into another intensity
For a further union, a deeper communion
Through the dark cold and the empty desolation,
The wave cry, the wind cry, the vast waters
Of the petrel and the porpoise. In my end is my beginning.

So here's to you, Mac. You cast a pretty long shadow over the rest of us these days. I don't agree with how you handled things. But maybe you've found forgiveness and new life on the other side of it. May your end be your beginning, old man.

Acknowledgements

The process of writing a book makes you see your dependence on other people. This novel is no exception. I am so grateful to:

- The crew that made a summer 2021 trip to Disappointment Mountain while this story was taking its final form. It was a joy to hike and paddle through the story with you: Scott, Scott, Matt, Matt, Sarah. Thanks for enduring indignant bees, a stowaway mouse, pirate shanties, and cream cheese frosting to make that trip a reality.
- A handful of people who have read and offered insights into various parts of the manuscript. Thanks to each of you for helping me see this book through your eyes.
- Lisa, you listened to each word of the final story with such engagement. Your encouragement for me and your partnership in this project have kept me moving forward.
- Mathea and Erica: from paddling together to critical edits to cover design, you both give me such great joy. You've been there in every way since this story was first imagined on Gaskin Lake years ago.
- Thanks to the folks at Ingram Spark who make it their business to streamline the process of publishing. That world, like so much else these days, has changed significantly over the past couple decades. As an author, getting a book in print is an impossibly daunting task. You take down so many barriers and make it possible for readers to hold this book in their hands.

Printed in the USA
CPSIA information can be obtained
at www.ICGtesting.com
JSHW030852241024
72290JS00006B/278